Joseph Edward Keller

The Life and Acts of Pope Leo XIII

Joseph Edward Keller

The Life and Acts of Pope Leo XIII

ISBN/EAN: 9783744659758

Printed in Europe, USA, Canada, Australia, Japan

Cover: Foto ©Raphael Reischuk / pixelio.de

More available books at **www.hansebooks.com**

THE LIFE AND ACTS

OF

POPE LEO XIII.

PRECEDED BY A SKETCH OF

THE LAST DAYS OF PIUS IX.

AND

THE ORIGIN AND LAWS

OF

THE CONCLAVE.

Compiled and Translated from Authentic Sources.

EDITED BY

REV. JOSEPH E. KELLER, S. J.

PRESIDENT OF ST. LOUIS UNIVERSITY, ST. LOUIS.

With the Approbation of His Eminence, the Cardinal, Archbishop of New York.

New York, Cincinnati, and St. Louis:

BENZIGER BROTHERS,

PRINTERS TO THE HOLY APOSTOLIC SEE.

1879.

Imprimatur.

† JOHN, CARDINAL McCLOSKEY,

Archbishop of New York.

TO

LEO XIII.,

KING AND PONTIFF,

CHOSEN BY THE SUPREME PASTOR AS A WORTHY SUCCESSOR TO

PIUS THE GREAT:

LUMEN IN CŒLO AFTER *CRUX DE CRUCE,*

WHOSE BRILLIANT DAWN

HAS GIVEN PROMISE OF A GLORIOUS DAY,

THIS BOOK

IS OFFERED AS A TRIBUTE OF HOMAGE—

A TOKEN OF FILIAL DEVOTION.

PREFACE.

THE title-page of this compilation sufficiently indicates its nature, and a preface would be superfluous were it not the editor's duty to give the public some information in regard to the sources from which he has drawn his materials, and the manner in which the book has been put together.

That a book of this kind was needed is evident from the very greatness of the names which form our title-page ; but that the need is supplied only now, when nearly a year has elapsed since the death of Pius IX. and the election of his successor, seems to require some explanation.

Letters from Roman correspondents to newspapers in the various countries of the Old and the New Worlds ; pamphlets purporting to give correct information on the great events which form our subject ; books, large and small, entitled " Life of Pius IX." and " Life of Leo XIII." were hurriedly poured from the press ; and it was to be expected that mere rumors would, in many instances, be stated as facts, and that the haste of the writers would betray them into many errors and exaggerations. It was, therefore, necessary to wait till the fermentation had subsided, and we could obtain a clear view of the subject in hand. It was necessary to compare the several writings, and to correct or supplement one by another.

It was necessary, moreover, to combine the various parts into something like an homogeneous whole. Then came the laborious task of translation from the German, French, and Italian originals. All this would be more than sufficient to account for the delay ; but it is not all. The manifold and never-ceasing duties of college life rendered it impossible to devote to this work any other time than that of the summer vacation, which of itself is not favorable to such a task.

But the editor knew that he could call to his aid a number of willing assistants among the young professors of several colleges, who would come together during that season of repose. And it is to their good-will and to their diligent pens that this book owes its existence. The editor, therefore, as in duty bound, here places all the merit of this production where it justly belongs, and takes no credit to himself beyond what is implied in the act of suggesting this manner of relieving the sports of vacation by an occasional hour of literary labor.

In the choice of our materials we have gone to the best sources within our reach. The writings of men who were present in Rome and well versed in the ceremonial of the Papal Court, have been our chief contributors.

The first part of our volume is taken from a pamphlet in German by the Rev. G. Schmid von Grüneck, a resident of Rome. The second part is from a book by Philippus Laicus, a writer of considerable research. The Life of Leo XIII. was gathered from several French writers, the chief of whom is A. Chaulieu, some of whose statements, however, we have deemed it proper to correct and others to amplify, with the aid of the German Life of Leo XIII., by Dr. A. de Waal, rector of the German Campo Santo at Rome. For the acts of the new Pope during the first year of his reign, we have drawn from the *Civilta Cattolica* and other foreign and domestic periodicals of known merit.

We feel that our work has been done very imperfectly; but the public, now informed of the difficulties under which we undertook it, will be lenient in their judgment, and will overlook the deficiencies of the style, in consideration of the interesting and useful matter which has been gathered for their benefit.

THE EDITOR.

St. Louis, Mo., Nov. 1, 1878.

TABLE OF CONTENTS.

PIUS THE NINTH.

A SKETCH OF HIS LIFE, HIS LAST DAYS, HIS DEATH AND BURIAL.

PIUS THE NINTH.

CHAPTER I.

A SKETCH OF HIS LIFE.

IUS THE NINTH presents in his life a picture so grand, so richly set, that he who attempts to write his biography is at a loss as to what should be made most prominent, and what may be passed over, without injustice to the subject.

We will once more call briefly to mind his life so fraught with good works, and, viewing his great deeds, try to soothe the sorrow caused by his departure from this world.

John Mastai-Ferretti was born on the 13th of May, 1792, in a little village in the Marches. He was the son of the Count Girolamo Mastai and the Countess Solazzi. In 1803, at the tender age of eleven, he began his studies in the college at Volterra, at that time under the direction of the Reverend Father Inghirami. In this institution he received the tonsure from the hands of Monsignor Incontri, Bishop of Volterra. In 1807 he had an attack of epilepsy, and this was the reason of his being declared unfit to be received into the Guard of Honor instituted by Napoleon I. And to this likewise the rumors that John Maria Mastai had wished to enter the Pope's Noble Guard owe their origin.

These reports, however, are unfounded. For the young count had, from his earliest boyhood, resolved to consecrate his life to the clerical state. But as his sickness stubbornly clung to him, he was permitted to carry out his idea only on condition that while celebrating mass he would have another priest standing by his side.

On Easter Sunday, 1819, he celebrated his first mass in the little church of St. Anne dei Falegnami, the church of the Joiners' Guild, situated near the boys' orphanage of Tata Giovanni, to which he was to be afterwards so closely attached. The restriction to which he was bound at his ordination was, a short time after, removed by Pius VII., and in fact from 1818 to 1878 he was ever spared from epileptic attacks.

In 1823 the young priest Mastai, together with Mgr. Muzi, was sent to Chili in South America to investigate and regulate church affairs. Thence he soon returned, and in 1825 he was appointed by Leo XII. director of the great hospital San Michele, and twenty months afterwards Archbishop of Spoleto. It would lead us too far to enumerate all the advantages the diocese of Spoleto enjoyed under his administration. Even now, after the lapse of half a century, old people speak of their archbishop Mastai with an emotion that moves to tears. Let it suffice to mention here how, by his singular prudence and the force of his eloquence, he subdued four thousand insurrectionists who had forced their way into Spoleto, so that of their own accord they submitted to lawful authority.

In 1832 he was removed by Gregory XVI. to Imola, and on the 14th of December, eight years later, he was raised to the dignity of cardinal. We will pass over the innumerable benefits bestowed by his charitable hand during his episcopate ; for the two dioceses are living tongues bespeaking his mildness and benevolence.

In the beginning of June, 1846, Cardinal Mastai was called to Rome for the election of a successor to Gregory XVI. The Conclave began on June 15th, and on the evening of the following day Cardinal Mastai was unanimously declared pope. The morning of the 17th announced to the Catholic world that Cardinal Mastai had ascended the papal throne, under the name of Pius IX.

He gave himself, heart and soul, to the high task now imposed upon him. Indeed he not only turned his attention to the government of the Church of Christ, but he wished also to withdraw Italy from the abyss into which it was rapidly falling. He earnestly endeavored to win by mildness those who had gone astray under the reign of Gregory XVI.

Having entered upon office on the 16th of July, his first act was to grant an amnesty to all political criminals, who in course of time repaid this act of mildness with the blackest ingratitude. To promote the welfare of Italy, he proposed a union of States ; but Piedmont, according to the historian Farini, opposed the proposition. To remove every ground of complaint advanced by the sects, the implacable enemies of absolute monarchy as it had hitherto existed in the States of the Church, Pius, ahead of all the princes of Italy, gave his provinces a constitution.

He called to the first seat in his ministry the somewhat liberal-minded but faithful and blameless Pelle-
grino Rossi, who by reason of his uprightness was
the terror of the secret societies that were under-
mining Italy.   They plotted his death.   Three assas-
sins were hired. In the night of the 14th of November,
1848, they dragged a corpse from the hospital St.

THE CAPITOL.

Giacomo, and practised on it for the intended murder.
On the 15th of November, when Rossi was about to
enter the council of ministers, some one pushed him
slightly, just as he put his foot on the first step of the
staircase leading to the ministers' hall.   He turned
round, but at the same moment the deadly steel inflicted the mortal wound.   He ascended two more
steps and fell a corpse.

We will not rehearse the fearful days when cannon were mounted before the Quirinal Palace ; we
will pass over the assassination of Monsignor Palma,
at the very side of the Pope, and the other excesses
which branded this period as one of the bloodiest in

the annals of Italian history. On the 24th of November Pius IX. was besieged in his own palace of the Quirinal. He succeeded, however, with the assistance of the Bavarian minister, Count Spaur, in making his escape from the hands of those to whom but a short time before he had given liberty.

The fugitive received the most cordial reception from Ferdinand II., King of Naples. His stay in Gaeta lasted until the republic under Mazzini and Garibaldi had sufficiently spent its rage ; and on the 12th of April, 1850, he returned to Rome amid the repeated acclamations of the people. He adhered to many of the measures he had adopted in 1846. And then, during the quiet and happy period from 1850 to 1859, he turned all the energies of his great mind to the welfare of his people and to the advancement of religion. In proof of this we may mention the many memorials, the countless monuments, the magnificent institutions, which remind us of the munificence of the great pontiff, and also the crown of lilies with which he encircled the brow of the august Mother of God in declaring her immaculate.

When in 1859 the war between Italy and France broke out, Pius IX. adopted without opposition the plan of an Italian confederacy as proposed by Napoleon III. Sardinia, however, opposed its execution. When the best provinces of the Church were lost at Castelfidardo, where the noble Pimodan renewed the spectacle of Leonidas at Thermopylæ, Pius IX. paid all his officers, and liquidated the debt that weighed heavily upon the States of the Church, without making an assessment on the subjects of the patrimony of St. Peter or on the provinces of Civita Vecchia, Frosinone, and Velletri. He was just engaged in carrying out one of his grandest designs by the work of the General Council, when the storming of the Porta Pia put an end to its deliberations. In virtue of the principle of " accomplished facts," the last remnant of royalty was torn from him, and that, too, without protest from the Catholic powers. But that which in those days suffered a greater defeat than the Pope's temporal power, was the justice of united Italy.

But the steadfastness of Pius IX., without ever giving way, defied every storm. For no skill in war, no bayonets, not even the cannon's dreadful roar, ever silenced his *Non possumus.* He persevered in the Vatican as a faithful general at his post. Without accepting the Guaranty Laws and the millions of dollars offered him by the King of Italy, he supported with the money which the faithful of their own accord had contributed, as a token of their love for St. Peter, not only the great number of officers faithful to the last, but also many bishops who had been robbed of their income. Many schools, institutions, and private families in and out of Rome are indebted for a very considerable assistance to the liberality of Pius IX. In the Vatican, which he left but once to give solemn audience to eight thousand Spanish pilgrims, he celebrated his jubilees, days of joy for the whole Catholic world. From the Vatican he published his grand encyclical letters, and there delivered the animated allocutions which like the voice of thunder were heard throughout Europe. There he received the pilgrims who came in vast numbers from every clime to see Pius IX., to hear his voice, and to return to their homes with new hopes animating their breasts. And in the Vatican, too, he ended his days, and entered, on the 7th of February, 1878, into the peace of the Lord.

To give light and color to the general outlines which we have drawn of the life of the great Pius, we feel it our duty to introduce what was written óf him by a Catholic of great erudition, but who now, for the empty praises of men, has left the Church he once loved so ardently and defended so heroically : " Whatever can be expected of a loving monarch who finds relief only in conferring benefits, that is shown forth brilliantly in the life of Pius IX. *Pertransiit benefaciendo.* He went about doing good. These words, though spoken of a higher One, may be truly applied to him. As far as a princely person is concerned, it is plainly apparent in him how the papacy, even in a worldly state, can, by suitable elections, be the most noble of all human institutions. Here is one in the full vigor of manhood whose youth was spent in innocence, whose episcopal duties were conscientiously performed, and who is now raised to the highest honors and to princely power. He is a stranger to extravagance. He has no desire but to do good. He has no ambition but to be loved by his people. His daily occupations are divided between prayer and the work of a ruler ; his recreation is a walk in the garden, a visit to some church, prison, or benevolent institution.

" Without personal want, free from all earthly ties, he has no relatives to advance, no favorites ; all have like claim, like access to him. He exercises the rights and powers of his office for no other end than to do his duty. The sparing and economical management of his court affords him ample means for supplying the wants of the needy and the suffering. He too, like other popes, has buildings erected, not indeed gorgeous palaces, but structures of public utility. Severely wounded, maltreated, and repaid with ingratitude, he has never nourished a thought of revenge, never committed an act of violence, but has always forgiven and pardoned.   He has not only tasted of the cup of sweetness and of bitterness, of the cup of the favors and disfavors of men, but has drained it to its very dregs ; he has heard the ' hosanna' and the ' crucify him.'   The man in whom he placed his confidence, the greatest mind of his nation, fell by the dagger ; the ball of a revolutionist pierced his friend by his side.   No feeling of hatred, no passing breath of bitterness, has tarnished the mirror of that pure soul.   Not led astray by human folly, nor drawn by human scheming, he moved on in his course with a firm and constant pace like a star in the heavens.''

CHAPTER II.

THE 2d of February, 1878, was for the true subjects of the holy father what the 17th of January, on which day Victor Emmanuel was buried, had been for the minions of the invader. Notwithstanding the corruption which set in with the storming of the Porta Pia, it was plainly apparent, on the feast of Candlemas, that love towards Pius IX. could not be torn from the hearts of the true Romans.

The 2d of February was the seventy-fifth anniversary of the holy father's first communion. Even at early dawn all the churches of Rome were crowded by the faithful, from the rank of the poor carter up to that of the Roman patrician, all offering up their holy communion for the preservation of Pius IX. The Roman youths met at the Gesù (church of the Jesuits). Here his Eminence the Cardinal-Vicar, Monaco la Valetta, distributed holy communion without interruption from early morning till ten o'clock. The faithful Romans returned from the altar, their eyes glistening with tears of emotion, their hearts bounding with courage to fight the battles of God and his Church.

On the same day the holy father received at the

Vatican the representatives of the chapters, the generals of the different orders, the pastors of Rome, and the rectors of the ecclesiastical institutions. This being the first public audience since November, many dignitaries of the Church from far and near were present, viz., Monsignor Perraud, Bishop of

CARDINAL MONACO LA VALETTA.

Autun in France, Mgr. Elloy, Vicar Apostolic of Oceanica, Mgr. Clifford, Bishop of Clifton, England, Mgr. Strain and Mgr. Eyre, apostolic delegates for Edinburgh and Glasgow, Mgr. Sallua, Commissary of the Holy Office, and others.

Towards one o'clock, the holy father, accompanied by the court, was carried in his chair to the audience chamber. Kindly receiving the blessed candles, which according to custom were presented on that day, he addressed those present in an earnest and sonorous voice as follows :

" It affords me unwonted consolation, dear children, to see you on this day assembled here about me. I thank you for the noble energy which you have ever manifested for the protection and salvation of souls entrusted to your charge. I thank the pastors who are leaving nothing undone to urge on the faithful perseverance in prayer and in the frequent reception of holy communion.

" My thanks also to all the pastors, both secular and regular, for the many prayers which by their counsel, and under their direction, the faithful have unceasingly offered up for me. I request you to thank in my name all under your care for these kind offices. Thank them, and tell them that I pray to God that he may shower down upon them three graces : perseverance in prayer and in the reception of the holy sacraments, and an unshaken fidelity towards the head of the Church. Tell them that I remember them, and beseech God to preserve them graciously under the kindly hand of his providence. I am not ignorant of the fact that in the different parishes there are some so ill instructed as not to be acquainted with the necessary truths of our holy religion. I know, too, that there are parents who have incurred fearful responsibilities for having brought up their children in religious ignorance. But, on the other hand, I know that we must go in search of sinners to correct them, and follow the ignorant to instruct them.

" Go then, seek out the ignorant, instruct them with all fervor, that it may no longer be said that in the centre of the Catholic world there are souls unacquainted with the principal mysteries of our holy religion.   Exert all your energy to take away this stain from Rome ; cease not until, by your efforts and your prayers, souls be converted and the truth shine forth brilliantly everywhere in the holy city.

" 'And I trust that he who hath begun a good work in you will perfect it unto the day of Christ Jesus.'   (Philip. 1 : 6.)

" This is what I wish to exhort you to on this occasion, my extreme weakness not allowing me to say more.

" And now I give you all my blessing.   I bless you, your institutions, and all the souls committed to your care.   May this blessing accompany you through your whole life, and be the object of your prayer, and the key-note of your songs of praise, when God will call you away to your heavenly country !

" May the blessing of Almighty God, the Father, the Son, and the Holy Ghost, descend upon you and remain with you forever !"

This is the last address of Pius IX., not a composition of artistic words and high-sounding phrases, but the language of truth, which, as Cicero says, can defend itself.

This is the last will of Pius IX. to the society of the nineteenth century.   The dangerous disease with which it is infected first manifested itself when Luther unfurled the standard of rebellion in matters of religion.   Its symptoms became more alarming at the outbreak of the revolution in philosophy, for which Descartes gave the watchword, and came to a crisis in the social revolution of 1789.   For a whole century the symptoms of this disease have been carefully studied.   The world outside of the Church has administered various remedies, but humanity lies prostrate as sick as ever. And no change for the better will be effected until the Church obtains the free exercise of all her powers and undisputed sway in what belongs to religion, and until the family is again animated by the spirit of a Christian training in which precept and practice are considered of equal importance. These are the means which Pius IX. in his last speech proposed for the regeneration of modern society, and they are the only efficacious ones : prayer for the conversion of those who have gone astray, diligence and ability for instructing and forming the minds of the ignorant, and a practically Christian education of youth given by father and mother.

This is the will of Pius IX. to all the Catholics on the face of the world. And we, as faithful sons of the great Pius, cannot show our fidelity and reverence better than by earnestly endeavoring to execute with conscientious exactitude this his last will. It is needless to ask what good will be obtained by it, and when and where the results will show themselves. We do not respect the effects so much, nor do we judge by them alone. The standard for judging the work of a man is the greatness and the purity of his intentions, and his conscientiousness in the fulfilment of duty. Thus history has thrown open the portals of the hall of fame to Leonidas, who fought without success in the very shade made by the Persian arrows, and branded with ignominy the noble Ephialtes, who successfully betrayed the Spartans. Let us do our duty, and God will take care of the rest. The last words of Pius IX. were : " I place my trust not in men nor in princes, nor in fleets nor in armies, but in Him who, when he has begun the work, knows how to perfect it."

In Pius IX. we have lost a great pilot, but the

helm of the bark of Peter is still steady. Another has taken it, and will direct it with a strong arm to the day of Jesus Christ, when a just Judge will take away the diadem from the brow of him who was successful on earth, to adorn him who, though he met with no success, stood up for the cause of right and truth.

CHAPTER III.

THE words of our blessed Redeemer were to be applied to his representative upon earth : " Ye know not the day nor the hour." Pius IX. was always ready for death ; his life, so pure, so holy, was one unbroken preparation for death.

But to the faithful, to his children, the death of Pius IX. came like a flash of lightning from the clear sky, like a thief in the night. They had a well-founded hope that the holy father would be preserved to the Church and her love for at least one more year. For he had safely passed through the winter, and revigorating spring had already set in.

When in the spring of the previous year pilgrims from all parts of the globe went to Rome, spending many instructive and at once pleasant evenings in the Palazzo Altemps, seeing the holy father in the Sala Ducale or in the Hall of the Consistory, hearing his strong and sonorous voice, and receiving his blessing —no one suspected that they were the last great band of pilgrims whom Pius IX. was to bless. No sooner had the pious travellers returned to their homes than a strong desire awakened within them to return once more to the gray-haired pontiff, and to give public testimony of their love for him to the whole world.

But Divine Providence, whose ways are not the ways of men, had determined otherwise. Even at the time when the holy father gave those imposing audiences his feet refused to render service, although in other respects he was in excellent health. This condition continued during the great heat of summer, which always had a wholesome effect upon him. From the end of November till Christmas he lost in bodily strength, while his mental faculties continued in full vigor despite the burden of old age.

At the opening of the new year, the health of the holy father seemed to undergo a change for the better. To the joy of all who had the good fortune to see him, his vital power seemed to increase day by day. The wound, which in the beginning of his sickness had closed, now assumed its unalarming aspect, and his health was wholly satisfactory. He rose from his bed, to which he had been confined for many weeks. To go to his private library he no longer made use of his movable bed which had been sent to him as a Christmas present by a lady of Paris, through Cardinal de Falloux, but of the sedan-chair in which, a summer before, he allowed himself to be carried into the Loggia of the court of St. Damaso, or into the Hall of the Consistory, to give audience to the faithful Romans and to the pilgrims from far and near.

It was about the middle of January when a Roman paper, edited by a Jew, published the sensational report that the Pope had died. This paper, which the holy father usually read, came within his reach. He read the notice of his own death, smiled, and said, " If that had been written about my feet, it would not be altogether wrong ; but of my head it cannot as yet be said."

The famous Professor Ceccarelli, the Pope's physician in ordinary, had hopes even of gradually curing the trouble in his feet. And truly the realization of these hopes seemed to draw nearer when on Candlemas-day the holy father was able to give audience, and when on the 3d of February he succeeded, with the support of two domestic prelates, in taking a few steps. Great was the astonishment of the bystanders, and greater still their joy at the happy result of the attempt ; for many of them had abandoned all hope of his ever again obtaining the use of his feet. The holy father, too, was overjoyed at this unlooked-for result. "And now," he said, raising his eyes to heaven, " now I pray God for one thing more : that in his infinite generosity he would grant me strength enough to fall down on my knees to thank him."

On the same day he received in his private library, adjoining his sitting-room, some few representatives, several cardinals and prelates. The same happened on Monday and Tuesday, when many persons of high rank congratulated him on his recovery. On Wednesday, too, he continued to give audiences, although the first symptoms of a relapse began to show themselves. On Wednesday evening he took a frugal supper as usual, and, according to his physician's advice, he went to his night's rest at an hour somewhat earlier than he had been accustomed to when he enjoyed good health.

The room in which Pius IX. exchanged the temporal for the eternal is the one in which he had lived since 1870. It is small and of rectangular form. Everything in it is most simple. The tapestry and carpets, as also the furniture, show anything but luxury and splendor.   Near the wall stand two beds, which the holy father used alternately.   In the middle of the room is a writing-table of dark wood, which has much the appearance of a piano.   On it lay a few objects of devotion.   On the wall near the bed are hung two little oil-paintings, one of them representing St. Joseph, the other a madonna, which he had brought with him from his native city, Sinigaglia, and to which he had a special devotion.

At ten o'clock in the evening, Professor Ceccarelli, to whom the precious health of the holy father was entrusted, paid him a visit.   He found nothing in the pontiff's condition that might cause anxiety. His pulse, however, was somewhat slower and more feeble ; but to this he attached no importance. The Pope, it is true, was a little exhausted, but, as ever, he received and dismissed his physician in a cheerful manner.   After a few hours of restless sleep he awoke with a fever.   He called his chamberlain, who slept in an adjoining apartment, and complained of a heavy pressure on the chest and of great exhaustion.   The attendant sent in haste for Doctor Ceccarelli, who came and found the holy father in a chill and in danger of a stroke of apoplexy.   His Holiness could speak but with great effort ; the beating of his pulse was faint and so rapid that it could hardly be counted ; the breathing was laborious. The wound on his foot had healed up.   The few words which the Pope uttered showed that he had fallen into a slight delirium.

A few moments later, the doctors Valentini and Antonini and a few domestic prelates of his Holiness made their appearance in the sleeping-apartment. Gradually the Pope came again to the full use of his senses ; he cast a glance about him, recognized the prelates, and attempted to say something, but the asthma rendered his effort vain. At two o'clock the fever increased ; the Pope fell into a gentle slumber, which seemed to strengthen him somewhat. Many of the courtiers knelt at his bedside, sending fervent prayers to God to preserve their beloved father.

At three o'clock they brought to the sick pontiff a little refreshment, which for some time seemed to give him new life. Two hours later critical symptoms manifested themselves ; the pulsation became rapid and the breathing laborious, to the grief and alarm of those who were present.

CHAPTER IV.

On the morning of the 7th of February, when the sun lit up the sick-room of the holy father, the silver-haired sufferer knew that on the next day not the sun of time but that of eternity would rise for him.

At half-past six o'clock a violent fever again seized him, lasting but for a short time, and not as long as on the previous occasion. The lethargy into which he had fallen during the last hours of the night had entirely disappeared and given place to a full consciousness. The pulse was rapid and faint ; the bronchial tubes were impeded ; his condition became at every moment more critical.

Those who knelt at his bedside prayed with sobs and tears, and clung to the last ray of hope ; their hearts so devotedly attached to Pius IX. could not harbor the thought of the possibility of losing him.

The holy father, however, to whom, together with a clear consciousness, was given the use of his speech, felt that his last day had dawned, and that when night would come over the Eternal City he would be able to say with the Apostle of nations, " I have finished my career." This he clearly expressed in a manner free from all ambiguity. When Cardinal de Falloux inquired about the state of his health, and endeavored to inspire him with hopes of recovery, the sufferer replied : " Questa volta bisogna andarsene" (This time I must go).

He asked at once for his confessor, Monsignor Marinelli, pastor of the papal palace, made his confession, and requested that the sacraments for the dying should be administered to him. At half-past eight o'clock Mgr. Marinelli brought him the Holy Viaticum. What an auspicious moment! The dying saint once more gathered all his strength, raised himself up as he was wont during his former sickness, said the usual prayers himself, and received the Body of our Lord with such devotion and such fervor that he seemed more an angel than a man. The invisible and the visible heads of the Church for the last time embraced one another here below.

He fell back on his pillow ; a sweet seraphic smile played about his lips, a celestial brightness lit up his countenance. He prayed ; prayed for himself and for his Church : for himself for strength and vigor against the powers of darkness, that in the last moments he might not succumb to those against whom he had stood like a hero during his whole life ; for his Church that she might be firm in her trials, and that she might be enabled to serve God in peace and liberty.

At nine o'clock Mgr. Marinelli administered to him Extreme Unction. The holy father had the full use of his senses. The beating of his pulse now became weaker at every moment, and at eleven o'clock it was no longer noticeable in the right arm.

Meanwhile the Cardinal-Vicar, Monaco la Valetta, had given orders to all the parish churches in Rome to expose the Blessed Sacrament, and to offer up prayers for the preservation of the beloved head of the Church.

All Rome repaired to the churches and to the Vatican. But God left the prayers unheard ; for in the decrees of infinite wisdom, the life of Pius IX. had come to a close. The silver-haired Pius was ripe for the harvest, for the crown of the confessor and the palm of the martyr.

His last lingering hours upon earth were wholly absorbed in God. He uttered but few words, and not without great pain, pausing frequently. They formed his last religious exercises, so highly edifying not only on account of the great exertion with which they were spoken, but especially because of the great and unshaken confidence in God by which they were dictated. He to whom it was given to hear his last words could but take them as flames ascending from the heart of a saint—all resignation, all patience, all deeply-rooted piety, to the very last.

The last hour was at hand. The remedies which had been administered to rouse nature had but momentary effects ; the skill of the physicians could no longer stay the disease in its course. A paralysis of the lungs now threatened the life of the august sufferer. Towards eleven o'clock, the pulse in the left hand died away ; the hands and feet turned cold. At half-past eleven he cast a long and loving glance at those kneeling in the apartment, as if he would bid them a last farewell. Then he took his crucifix from under his pillow, blessed all, and holding the image of the Saviour in his hand, he sank back.

CHAPTER V.

ABOUT twelve o'clock, the medical attendants of his Holiness declared that his breathing had become abnormal. The hands were swollen with blood, and his feet were cold and motionless. The eventful moment which like a double-edged sword pierced the hearts of nearly three hundred millions of Catholics was rapidly approaching. His Eminence Cardinal Bilio, who in his capacity of Grand Penitentiary of St. Peter's had the privilege of reciting the prayers over the dying pontiff, began the recommendation of the noble soul of Pius into the hands of its Creator. The holy father, whose strength was fast ebbing away, answered, and with difficulty succeeded in repeating distinctly the words, " Col vestro santo ajuto" (With thy holy help), which occur in the act of contrition.

Whilst Cardinal Bilio interrupted for a moment the recitation of the prayers, the holy father said, with an expression in which the whole of his great soul seemed to be concentrated : " In domum Domini ibimus" (We shall go into the house of the Lord), which was verified a few moments later.

The Grand Penitentiary then continued, amid the loud sobs and weeping of the bystanders, the touching prayers of the Church. When he came to the prayer which begins with the words "Proficiscere, anima christiana" (Depart, Christian soul), he paused and cast an inquiring look towards the holy father, who then spoke for the last time and said, "Si, proficis-

CARDINAL BILIO.

cere" (Yes, depart), by which he wished to indicate his desire of having also this last prayer recited over him. The cardinal then pronounced, in a voice which plainly betrayed the deep emotion of his heart, the "Proficiscere," by means of which the Church delivers into the merciful hands of God the soul standing on the brink of eternity, and which is at the same time a recommendation of the Church militant to the Church triumphant. The solemnity and impressiveness of this moment beggars all description. The

THE LAST BLESSING.

Page 37.

angels themselves, were they to attempt it, could but say in angelic accents, " Pius IX. is dying." It was now three o'clock in the afternoon. Cardinal Bilio and Mgr. Marinelli remained constantly at the bedside of the holy father, suggesting pious ejaculatory prayers. Once more he lifted his consecrated hands in benediction over the bystanders. It was the last blessing of Pius IX.

About four o'clock the agony began ; a thick clammy perspiration covered the brow of his Holiness, and a rapidly increasing rattle announced in unmistakable language that the end was near at hand. The death-chamber now presented a most harrowing spectacle.

At five o'clock the attending physician, Professor Ceccarelli, called upon Cardinal Bilio to recite once more the prayer " Proficiscere" over the dying pontiff. Pius IX. was expiring. A few moments after the recitation of this prayer, the Grand Penitentiary began to recite on bended knees the sorrowful mysteries of the rosary, to which the attendants answered with sobs and weeping. The eyes of the holy father, which can never be forgotten by those whose happiness it has been to behold them, on account of the indescribable mildness which beamed from them, were raised towards heaven, and remained fixed as if in ecstasy till the shadows of death clouded their earthly vision forever.

When they had reached the fourth mystery, the rattle ceased, and the last clear pearly tear appeared in the eye of the venerable father. Pius IX. had run his course ; he had finished the battle, and exchanged this vale of tears for the happy abode of the heavenly Jerusalem. It was 5.40 in the afternoon, and the Ave Maria rang in silvery peals from the dome of St.

Peter's. Whilst the faithful on earth saluted at the close of day the virgin spouse of the Holy Spirit, the angels in heaven imprinted upon the brow of the great Pius the kiss of glad welcome. After a struggle of more than half a century, he departed this life like the sun which just then greeted the cross of St. Peter's with his last golden beams. He disappeared from the sight of men with that serenity of soul, that peace and amiability, characteristic of favored souls, in full consciousness of the important step he was about to take, and with a heart full of the love of God, and as resigned as if there were but a step between heaven and earth.

Pius IX. was no more. But his death could not be realized by those who had seen him dying. All seemed like a dream. When, however, Cardinal Bilio, in low and mournful accents, intoned the " Requiem æternam dona ei Domine," etc., the whole weight of grief which till then had almost crushed the hearts of the bystanders was made manifest in all its intensity. The more fondly they had clung to hope, the more bitter proved their disappointment. They covered their faces with their hands and wept bitterly. In the antechamber of the papal palace the representatives of the foreign powers accredited to the Holy See, many prelates and the foremost of the Roman nobility, and others who had access to the papal court, had gradually gathered. Here knelt, side by side, ambassadors and servants, cardinals and simple citizens, Roman princes and Scopatori Secreti, without distinction of rank or title. Love and sorrow ignore ceremonies ; they are the language of the heart. Mgr. Clifford, Bishop of Clifton in England, recited the rosary, to which the bystanders answered with deep emotion. The door which led to the private chamber of the holy father now opened. A private chamberlain of his Holiness stepped forward and breathed with faltering voice over the assembled multitude the words, "Il papa è morto" (The Pope is dead).

This announcement had an effect similar to a spark of fire cast into a mine. The tears hoarded up

CARDINAL AMAT.

during many a long hour now burst forth with the impetuosity of a torrent ; none could resist them. Some sprang to their feet and ran hither and thither as if their hearts would break ; others remained standing as if petrified, while others again rushed into the death-chamber in order to cover the cold hands of the holy father with kisses.

Pius had ceased to live. The ambassadors left

the Vatican ; the Camerlengo, Cardinal Pecci, Bishop of Perugia, entered upon his office of temporal ruler during the vacancy, while the oldest of the cardinal-bishops, Amat, the oldest cardinal-priest, Schwarzenberg (in his absence, Asquini), and the oldest cardinal-deacon, Caterini, divided among themselves the spiritual government of the Church.

The announcement of the Pope's death was communicated to all foreign cardinals and nuncios, as also to his relatives, by telegraph from the office of the Vatican.   His Eminence the Cardinal-Vicar ordered that the exposition of the Blessed Sacrament, before which the faithful of Rome were still kneeling in supplication, should cease.

At six o'clock, the physicians who had had the privilege of assisting the holy father during his sickness approached the bed of the dead pontiff, and testified to his decease by the following document :

" We, the undersigned, certify that his Holiness, our holy father, Pope Pius IX., for a long time affected with a lingering bronchitis, died of pulmonary paralysis this 7th day of February, 1878, at 5.40 P.M.

> " Doctor ANTONINI, Physician.
> "   CECCARELLI, Surgeon.
> "   PETACCI, Assistant.
> "   TOPAI, Assistant."

A few moments later, the body of the deceased pontiff was conveyed to a larger apartment that had a northern exposure, where it was given in charge of the Noble Guards.   Meanwhile the penitentiaries of St. Peter's chanted the office of the dead in the adjoining rooms.

On the same evening the Cardinal-Vicar an-

CARDINAL SCHWARZENBERG.

Page 43.

nounced the death of Pius IX. in the following circular :

" *To the Clergy and People of Rome :*

" Raphael, of the title of Santa Croce in Gerusalemme, Cardinal-Priest of the Holy Roman Church, Monaco la Valetta, Vicar-General, Judge Ordinary of Rome and its district, and Abbot Commendatory of Subiaco. The majesty of the omnipotent God has recalled to himself the sovereign pontiff Pius IX., of blessed memory, according to the sad news just imparted to us by the most eminent Camerlengo of the Holy Roman Church, to whom it belongs to make known to the public the death of the Roman pontiffs. At such an announcement, the Catholic people in every part of the world, devoted to the great and apostolic virtues of the immortal pontiff and his sovereign magnanimity, will weep. But, above all, are we most supremely sorrowful ; we, O Romans ! since to-day has unhappily terminated the most extraordinary and glorious pontificate which God has ever conceded to his vicars upon earth.

" His life as pontiff and as sovereign was a series of widespread benefits as well in the spiritual as in the temporal order, diffused over all the churches and nations, and in a most particular manner upon his Rome, where at every step monuments of the munificence of the lamented pontiff and father are met with.

" In accordance with the sacred canons, in all the cities and important places solemn obsequies and suffrages for the soul of the departed pontiff should be made until the Holy Apostolic See be provided with a new head, and prayers should be made to the Divine Majesty for the speedy election of a successor to the deceased, whom we can never sufficiently lament.

" For this purpose—

" (1) It is made known that the public and solemn funeral will be celebrated by the canons of the Patriarchal Basilica of the Vatican, to which the body of the immortal pontiff will be brought and placed, as is customary, in the Chapel of the Most Holy Sacrament.

" (2) It is ordered that in all the churches of this holy city, the clergy, secular as well as regular, whatever be their privileges, shall toll all the bells for the space of one hour, from three to four in the afternoon of to-morrow (Friday).

" (3) As soon as the precious remains of the sovereign pontiff are brought into the Vatican basilica, the solemn obsequies will be celebrated in all the churches already mentioned.

" (4) The reverend clergy, secular as well as regular, are exhorted to offer the unbloody sacrifice in suffrage for the soul of the august departed, and the religious communities of both sexes, as well as the faithful, are invited to recommend his blessed soul in their prayers.

" (5) Finally, it is prescribed that in each of the churches mentioned, in the mass and other functions, there be added the collect *Pro Pontifice eligendo* as long as the vacancy of the Apostolic See shall continue.

" Given from our residence, the 7th of February, 1878.

"R. CARD. MONACO, Vicar.
PLACIDO CAN. PETACCI, Secretary."

CHAPTER VI

WHEN on September 20th, 1870, the Bersaglieri had entered Rome through the breach of the Porta Pia ; when Rome, after a short but heroic resistance, had fallen into the hands of the revolutionists ; when the Pope, robbed of his estate, sat a prisoner in the Vatican—the enemies of the Church rejoiced and hoped that the Roman people would in a short time forget their lawful sovereign, and would hail as their deliverer him to whom the irony of fate had given the surname of the man of honor, or " the gentleman-king."

That the boasting of these infidels proved futile is proved by the late events in Rome with such evidence of facts as madness and total blindness alone could deny. Such is the power of great events that by their means the thoughts, sentiments, and secrets of the heart, which otherwise would not have assumed a visible and tangible form, become manifest to the eyes of all. This power the death of the great pontiff Pius IX. exercised over the hearts of the Roman people. When we speak here of the Roman people, we mean those of " royal " Rome in opposition to " legal " Rome, which emigrated from Upper Italy, Sicily, and Naples, and tarries in the city of the seven hills, but through whose veins no Roman blood courses.

The sword of sorrow which pierced the heart of the Roman people at the death of Pius IX. has revealed the innermost secrets of their hearts. When on the morning of February 7th, at about ten o'clock, the bells of Rome rang for the exposition of the Blessed Sacrament, anxious inquiries were made by every one as to its significance. The faithful entered the churches and saw the Blessed Sacrament covered with a veil, as is prescribed when devotions for the dying are taking place. Who could this dying person be?

Like wildfire the news of the dangerous condition of the holy father spread from St. Peter's to the Porta Pia, and from the Piazza del Popolo to the Lateran. But as the Roman people, even more than those of other countries, had been so frequently alarmed by false reports of death, the news at first found but few believers. When, however, the rumor was confirmed by the announcement of the pastors, who had been ordered by the Cardinal-Vicar to hold these devotions, every one flocked to the church in order to beseech the Lord to prolong the precious life of the holy father. Scarcely an hour had elapsed, before the churches were crowded to excess with weeping and sobbing people.

Others, however, could find no rest at the thought that the life of the holy father was seriously endangered. They left their work and hurried towards St. Peter's, where, alas! the sad news was but too soon confirmed. The Roman nobility, who during the Piedmontese government had manifested a loyalty towards their legitimate sovereign, the holy father, which entitles them to the gratitude of the whole Christian world, now hurried towards the Vatican in order to obtain more definite information with regard to the condition of the holy father, and to convey to his Holiness the expression of their heartfelt sympathy. The number of princely carriages wending their way towards St. Peter's was so great that the passage across the bridge leading to the castle of St. Angelo was for a time impeded. The multitude in the church of St. Peter's and in front of the gate which leads by the colonnade of Bernini into the Vatican increased momentarily. Every one who came out through this gate was detained and overwhelmed with questions concerning the condition of the holy father. The Swiss Guard had closed the larger gates and permitted the smaller ones only to remain open, in order to avoid all disturbance in the crowd. One of the highest officers of the guard was constantly present to give the necessary commands. All who belonged to the papal palace were allowed to enter ; to all others admittance was strictly refused. Whoever had reached the antechamber of the papal palace was unable to leave the Vatican until the death of the holy father had taken place.

As early as three o'clock the Secretary of the Italian Cabinet, Della Rocca, informed the ministers that the Pope had died at 2.30, and the " Agenzia Stefani," which claims to receive its information always from the most reliable sources, was guilty of the unqualified silliness or wickedness of announcing the death of his Holiness to the world three hours before it had taken place.

But the Roman people did not credit any of these reports. They went by thousands to St. Peter's, and would not believe the sad news until they had heard it from one who came out of the Vatican, so strong was their attachment to Pius IX.

The news of the death of the beloved pontiff spread during the same evening throughout the greater part of the city, and was everywhere received by the populace with the same manifestation of sincere sorrow and sympathy. The theatres, which during the carnivals are constantly filled, were now empty and deserted. The mourning was universal.

As soon as the morning of the 8th February dawned, small groups might be seen in front of every church. What were they doing? They read the official announcement of the death of Pius IX. by the Cardinal-Vicar Monaco. We have already given the text of this document. Rome gave on this day— we refer to it with pride and joy—a most brilliant testimony in favor of Pius IX., a testimony the more valuable as it was a spontaneous outpouring of its heart, not urged by any worldly consideration. During the whole of February 8th, and also during part of the following day, all the stores and shops of the city remained closed, and this without any order from the police, as had been the case at the death of Victor Emmanuel. The signs of mourning were visible in all the great streets of Rome; even the Jews in Ghetto would not allow themselves to be out· done in their manifestation of attachment to his Holiness. Their doors remained closed during two whole days.

Even the royal court in the Quirinal interested itself in the condition of the holy father. King Humbert I. as well as Queen Pia of Portugal, who had come to Rome to assist at the obsequies of her father, Victor Emmanuel, sent their attendants to the Vatican to inquire about the health of the holy father.

The king, as soon as he had learned the death of his Holiness, broke off a soirée with the ambassador of Austria.

The conduct of the government, on the other hand, though not positively hostile, was indifferent in the highest degree. It did nothing but what it was obliged to do by the laws of the guarantees, and this in such a manner as to render evident the baseness of its sentiments. It did not close the theatres until the evening of February 8th, although it had learned the death of the holy father on the previous evening at six o'clock. It closed the Exchange but for one day, and ordered that the public military concerts which took place for the amusement of the pleasure-seekers, in the gardens on the heights of the Pincio, should be suspended till further notice.

From three to four o'clock of February 8th, all the bells of Rome were tolled as if they would plead for prayers for the eternal repose of the great Pius. This sad and melancholy ringing of the bells was the expression of universal mourning which the death of Pius IX. had caused throughout the Eternal City. Pius IX. had, during his life, created an enthusiasm far more widespread than that created in France by Napoleon I. during the first decade of the present century. The sorrow, however, with which his death was lamented was, if possible, still more universal ; since every heart which can value magnanimity and true worth lost in Pius IX. its most perfect model and ideal.

CHAPTER VII.

AT eight o'clock on the evening of February 8th, the members of the papal palace and other officers of the Holy See called on his Eminence Cardinal Pecci, Camerlengo of the Holy Roman Church. He immediately left his room and went to the hall where the dead pontiff lay, in order to perform the act of the recognition of the corpse. His Eminence was followed by the clerics of the Apostolic Chamber; the Major-domo, Monsignor Macchi, Monsignors Casali del Drago and della Volpe, private chamberlains of his Holiness.

When they had arrived in the hall, they threw themselves on their knees at the bed upon which rested the mortal remains of Pius IX., and adored in all humility of heart the inscrutable disposition of Divine Providence. After his Eminence Cardinal Pecci had finished a prayer, he arose, approached the bier, and struck the brow of the dead pontiff three times with a silver mallet, pronouncing each time the following words: "Holy father, Pius IX.;" then he turned to his attendants and declared that Pius IX. was dead, and forthwith intoned the "De profundis," to which the attendants responded with deep emotion. He repeated once more the absolution, and sprinkled the countenance of his Holiness with holy water.

Then Mgr. Pericoli, Clerk of the Chamber and Dean of the College of Apostolic Protonotaries, knelt at the bedside of the dead Pontiff and read the following recognition of the corpse, which we translate from the original :

THE CAMERLENGO WITH THE SILVER MALLET.

"This morning, February 8th, at eight o'clock, Cardinal Pecci, Chamberlain of the Holy Roman Church, accompanied by the clerks of the chamber, by Mgr. Vice-Chamberlain, by Mgr. Auditor of the Reverend Chamber, by the Advocate-General of the Apostolic Chamber, by the Procurator-General, and by the secretaries and chancellors of the above said chamber, was conducted into the private rooms of his Holiness, in one of which he found upon the bed of death the corpse of his Holiness.   The death of the holy father being established, and the prayers for the occasion recited on behalf of his blessed soul, his Eminence demanded of Mgr. Macchi, his Holiness's Master of the Chamber, the Ring of the Fisherman, which by the same Mgr. Macchi was immediately delivered to the Chamberlain, who received it, hereafter to present it in the first congregation of car-

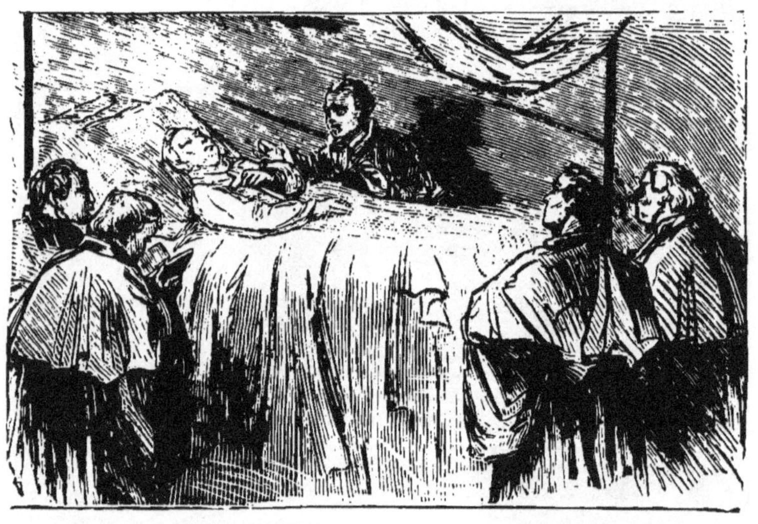

THE INSPECTION OF THE CORPSE.

dinals, for which ring his Eminence gave a receipt to the aforesaid Monsignor, Master of the Chamber.

"After that, at the request of the Cardinal Chamberlain, a solemn act of these proceedings was drawn up and signed by Mgr. Pericoli, Clerk of the Chamber and Dean of the College of the Apostolic Protonotaries ; the said act being attested by the Most Eminent and Most Reverend Chamberlain, by the others above named, and by two of the private chamberlains of the late pontiff, the Rev. Mgrs. Casali del Drago and della Volpe being witnesses thereto.

" Adhering to the injunctions of the Most Eminent and Most Reverend Chamberlain to the clerks of the Apostolic Chamber, these have met together before the same Most Reverend Eminence, and, in accordance with the ancient customs, divided the different duties between them."

At this solemn act there were present, besides the above-named personages, Mgr. Vanutelli, substitute of the secretary (brother of the Nuncio in Belgium), the Princes Barberini and Altieri, commanders of the Noble Guard.

His Eminence Cardinal Pecci hereupon left the death-chamber and returned to his own apartments.

The cherished remains of the holy father rested upon an iron bed, covered with red silk and a white coverlet, so that only his head could be seen. The countenance, which during the last few hours of his life had been somewhat contracted on account of excessive pain, took again all the expression of superhuman kindness with which it had shone in life, and, instead of inspiring terror, drew to itself with irresistible force every one who approached.

During the night between the 8th and 9th of February the process of embalming took place. Professor Ceccarelli, to whom this function had been intrusted, was attended by the three physicians who had assisted him during the sickness of the holy father. The other medical attendants of the palace, Drs. Battistini, Melata, Sciarra, Capparoni, and Prima, also took part. The embalming began at eight o'clock, and was completed at four o'clock next morning. It was performed by means of injection, as also by means of preserving the separated viscera.

The result was so favorable, that even on the sixth day not the slightest sign of decay could be detected. This was the more desirable, since the entire failure of the embalming of Victor Emmanuel was still fresh in the memory of all.

About ten o'clock the investment of the dead pontiff began. One hour afterwards the rooms were opened, and the body of the great Pius was offered to the veneration of his faithful children. Long ere this many persons who had access to the Vatican had waited in anxious expectation in the antechamber. They entered and crowded around the dead pontiff, touched his body with sacred objects, and knelt in prayer at his side. The tears, which trickled down the cheeks of all, spoke more eloquently than words of the love felt for Pius IX.

There he rested upon the bier, decorated with red silk, clothed in his ordinary white garments, and in the mozetta, a dark red cape ; the head was covered with the camauro, a dark velvet beretta. His arms were crossed upon his breast, his hands were white as snow. A heavenly peace shone from his countenance. Mildness, amiability, attractiveness, seemed to have descended from heaven upon the countenance of Pius IX. His features were those of the just man who has fallen asleep in the peace of the Lord, enjoying a foretaste of the heavenly glory ; his cheek was transparent as wax, and around his lips played a heavenly smile. The hand which had never tired of doing good, and had never trembled in defending the rights of the Church, rested cold and lifeless on his breast ; but the crucifix, the last hope and refuge of him who believes and loves, was still clasped in sacred embrace as an assured pledge of a glorious resurrection,

THE BIER.

Page 57.

The bier of Pius IX. was surrounded by every thing symbolic of love and veneration, as well as expressive of sorrow and grief. In the streets and public places of Rome, as in the Vatican, the 8th and 9th of February beheld an unbroken succession of testimonials of love and veneration for Pius IX. His mortal eye could no longer see them, but with the eyes of the spirit he looked down upon his devoted children from the heights of heaven, and poured into many a sorrow-stricken heart the balm of consolation and hope.

Words cannot express the grief which was manifested around the bier of the holy father, when, at four o'clock, the Duke de Witten announced the order of the Major-domo, Mgr. Ricci, that all should leave the death-chamber. It became almost necessary for the Guard of Honor, which watched over the sacred remains, to use violence in order to execute the command. The doors were closed and entrance refused. Yet every now and then distinguished persons, Romans as well as foreigners, called and begged to be allowed to kiss once more the feet of his Holiness. How sad was their disappointment when they found the doors closed! Slowly, silently, and with weeping eyes they went home, as if the cherubim had closed to them the gates of Paradise.

CHAPTER VIII.

THE TRANSLATION OF THE REMAINS.

AT four o'clock on the evening of February 9th, the venerated body of the great Pius was clothed in the episcopal vestments, and placed upon a bier provided for the purpose of conveying the body from the Vatican palace to the adjoining Basilica of St. Peter.

After the lapse of one hour, admission to the consistorial hall was again granted. There the holy father was, for a few hours longer, the object of veneration for many persons of high rank, who had hitherto been prevented from kissing his feet in loving remembrance.

Here he rested, the golden mitre upon his head, the hands folded upon his breast, and the image of his Lord and of his own life clasped in loving embrace.

In the meantime those who were about to take part in the procession had gathered in the hall and in the adjoining chambers. The clock of St. Peter's struck half-past six, when the pall-bearers took up the venerated remains of the beloved holy father, and the procession began to move.

At the head marched the pages, clothed in red velvet ; these were followed by the clergy, bearing

FUNERAL PROCESSION.

Page 61.

fighted tapers in their hands. On both sides the Swiss Guards, the most devoted attendants of Pius IX., marched with slow and solemn step, dressed in their peculiarly striking uniform. After these came the mace-bearers, dressed in Spanish costumes, and the officers of the Swiss Guards.

Then followed the bier upon which rested the remains of the immortal Pius IX., borne by the Palafrenieri, clothed in red velvet, surrounded by the Papal Guard of Honor, and the Penitentiaries of the Vatican Basilica, also bearing lighted tapers in their hands.

Behind the bier followed his Eminence Mgr. Ricci, Major-Domo ; Mgr. Macchi, Maestro di Camera ; Mgr. Saminiatelli, Papal Almoner ; the Mgrs. Negrotto, Casali del Drago, di Bisogno, and della Volpe, private Chamberlains, and Mgr. Vanutelli, substitute of the Secretary of State. These were followed by the laics, functionaries at the Vatican palace ; the Marquis Sachetti, Lord High Steward, the Marquis Serlupi, and Commendatore Fillipani, Chief Cup-bearer.

The next group consisted of the Duke of Castelvecchio, General of the Noble Guard, Prince Altieri, Colonel, and the rest of the officers of the same corps.

After these might be seen, in great numbers, the cardinals of the holy Roman Church, clothed in violet gowns, capes fringed with ermine, and berettas of red silk ; these also bore lighted tapers, and at the same time recited the Psalms.

The College of Cardinals was followed by his Excellency Filippo Orsini, prince assistant at the throne ; Prince Marco Chigi, Marshal of the Conclave ; Prince Ruspoli, Master of the Sacro Ospizio ; a long file of Roman patricians of the highest rank, and by many other noble personages from abroad. The close of the procession was formed by a number of private chamberlains of his Holiness, and a division of the Palatine Guard of Honor.

The overwhelming effect produced by this solemn procession exceeds anything that can be pictured by the most lively imagination. The earnest bearing of the participants, the tapers glimmering through the darkness of the night, the sounds of the prayers dying away in the long corridors and broad vaults of the Vatican palace, the mourning—deep, though resigned—which spoke from every countenance ; all this made a spectacle which took possession of the inmost recesses of the heart ; it was, in a word, a procession such as Torquatus may have seen in the vaults of the Catacombs.

The solemn funeral procession passed along the spacious halls of the Vatican, then through the far-famed galleries of Raphael, through the royal hall, and thence down the broad marble steps, as over so many grand monuments that proclaimed the greatness of the Roman pontiffs.

A great number of Roman citizens who, by a special favor, had obtained admission to the Vatican, had stationed themselves along the walls of the corridors, where with tears in their eyes and with audible sobs they bade a last farewell to their beloved father and king.

At seven o'clock the funeral cortege reached the Chapel of the Most Blessed Sacrament in St. Peter's. The sacred species had been removed to the altar of the crucifixion of St. Peter, situated in the left aisle. The corpse was received with impressive solemnity by the Chapter of the Vatican Basilica, and placed upon the catafalque erected for that purpose.

All the cardinals and ecclesiastical dignitaries who had taken part in the procession arranged themselves in a circle around the catafalque. The choir of the Capella Giuglia intoned the " Libera me Domine ;" the tones burst forth slowly and solemnly, re-echoing from the gigantic pilasters that stood opposite, and, like unto distant thunder, died away in the vaults of St. Peter's. Mgr. Folicaldi, Archbishop of Ephesus and Canon of the Basilica, performed the sacred ceremony of absolution.

All withdrew after taking one more long and affectionate look at the illustrious dead ; the last step died away in the spacious hall ; deep and still deeper the night enveloped the sublime dome of Michael Angelo. Deathlike silence reigned supreme at St. Peter's, interrupted ever and anon by the clank of swords when the detachment of the Papal Noble Guard who kept watch around the bier of their beloved sovereign Pius IX. were relieved.

CHAPTER IX.

THIS silence was but of brief duration. Pius IX., whose life had fallen upon stormy times, was destined to enjoy but a brief repose even in death. The hour of midnight had scarcely sounded from the tower of St. Peter's when voices were heard at the gates. Who dares disturb the rest of the venerable dead, who while alive could have insured silence by a single look? The murmurs grow louder, the voices become more audible. Do they intend to offer violence, to break through the railing and force open the gates?

Yes, they mean to offer violence, but not that rude violence which works only destruction ; but gentle force prompted by great and deep-seated love. Already at the midnight hour the devoted children of Pius stand in front of the bronze gates of St. Peter's, demanding entrance, in order to gaze upon their beloved father, to pray for his repose, to kiss reverently his sacred feet, and to draw courage and hope from his very countenance, though no longer glowing with that fire and animation which illumined it in life, in order to renew their resolve to live and suffer according to his noble and heroic example.

Standing in front of the grated entrance, or seated on the steps of the terrace, the Romans waited from midnight till the break of day, in order to be at the bier of Pio Nono.

Under the left colonnade of Bernini a battalion of infantry was stationed ; the police and a number of carabinieri stood on the terrace in front of the church to insure public order.   However, this demonstration of the Romans in favor of the papal sovereignty was, in its very nature, too peaceable to cause any apprehension of disturbance.

When the dawn of February 10th broke upon the spray of the fountains in the square of St. Peter's, the grated gates of the church were thrown open, and, like a living stream, the assembled mass poured into the spacious vestibule.   This square, which can easily contain two hundred thousand persons, was thronged with hackney coaches and the carriages of nobles ; and along the three avenues which lead to St. Peter's might be seen cabs and escutcheoned carriages, three abreast, winding slowly towards the church.   The whole scene, as viewed from the steps of the terrace, was grand and affecting ; and the thick fog, which seemed to challenge the breaking dawn, was a faithful picture of the deep mourning with which the death of Pius IX. had filled the hearts of the Romans and of the entire Catholic world.   Though the multitude had long to wait, and the morning breeze was chilly, not a word of complaint nor a sound of impatience escaped their lips. The countenances of men and women, of peasant and citizen, of priests and laymen, presented an expression of sincere and deep sorrow, as if they would say to the stranger, who happened to lean against the base of one of the colossal pillars of the façade, view-

ing them with inquiring looks: " Weep with us ;
for our father is dead."

A few minutes before seven o'clock, the bars
were removed, and a prolonged murmur of satisfaction arose from the crowd. The outer door on the
left turned on its hinges ; every one crowded towards it ; but immediately after the door next to it
opened, and thus a part of the multitude found entrance there. At the same time the doors at the
right of the main entrance were thrown open. The
janitors deserve all praise for the great prudence
which they exercised on this occasion ; for it was by
this means that the danger attendant on a crowd of
the kind was averted.

As the multitude entered they beheld at first the
blinding light that streamed from the Chapel of the
Blessed Sacrament into the yet partially dark nave of
St. Peter's. Riveting their gaze upon the spot where
the precious remains rested, they passed by the great
works of art, not deeming them worthy of even a
passing glance, and proceeded to the chapel. There,
towards the left of the grated door, they beheld the
bier of their beloved father.

Upon a bed of state, hung with red velvet, lies
Pius IX., vested in his episcopal robes. The upper
part of the body is somewhat raised, and can be
seen from the middle aisle. He wears violet gloves
interwoven with silver. The bishop's ring glitters
on his finger. Even in death, he clasps in fond embrace the cross, the sign of our undying hopes, which
had ever accompanied him during life. The mitre,
inlaid with gold, adorns his sacred brow. His countenance, whose lineaments death itself could not dis-
tort, beams with majesty and grandeur, and retains
that amiability and sweetness which makes one imag-

THE REMAINS IN THE CHAPEL OF THE BLESSED SACRAMENT.

Page 67.

ine that he stands before the shrine of a saint. His eye, which had so long kept faithful ward from the watch-tower of the Church, to guide the storm-tossed nations from the foaming sea to the rock on which he stood, is closed as if in sleep. The lips, that had uttered the word of forgiveness to many an erring soul, are mute ; but the smile, which in life enchanted all who saw it, still plays around his lips, and even now captivates the beholder ; for it is the expression of his great and loving heart.

On either side of the catafalque hangs a cardinal's hat, adorned with heavy tassels of silk. Four soldiers of the Papal Guard, dressed in a uniform of light and dark blue, a shining helmet surmounted with a white cockade, stand motionless with drawn swords at the four corners of the bier. One of the Swiss Guards, with helmet and halberd, is stationed at the grate which separates the Chapel of the Blessed Sacrament from the grand nave.

The feet of the Pope, covered with slippers of red silk, were extended through the bars of the grate in such a manner that the pious faithful were enabled to kiss them. It was affecting to the highest degree to witness how the devout assembly endeavored to touch the vestments of the holy father with medals, chaplets, crucifixes, rings, and pictures, in order to carry them away in loving and perpetual remembrance.

However, the multitude swelled like a mountain torrent. The carabinieri, who had been stationed in the church, outside the grating of the chapel, were no longer able to withstand the throng. Reinforcements were called in. The people were allowed to enter at one of the two gates on the left side ; a semicircle was formed by the police in front of the grating, so that only two or three persons at a time had room to pass and kiss the feet of his Holiness. They were allowed to tarry for a moment at the bier, to take one sorrowful glance at the beloved features of their dead pontiff, after which they issued from the church at the door on the extreme right. The door on the extreme left, as you enter, was left open for those whose time was too limited to make the pious yet tedious pilgrimage to the feet of the holy father.

To express the exclamations of love and sorrow which escaped from the lips of the faithful as they arrived at the grating, to portray the devotion with which they kissed the feet of their departed father, would require the pen of a Dante and the pencil of a Raphael.

At ten o'clock it was evident that the arrangements made for the preservation of order were insufficient. The multitude grows from minute to minute, and has become a rushing torrent. The carabinieri are powerless to oppose it ; they are swept away by the billows of living beings. At this stage a numerous division of soldiers of the line enter through the door of the sacristy, by permission of Mgr. Theodoli, rector of the church ; these troops separate the multitude, and form in front of the grate behind which the catafalque looms up. All the entrances to the vestibule are closed, with the exception of the second, which answers as an exit. The last grated door to the left is opened from time to time, allowing several thousand people to enter at each opening. From the choir chapel, opposite that of the Blessed Sacrament, where the canons of St. Peter's celebrated divine service, are heard in tones at once earnest and solemn the sounds of the requiem.

At eleven o'clock, St. Peter's place, the adjoining Piazza Rusticucci, the avenues, the bridges, the public squares, all the streets of the Leonine City are closely packed with people and vehicles. All Rome moves towards St. Peter's, in order to bestow a last tribute of veneration upon her father, benefactor, king, and pontiff. The inhabitants of the neighboring cities and villages, who had come to Rome in great numbers, mingled with the throng.

At noon the multitude who have flocked to the bier of Pius IX. exceeds all belief. Perfect order, however, is observed; the behavior of the Roman people is calm and dignified. The solemn requiem mass is over. The bronze statue of St. Peter and the tomb of the Prince of the Apostles are surrounded at all hours by the faithful of every age and condition of life, who, on bended knees, remember in pious supplication their dearly beloved deceased father.

Three o'clock witnesses in the great square of St. Peter's and its surroundings a scene similar to that which was exhibited in former and better times on all the great festivals of the Church. An interminable procession of hackney coaches and princely carriages moves in front of St. Peter's towards Borgo di Santo Spirito and Ponte Sisto, in order to disperse themselves from these points in all directions.

At four o'clock, the throng in front of the grating of the vestibule increases to such an extent that it is resolved, in order to avoid accidents, to close the church. This decision causes great dissatisfaction among the assembled people, since many who had come from Frascati, Albano, Tivoli, and other distant cities, and who had intended to return on the same evening, found themselves disappointed in their hopes of kissing the feet of the holy father.

It would seem as if the number of people flocking to the bier of Pius IX. should have decreased after the first day. But the same spectacle, more imposing even, if possible, took place on the three following days. The soldiers, in order to keep the multitude in check, were obliged to form a double line, extending to the second flight of stairs, and thus let the people file into the church. The terrace and the piazza of St. Peter's were taken possession of, from early morn till late at night, by a vast concourse of people. Even the rain, which fell in great abundance on the 12th of February, was not able to disperse the crowd whose attachment to Pius IX. was unconquerable.

There were witnessed at the bier of the immortal Pius IX. many things calculated to console and edify ; for the days between the 7th and 23d of February were days of a solemn recognition of the papacy. On the other hand, many things caused deep sorrow and grief. The pen is loath to describe them, but truth demands it imperatively.

As the life of Pius IX. had been a portrait of the life of our Lord, Crux de Cruce, so also his bier in St. Peter's presented many striking points of similarity to the sepulchre of our Lord on Mount Calvary.

Victor Emmanuel, King of Italy, had died, on the 9th of January, in the palace of the Quirinal, and was buried in the Pantheon, both usurped from his Holiness. On his deathbed he implored forgiveness of the Pope for all the wrongs · inflicted on the Church. He died with sentiments of sincere contrition, like the penitent thief on the cross. Pius IX. uttered in his behalf the following consoling words :

" May God pardon him, as I also pardon him from the bottom of my heart." After the lapse of one month, the noble Pius followed him to the grave. And now the days of the hero of the island of Caprera, Garibaldi, seem to be numbered. But even if Pius IX. should not, according to the example of his Lord, die in so striking a manner, between two thieves, it will remain true, nevertheless, that the

THE PANTHEON.

tomb of Pius bears unmistakable points of similarity to the sepulchre of our Lord in Jerusalem.

Pilate said to the Pharisees, " You have a guard : go, guard it as you know ; but they going, secured the sepulchre with guards" (Matt. xxvi. 65).

This bier, these guards, carabinieri and sol-diers, whom the government of Italy sent to guard in death him whom during life they had robbed of his royal diadem, remind us vividly of the guard which Pilate stationed at the sepulchre of Him whose vicar Pius IX. had been upon earth.

Insults and rudeness were not wanting around

the bier of him whom the whole world venerates.
Some Italian soldiers, and not a few Italian officers,
conducted themselves, on this occasion, in St. Peter's,
in such a manner as to call upon them the condemna-
tion of all Europe. They used such words to the visitors of the bier of Pius IX. and took such unbecoming liberties as were by no means in conformity
with the decency we naturally expect from officers of
the crown, and were altogether inexcusable when the
sanctity of the place in which they happened is taken
into consideration.

Even a Judas was not wanting at the death of
Pius IX. Marco Minghetti, who, as minister of Pius
IX., had received the Blessed Sacrament from the
pontiff's hand, in confirmation of his oath of loyalty,
and who, a short time afterwards, betrayed him so
shamefully, was also at the bier of Pius IX. Who
knows what sentiments the lifeless countenance of his
sovereign engendered in his soul?

But the consoling personages of the sepulchre
of Christ were also found in St. Peter's on this occasion. During the night many of the Roman nobility, by a special favor of Mgr. Theodoli, approached, like Nicodemus of old, to pay their respect
and veneration to Pius, the Vicar of our Lord. Even
the pious women were not wanting. They touched
the precious remains of the holy father with sacred
objects, which, like Veronica, they carried off, as a
precious souvenir of their beloved pontiff.

Such are the impressions received in these days
at Rome—impressions calculated to cheer the gloomy
hours of a whole lifetime—impressions the more valuable because they proved, with irresistible force, that
the heart of the Roman people points towards St.
Peter's, as the magnet turns towards the pole.

CHAPTER X.

THE entrance into the grandest temple which man has erected in honor of his Creator, is always elevating and impressive. But he who, on the evening of the 13th of February, entered St. Peter's through the small side-door, would be overpowered by a feeling which he himself would not be able to describe. Upon slender iron candlesticks, placed here and there, burned small wax tapers, which lit up the marble floor of St. Peter's with a melancholy effect. Further on glimmered the lamps of the " Confessio," where the sacred body of the Galilean Fisherman reposes, to whom Christ entrusted the guidance of his Church. On either side of him repose many of his glorious successors, whose epitaphs are a compendious history of the world. To these was about to be associated one of the " best hated," but at the same time most affectionately beloved, of Roman pontiffs.

The bier upon which reposed the mortal remains of Pius IX. had been moved into the middle of the Chapel of the Blessed Sacrament. In front of the railing a great number of the Roman nobility and many distinguished foreigners, who had obtained an entrance-ticket, waited anxiously.   They numbered from four to five thousand.

The shades of the approaching night had already begun to shroud the magnificent basilica, when the cardinals, who had assembled at six o'clock in the Hall of the Consistory, entered the chapel.   In passing they kissed the feet of the dead pontiff, as is prescribed by the ritual, making a genuflection at the bier, and then ranged themselves in a circle around the catafalque.   From the sacristy the canons and beneficiaries, together with the choir of the Capella Giuglia, issued two by two.   Having arrived at the bier, Mgr. Folicaldi, Archbishop of Ephesus, clothed in black cope and surplice, besprinkled the venerable corpse with holy water, recited the prescribed prayer, and intoned with faltering voice the " Miserere."   The singers of the Julian Chapel, under the excellent direction of Salvatore Meluzzi, answered with those deep sonorous tones, so characteristic of genuine church-music, and so well calculated to touch the heart and raise it heavenward.

The solemn moment had arrived in which the mortal remains of Pius IX. were to be translated to that place in which every Pope is buried until the death of his successor.

The great silver cross, which headed the procession was followed by the alumni of the Vatican Seminary, bearing lighted tapers and chanting the "Miserere."   The chapter of St. Peter's, with the Arch-priest of the Basilica, Cardinal Edward Borromeo, followed.   Then came the bier, surrounded by the Guard of Honor and a division of the Swiss Guard. The clergy of St. Peter's, the officers of the Guard of Nobles, and the members of the archconfraternity of St. Michael in Borgo, had divided among themselves the honor of carrying the sacred remains of the great Pius to the grave.   Behind the coffin followed their Eminences the Cardinals, the officers of the Vatican Palace, the private chamberlains, and many others whom special ties of love and gratitude

CARDINAL BORROMEO.

had attached to the venerable deceased.   A division of the Palatine Guard of Honor, composed of Roman citizens, closed the solemn funeral cortege.

The procession having issued from the Chapel of the Blessed Sacrament, turned towards the right, in the direction of the tomb of the Prince of the Apostles.   The sounds of the " Miserere" re-echo from the gigantic pillars of the church ; the multitude is on bended knees; the procession moves more and more slowly; the bier stops for a moment in front of the

bronze statue of St. Peter. The first of the long line of popes seems about to bless in his march to the grave the dead Pius, the only one who has surpassed the years of St. Peter.

PIUS IX. LAID IN THE COFFIN.

Page 81.

At the "Confessio," the procession turns again towards the left, going down the middle aisle, and enters the chapel of the choir. The bier is turned in such a manner that the dead pontiff is carried as is prescribed, the head first entering the chapel. There he is placed in the middle, surrounded by numerous clerks. After Mgr. Folicaldi has recited the prayer prescribed in the ritual for such occasions, Mgr. Ricci, Chief Chamberlain, approaches the bier and covers the face of the deceased with a white cloth ; the attendant taking one long fixed look at the amiable features of Pius IX. Many sobs are heard during the pauses which the singers of the Capella Giuglia are wont to make from time to time. Mgr. Martinucci, Papal Master of Ceremonies, spreads a large red silk veil over the entire body of the deceased, whereupon the pall-bearers place the corpse in the first coffin, made of pine wood. The chief steward approaches and deposits in the coffin three red velvet purses containing, respectively, thirty-two golden, thirty-two silver, and thirty-two copper medals, corresponding to the number of years of the reign of Pius. At the feet of the dead pontiff lies enclosed in a metal case a eulogy written on parchment, the work of Mgr. Mercurelli, describing the deeds of his pontificate. A silk ribbon is placed crosswise upon the coffin, sealed with five different seals. Archbishop Folicaldi pronounces the last absolution, the lid of the coffin is put on, and the mortal remains of one of the most glorious Roman pontiffs are hidden forever from the sight of his mourning children.

Whilst Filiberto Pomponi, the chancellor of the chapter of St. Peter's, read a document in which he described all that had transpired since the death of the Pope, the first coffin was placed in a second one made of lead, and the cover was sealed with seven seals. The leaden coffin was adorned with a cross, the coat-of-arms of the Pope without the keys, for these emblems are the signs of a living power, and with the following inscription :

CORPUS

PII IX. P. M.

Vixit. An. LXXXV. M. VIII. D. XXVI.

Eccles. Univer. Praefuit

An. XXXI. M. VII. D. XXIII.

Obiit. Die. VII. Febr. An. MDCCCLXXVIII.

Both coffins were placed in a third one, made of walnut, and were then conveyed from the chapel to their resting-place. This is above the door that leads to the vestry of the choristers, opposite the monument of Innocent VIII. The coffin was raised by means of a mechanical contrivance about twenty feet in the air, and whilst the choir sang the last verse of the Benedictus, *"* Illuminare his qui in tenebris et in umbra mortis sedent, ad dirigendos pedes nostros in viam pacis,'' the coffin disappeared in the wall. The masons began their work, and by nine o'clock the solemn service was concluded. , A simple sarcophagus, upon which rests a tiara, bears on the outside this short inscription :

PIUS IX. P. M.

The diplomatic corps, the wife of the President of the American Republic of Costa Rica, and the *élite* of the Roman nobility were present at the solemnity, and had their seats in the gallery of the chapel. Long after the ceremony the faithful were still seen kneeling before the newly-closed tomb, but their prayer for the repose of the soul of Pius IX. was involuntarily changed into prayer to a saint.

CHAPTER XI.

THE OBSEQUIES.

IT has been the custom for many centuries for the cardinals, before they commence the election of a new pontiff, to spend several days in prayer for the deceased pope. In the year 607, Boniface III. prescribed that no one should take any steps towards the election of a new pontiff until three days had elapsed from the death of his predecessor. This custom was made a law by Gregory X. in the General Council of Lyons, 1274, by a decree in which he prescribed that, after the death of the pope, the cardinals should wait ten days for the arrival of absent electors, and celebrate in the mean time the obsequies of the deceased during nine days. Pius IV. in the year 1562, ratified this funeral service of nine days by the bull "In eligendis," and Gregory XV. in the year 1622 by the bull "Decet Romanum Pontificem," fixed the sum of ten thousand ducats, which the expenses of the obsequies were not to exceed.

In virtue of the decree which the Cardinal Vicar, Monaco, issued on February 7th, masses for the dead were immediately said in all the churches of Rome after the death of Pius IX. They were celebrated with unusual solemnity in the Church of St. Appollinarius, at which the students of the Roman Seminary assisted ; in the German National Church, " All' Anima," where the students of the German College added to the solemnity of divine service by their melodious singing ; and in the church of the Jesuits, where the catafalque erected for the occasion was a real work of art. The requiem masses which the chapter of St. Peter's had ordered for the dead pontiff in the Vatican basilica were likewise conspicuous on account of the great display and numerous donations of the people. At the conclusion of every service the tomb of Pius IX. was surrounded by a throng of faithful, who on their knees prayed for his repose, or rather for his intercession at the throne of God.

The cardinals, for a well-known and obvious reason, declined to hold a solemn requiem in St. Peter's. But the obsequies which the College of Cardinals ordered to be held in the Sixtine Chapel in the Vatican were the more solemn. This chapel was built by Sixtus IV. in 1473, and embellished by the unrivalled paintings of Michael Angelo.

It is in the same domestic chapel of the pope that, before the entrance of the Italian troops into Rome, took place those grand ceremonies which attracted so many thousands of strangers to the Eternal City.

Formerly, during such solemnities, the far-famed tapestries or Arrazzi of Raphael were to be seen, which constitute the greatest art treasure of the Vatican Gallery. But since 1870 these ceremonies had ceased, and strangers were only admitted to admire the sublime productions of Michael Angelo. Even the director of the renowned choir has retired to his beautiful villa at Montefalco, in the much-praised valley of Clitumnus.

On February the 15th, the chapel, after having been closed for seven years, was again opened for the first time, not indeed for the celebration of a joyous and happy festival, but for the obsequies of him who had shown himself so often in this chapel in all his majesty. In the middle of the chapel rose a gigantic catafalque, on which reposed a tiara, the emblem of the papal dignity. The design was a production of the mind of the architect, Martinucci. A forest of candles surrounded the bier, and the following inscriptions adorned the four sides of the catafalque :

Petri Annos
In Romana sede
Unus Superavit.

Optimi Principis
Nomen et Famam
Est Meritus.

Mariam D. M.
Immaculatam.
Rom. Pont. Magisterium
Inerrans.

Beneficentia Ingenio Moderatione
Animos Omnium ad sui
Admirationem erexit.

On the side of the base on which stood the catafalque were exhibited four exquisite bas-reliefs. They represented the oath of allegiance of the Roman senator to the deceased pontiff ; the proclamation of the dogma of the Immaculate Conception ; the beneficence of Pius IX.; and the dead pontiff himself on the bier, in the Chapel of the Blessed Sacrament in St. Peter's.

THE CATAFALQUE IN THE SISTINE CHAPEL.   Page 89.

Towards ten o'clock the seats of the cardinals were almost filled. They appeared not in their scarlet garments, but in their violet mourning-suits and capes of ermine. The Monsignori, who took position behind their Eminences, were not dressed in their festive garments, but in mourning. On both sides of the catafalque stood a detachment of the

CARDINAL DI PIETRO.

Noble Guard in military attitude; whilst the Swiss Guard, under the command of their leader, the Baron Sonnenberg, formed their lines from the entrance to the balustrade. General Kansler, the hero of Mentana, represented, among the Roman nobility those magnanimous and zealous men who had hastened to Rome from all countries, ready to hazard their lives for the father of Christendom.

Outside the balustrade, which divides the Sixtine Chapel, the diplomatic corps took the seats on the left, whilst the ladies of the Roman nobility occupied those on the right.

The funeral service began. His Eminence Cardinal Di Pietro, was the celebrant of the mass. The

CARDINAL SACCONI.

choral song of the requiem was an expression of general mourning, which spread itself over every countenance. The Dies Iræ was a beautiful composition of the director, Mustafa, magnificently and nobly executed, and, with the exception of a few faulty passages, delivered in a masterly way. The sublime words of the Dies Irae, and the Last Judgment, painted by the master hand of Michael Angelo

CARDINAL SIMEONI.

Page 93.

as an altar-piece ; the hopes of the resurrection, which sound to the soul amidst the harmonies, and the ceiling of the Sixtine Chapel, with Buonarotti's preparation for the resurrection—all these must be seen and felt : words can not describe them. The five absolutions, as prescribed for the obsequies of the pope, were pronounced by their Eminences the Cardinals Di Pietro, Sacconi, Guidi, Bilio, and Schwartzenberg.

After the mass the cardinals proceeded to the Consistorial Hall, to receive in public audience the diplomatic corps accredited to the Holy See. The ambassadors of Austria and of Spain had the honor of precedence. They were surrounded by the entire body of their attachés. These were followed by the ministers plenipotentiary of Bavaria, Belgium, Brazil, Costa Rica, and Bolivia, who expressed the condolence of their respective governments to the College of Cardinals on the decease of Pius IX. His Eminence Cardinal Di Pietro, as acting dean of the Sacred College, in the name of his colleagues gave thanks for the sincere sympathy which the represented nations had taken in the general mourning felt for the loss of their chief pastor.

In the afternoon the public reading of the last will of Pius IX. took place in the apartments of Cardinal Simeoni, the late Secretary of State, in presence of the Cardinal Camerlengo, the dean of the apostolic protonotaries, and of some relatives of the deceased pontiff. It comprises twenty-eight pages, bears the date of the year 1875, and is in the Pope's own handwriting. Mgr. Cenni was appointed executor of his last will.

The first article in this testament regards the place of interment and the monument :

" My body shall be interred in the Church of St. Lorenzo, outside the walls, under the arch where the grating protects the stone on which are still to be seen the marks of the martyrdom of the Saint.

The expenses of the tomb shall not exceed the sum of four hundred scudi."

Then follows the direction that the coat-of-arms on the monument should consist of the Pope's insignia and a death's-head.   The epitaph which the holy father wrote with his own hand is the most faithful copy of his life.   It is simple, humble ; and if nothing were to remain for coming centuries to portray the noble character of Pius IX., it alone would be sufficient to reveal the characteristics of his life.   The epitaph reads as follows :

Ossa et Cineres Pii P. IX.
Sum. Pont. Vixit. Annos.
In Pontificatu Ann.
Orate pro Eo.

The mortal remains of Pius IX., Pope.
He lived —— years ; as Pope ——.

The second part of the will embraces the dispositions concerning alms, to be distributed at his death, as also the revenues of the future pope.   To the poor in Rome he left a sum of three hundred thousand francs, and to the officers who, by the fall of Rome, lost the necessaries of life, and had remained loyal to the pope, he left a fund to indemnify them for their loss. To the churches with which he had been connected during life, such as the Vatican and Lateran basilicas, the collegiate church of Sta. Maria in Via Lata, the cathedrals of Imola, Sinigaglia, and Gaeta, he gave especial memorials.   The persons who had remained faithful to him in the days of prosperity as well as adversity are remembered in the following clauses :

" I bequeath to his Royal Highness the Count de Chambord, the Madonna del Destino in mosaic. To her Royal Highness the Duchess of Modena, a Madonna in mosaic. To Queen Isabella of Spain, the Crucifix of Lucca. In token of fatherly benevolence, I leave to his Majesty the King of Naples a silver group representing the Holy Family. To his Imperial and Royal Highness the Grand Duke of Tuscany, a copy of Raphael, with silver frame. To his Royal Highness the Duke of Parma, a large miniature, ' Sinite parvulos.' To his Royal Highness Don Alfonso of Bourbon, formerly a pontifical zouave, a mother-of-pearl representation of the Resurrection. To her Highness the Princess of Thurn and Taxis, the silver cross adorned with diamonds, with two angels having in their hands the symbols of the passion, and with the relic of the holy Cross." In the third and last part of his testament he bequeathed the small remnant of his private property to his relatives in Sinigaglia.

Each word of this will bears witness of the great soul of Pius IX. Even in death he wished to be buried near those whom, not a desire of vain praise, but the power of conviction, had induced to take up arms and to fall with weapons in hand at the Porta Pia as martys of the papacy. Even in death his hand could find no rest till it had given consolation and succor to his favorite children, the poor. Immediately after his death, the sum of one hundred thousand francs was distributed by the Cardinal-Vicar. The rest of the bequest was distributed, by the agreement of the cardinals, among the different charitable institutions of Rome and its environs.

The same funeral services described above were also held during the next two days, the 16th and 17th of February, in the same chapel. In like manner the College of Cardinals received on the following days the ambassadors and plenipotentiaries of the other powers accredited to the Holy See.

CHAPTER XII.

THE following is the official record of the life of Pope Pius IX., prepared by Mgr. Mercurelli, Latin Secretary, and deposited in the tomb with the body of the deceased pontiff :

Here lies the body of Pius IX., sovereign pontiff. He whose body reposes here was born on the 13th of May, 1792, at Sinigaglia, and was the fourth son born of the marriage of Count Girolamo Mastai-Ferretti and the Countess Caterina Solazzi. He was baptized by the name of Giovanni-Maria. He was taught at first in the Seminary of the Fathers of the Scuole Pie in Volterra, and afterwards entered on more advanced studies in Rome. He was promoted to the priesthood in the year 1819, and celebrated his first mass on Easter Sunday in the Church of the Orphan Asylum of St. Anne, called after its founder, Tata Giovanni, and of which he was a director. Afterwards he was appointed as an assistant to Bishop Giovanni Muzi, who had been elected delegate and vicar apostolic for Chili and the other countries of South America, and he left Rome in 1823. But on his return in 1825 he was appointed director of the Apostolic Hospital by Leo XII., of holy memory, and two years later was preconized and consecrated Archbishop of Spoleto.

He was endowed with all the qualities of an excellent bishop, especially those of charity and wisdom, and gave brilliant examples of the fact when, in 1831, he was invested with an extraordinary mission to Spoleto and Perugia, and put an end to the rebellion in those provinces by his urbanity and by aiding the insurgents to quit the country and give up their arms, which he sent to Rome. Also in the following year, when he gave himself up entirely to the solace of the people who were sorely afflicted by the fearful earthquake in Umbria. His remarkable abilities led Gregory XVI. to believe that it would be advisable to transfer him to the See of Imola, then vacant, and there he showed himself in every way worthy of the pastoral charge entrusted to him. He was the first of the Italian prelates to establish canonically in his diocese the Society for the Propagation of the Faith, and to spread its utility. Among other proofs of his courage and episcopal charity he gave a brilliant example of those qualities when in 1846, one evening, as he was engaged in prayer in the cathedral, he saved single-handed the life of a man who was attacked by three brigands. The same pope reserved him *in petto* in the Consistory of the 23d December, 1839, and decorated him with the purple on the 14th December of the following year.

When he was informed of the death of Gregory XVI. he at once went to Rome to take part in the election of the new pontiff, but all the votes were united for him with a marvellous promptitude, and he himself was elevated to the chair of Peter. However, the enemies of religion and of perfect order soon changed into mourning the joy that was universally felt at the announcement of such an unaccustomed event, and arousing a revolt they surrounded the Pope in such a way that it was with difficulty, and only by the special help of God, that he was enabled to escape from their hands and reach Gaeta. The King of Naples received him there with many marks of courtesy and respect. While the whole Catholic universe came to him to testify their feelings of veneration and to lay their offerings at his feet, he turned his thoughts to the evils suffered by our holy religion, to the outraged rights of the Holy See, to the destructive errors which had misled the nations ; and in his allocutions and apostolic letters he bore witness to his feelings and made known to the faithful the deplorable state of religious affairs, implored the succor of Catholic princes, and laid plainly before the people the real nature of the plans designed by the foes of the Church. Besides that, he set about re-establishing in England the ecclesiastical hierarchy, which had for such a long time been destroyed ; and on account of his wondrous piety towards the Mother of God he announced to the episcopate that he had ordered researches to be made for the purpose of defining her Immaculate Conception, and he asked them all to pray for that object with him, and to inform him of the traditions on the point which obtained in their respective countries.

Brought back to Rome by Christians, amidst the acclamations of the city and of the whole world, he evinced no less care for the Eastern Church than for the Western. As in 1847, he had already re-established the jurisdiction of the Latin Patriarch of Jerusalem, and in the following year had confirmed the election of a Patriarch of Babylon for the Chaldeans ; so later on he set himself with an indefatigable zeal to protect, strengthen, and unite the Eastern Churches, torn by schisms, disputes, and dissensions, by framing new rules for their conduct, by increasing the number of bishops, by aiding them in all manner of ways through his liberality, and in sending them even an apostolic delegate and a legate *a latere*.

He left nothing undone in his efforts to stay the persecution of the Catholic religion in Russia, or at least to obtain its mitigation either by the conventions which he proposed, by appeals to the ministers of that empire, by public protests, by special letters to the emperor, or by sending delegates to him ; while during all this time he never ceased to defend and support the Ruthenians and to console the Poles. And as everywhere religious affairs were in dire distress, he used every diligence in stipulating with the greater part of the heads of nations for conventions by which the rights and liberty of the Church might be protected.

He never ceased from exposing, refuting, and condemning in encyclical letters, allocutions, public discourses, letters to bishops or private persons, the errors which are the cause of so much evil, and notably the machinations of the freemasons. He published the celebrated Syllabus, which will remain forever to crush all errors ; and, finally, he convoked and assembled the Œcumenical Council, so that by clearly setting forth and confirming the true doctrine as to God, the Church, and the authority and infallibility of the sovereign pontiff, no ground would be left for sophism.

While he was thus engaged in the struggle against the kingdom of Satan, he applied himself with the

same zeal to spread the kingdom of Christ, to en-
liven the faith and piety of Catholics, and to furnish
them with new celestial help. He re-established the
ecclesiastical hierarchy in England and Holland,
and he was considering its restoration in Scotland
when he became the prey of death. He sent missions to the extremities of the earth ; he approved of
the establishment of a great number of new religious
congregations devoted to the special necessities of
the people ; he particularly protected the Catholic associations instituted for the support of the Church and
the benefit of the neighbor ; to unite more closely
the universal Church to the Sacred Heart of Jesus,
he gave it St. Joseph as patron saint ; among the
Christian heroes whose acts might be an encouragement, and whose patronage might be an assistance,
he inscribed eleven on the list of the Blessed and
fifty-two on the list of the Saints ; and, finally, he
increased confidence in the Mother of God and
added to her glories by the dogmatic definition of
her Immaculate Conception. By these cares he ex-
panded the Church to such a degree that he had to
add, to those already existing, twenty-nine metropolitan sees, one hundred and thirty-two episcopal sees,
three *nullius diœceseos*, three apostolic delegations,
thirty-three apostolic vicariates, and fifteen apostolic
prefectures.

Although subject to a hostile domination, he
always vigorously defended the rights of the Church ;
with an apostolic liberty he censured the powerful for their sacrilegious usurpation, and proclaimed and renewed the censures which he pronounced
against them. He watched over the splendor
of divine worship, and rebuilt, repaired, and orna-
mented the temples with a royal magnificence, or
furnished the money and the sacred ornaments for

that purpose both at home and abroad. He proposed a new *Ratio Studiorum* for the advancement of true science, established Catholic universities, founded colleges, seminaries, and schools ; he left everywhere monuments of his munificence, and so great was his liberality that all that was offered to him seemed to be accepted not for himself, but for others.

As he combined with all these virtues a remarkable gentleness and affability, he charmed the minds of all who approached him in a manner that increased the respect and devotion due to the Vicar of Jesus Christ, until developed into the most ardent love. This is shown by the addresses offered to him, by frequent assemblages of pilgrims, and especially the celebrations in the jubilee years of his priesthood, his episcopate, and his pontificate, which furnished altogether unusual marks of the filial piety and warm affection of the entire Catholic universe.

Sole among the popes,* he sat in the chair of St. Peter thirty-one years, seven months, twenty-two days.   He died at the age of eighty-six years, on the 7th of February, of the year 1878.

---

* VARYING DURATION OF PONTIFICATES.—Three popes died within a day or two after their election and before they were consecrated ; eleven popes reigned less than one month each ; forty-four less than one year ; twenty-one less than two years ; twenty-two less than three years ; nineteen less than four years ; sixteen less than five years ; seventeen less than six years ; nine less than seven years ; seven less than eight years ; fifteen less than nine years ; twelve less than ten years ; fourteen less than eleven years ; eleven less than twelve years ; nine less than thirteen years ; six less than fourteen years ; seven less than fifteen years ; ten less than sixteen years ; one less than seventeen years ; one less than eighteen years ; six less than nineteen years ; three less than twenty-one years ; three less than twenty-two years ; two less than twenty-four years ; one less than twenty-five years ; and two, St. Peter and Pius IX. more than twenty-five years—St. Peter reigning as pontiff at Rome exactly a quarter of a century, and Pius IX. nearly thirty-two years.

CHAPTER XIII.

It is said that eight hundred years before his accession to the papal throne Pius IX. was styled "Crux de Cruce." It is not our intention to determine whether this prophecy, commonly attributed to St. Malachy, Bishop of Armagh, is genuine or not. What we wish to insist upon is that this motto finds a most striking verification in the life of the late sovereign pontiff. We need not go back to the first days of his pontificate, when the revolutionary party forced him to leave his capital, and to live an exile at Gaeta. We need not recall to our minds the faithlessness of the Piedmontese in 1870, nor the entry of the Italian troops through the breaches of Porta Pia. All worldly possessions had no value for Pius IX. He deemed it but small loss to be deprived of a country which cost him so much trouble and anxiety. But what he had very much at heart was the welfare of the Church, the independence of the Holy See, and the upholding of sound principles in faith and morals: and all these he defended ; for these he struggled in such a manner that, even when overpowered by material force, when compassed round about by false friends or declared enemies, he made use of the only means at his command—he protested. Upon his banner were emblazoned in characters of gold the words : " Rights divine and human ; rights ecclesiastical and civil." This his banner he held with a firm grasp ; he held it unfurled and steadfast to the end. Pius IX. has passed away, but his spirit will not pass away.

The full significance, however, of the words " Crux de Cruce" was revealed in a special manner during the last years of his life. Let us imagine for a moment that we are in the cabinet of Pius IX., and that we hear the sad tidings as they are pouring in from all sides. It is the New World which first engages our attention. The Empire of Brazil is the theatre of an anti-Catholic revolution. The bishops are put in prison, the priests are sent into exile, for no other reason than that they proved true to their charge. Adjacent to Brazil is the Republic of Ecuador. This country, which, under the wise and beneficent presidency of Garcia Moreno, the regenerator of his native land, had become at once a model for all Christian commonwealths and a source of consolation to the afflicted pontiff, witnessed a reaction at once anti-social and anti-Christian. The illustrious president falls a victim to the dagger of an assassin. And the same powers—the secret societies—which had directed the arm of the parricide, found means to pour poison into the chalice of the Archbishop of Quito while he celebrated the holy mysteries, thereby renewing a crime which for centuries had remained without an example among civilized nations. Who could picture to himself the grief of the aged pope when he saw that the seed of civilization and piety, which these two champions of the faith had sown with so

Page 107.

much labor, was rooted up and destroyed; when he saw that the faithful clergy were driven from their flocks, and that the schools were either deserted or turned into nurseries of infidelity and lawlessness? Even in the great and free States of North America much was done which might fill the heart of Pius IX. with sorrow, and might add to his cup of bitterness. True it is that as yet no decided step has been taken against the Church. Still there was the danger to be feared from the public-school system, a standing evil, and had there not been a change for the better, the peace of the Church might have been threatened. However, it cannot be denied that the events which most afflicted the Vicar of Christ took place in the Old World.

How many and how cruel were the persecutions to which the Church was subjected throughout the vast territories of Asia. On reading the relations of the missionaries, reaching us from Siam, from China proper, from Japan, from Cochin China, Corea, and Thibet, we are reminded of the bloody edicts of Nero and of the devastations of the Huns and the Tartars. Hardly had the blood of martyrs ceased to flow in one country when it began to be shed with renewed cruelty in another. The bishops were separated from their clergy, the priests were torn away from their flocks, whole villages were destroyed, entire districts were ravaged in such a manner that they retained not even so much as a trace of Christianity. The path of the Catholic missionaries has, indeed, at all times been marked with blood. They go forth to pagan countries like so many generals, sent by their king, the pope, to make conquests for Christ and His Church. The blood which they shed is not that which makes orphans and widows; but it is their own, which, in imitation of their Master, they give for the salvation of those that persecute them. Is it possible that the pope could hear all this and remain unmoved? Could he see his children in poverty, in anguish, in torments, without suffering with them?

Turning our eyes to Europe we find that the warfare waged against the Church in that part of the world was indeed less cruel, but far more perfidious. Fire and sword were not put into requisition, but what is worse—attempts were made to poison the atmosphere of the Church itself, to make the practice of Catholic rites an offence against the state, and thus to bring about, under the specious pretext of patriotism, the silent but gradual and inevitable destruction of the Church. There is, however, one country in Europe which throughout the extent of its immense territories displayed a hatred of the Church worthy of the bitterest tyrants that ever persecuted the early Christians. The reader understands that we are speaking of Russia. In fact, the attitude of Russia towards the Church exhibited at once the worst traits of Asiatic barbarity and the malicious cunning of the more refined nations of Europe. It is not an easy thing for us to imagine the heart-rending grief which filled the noble pontiff at the sight of the outrages perpetrated upon the unoffending Poles by the cruel officials and the barbarous soldiery of the Czar. Not only were the bishops exiled to Siberia, and the priests either expelled from their parishes or incarcerated, but also the faithful were visited with all sorts of molestations, and tormented even unto death. The scenes which but a few months ago were enacted in Poland are of such a nature, that while they make us shudder with terror they at the same time recall to our minds the worst days of a Nero or of a Taikusama. But let us take an example. The inhabitants of the village of N—— are assembled in their parish church to assist at divine service. On leaving the sanctuary they are attacked by a ruthless soldiery, who had stealthily come up and posted themselves in the neighborhood. The people were not allowed to pass on, and only after all had left the church they were called upon, in the name of the Czar, to apostatize from the faith of their fathers. Great favors were promised to those who would comply with the imperial mandate. But all this proved useless, the villagers one and all crying out that they would cling to their Catholic faith. Thereupon a scene ensued which we would fain pass over in silence. The Cossacks, mounted upon their wild horses, pranced in upon the people, and, without distinction of age or sex, lashed them with the knout and cut them with lances, and amid the wails of the wounded and the dying shot them down in great numbers. This tragedy was repeated in many other places with the same unheard-of cruelty on the part of the Russians, and with the same heroism on the part of the Poles.

In Germany the contest against the Church assumed a different character. There is in our time perhaps no country besides Northern Germany in which the Catholic Church had so rapidly developed all her powers, and had displayed in so striking a manner the divine efficacy of her organization. Institutions for the Catholic education of the higher classes were springing up on all sides ; the parish schools in the cities, as well as in the rural districts, were conducted in so satisfactory a manner that more than once they elicited the highest praises from the lips of the Holy Father himself. Societies for the relief of the poor were in great numbers. The young men of the laboring classes found in the admirable organization of the *Kolping-Verein* both a means to recreate themselves agreeably and innocently and an opportunity to perfect themselves in learning. The *Central-Verein*, too, was attended with the most happy results. \The meetings of this association, which lasted for a whole week, were held yearly in one of the large cities of Germany. There you might see, side by side, the bishop and the layman, the nobleman and the plebeian, the philosopher and the artisan. How much soever these persons might differ in education, in social standing, in the pursuits of life, they were united and equal in the communion of their faith. In these assemblies, popular in the best sense of the word, the poor had an opportunity to make known their wants, the clergy to remind the laity of their duties, and all could learn what rights they had to claim and what good works they had to perform.

The venerable pontiff was doomed to see all this either destroyed or changed in so far from its original purpose as to be incapable of producing any good fruits. The convents were suppressed one by one, and their inmates, models of edification and piety, were obliged to shake the dust of their native land from their feet, and to eat in tears the bread of exile. The aged Pope lived to see many bishops driven from their sees and wandering about in strange lands ; he himself offered shelter and hospitality to several of them, that he might learn from their own lips the sad story of the destruction wrought in their once flourishing dioceses. To enumerate all the cases in which both priests and laymen, because of their unswerving attachment to Rome, were sentenced to pay heavy fines, or to lie like felons in the prisons of the state, were indeed a difficult task.

And yet this was not all ; still greater evils were in store for Pius IX. Attempts were made to divide the seamless garment of Christ. A new heresy, abetted by an infidel government, sprang up in Germany. Doellinger, together with his party of priests and of proud laymen, rebelled against the voice of the pope and of the general council, by rejecting the dogma of Papal Infallibility. The prevaricators were few in number, and in face of the loyalty to the Church displayed by the Catholics all over the world, their influence melted away like snow before the rays of the sun ; still it cannot be denied that one drop of poison of this kind is enough to turn the whole contents of the cup into wormwood.

Germany, however, was not to stand alone in the sad renown of attempting to create a schism. If Germany had her Doellinger, France had her Loyson, Italy her Curci, and Switzerland her schismatic parish priests.

Where was there during the last years of the late pontificate any country from which news of the most distressing nature did not again and again reach the Eternal City? Even if we were to make abstraction from the world at large, and confine ourselves to the examination of Rome and its neighborhood, we should still find much to move a heart less delicate and sensitive than that of Pius IX. From the height of the Vatican palace he might see the devastation wrought in the Eternal City ; he might see religious men and women turned upon the streets, while their monasteries were changed into barracks or transformed into stables ; he might see many a pious foundation that had developed itself with the rise and the growth of Rome sold publicly at auction ; he might see many a beautiful church razed to the ground, while on the other hand lawlessness and irreligion and open blasphemy were taught as well in the school-room and public assembly as by the infidel press of the day. There stood in the centre of the Coliseum, that silent monument of pagan cruelty and of Christian heroism, a simple wooden cross, which for generations had been venerated alike by the inhabitants of Rome and by the pilgrims from distant lands. This touching emblem of the Crucified was removed under the very eyes of the pope and replaced by the statue of some revolutionary hero. And what was the Pope himself but a prisoner in his own palace ? There existed, it is true, the law of guarantees, so called, protecting the Pope against any personal insults. This law, however, inspired the pope with as little confidence as the power from which it emanated. Might not the same government which had made void so many treaties and had broken so many promises, annul this one too under any specious pretext and for any purpose ?

Being, therefore, perfectly conversant with the aims and tendencies of the revolution, and knowing that no compromise on eligible grounds could ever be effected between the Church and the Italian Government, he stood, like the prophet of old, upon the watch-tower of the Lord, protesting by day and crying out by night against the impious measures of the usurper.

Is it not true, then, to say that during the greater part of the Pope's life one cross followed fast upon another ? But as divine providence gave our departed pontiff so large a share in the ignominy of the cross, it bestowed on him an equal share in its glory.

THE CROSS IN THE COLOSSEUM.

Page 115.

For in ages past it had been foretold that the cross would be a sign not only of shame and of death, but also of salvation. Even the penitent thief caught a glimpse of that glory, and at the sight of it he begged to be admitted into the kingdom of Christ. The soldier who pierced the heart of Jesus with a lance recognized the hidden virtue of the cross, and being won over to it he became, as tradition tells us, a bishop of the Church, and died the death of a martyr. The centurion who, at the death of Christ, stood over against the cross, understood, at least to some extent, the mysterious greatness of the Crucified One, and exclaimed : " Truly, this man is the Son of God."

Throughout the pontificate of Pius IX., and more especially in the latter years of its duration, this glory of the cross was manifested in a most striking manner. What man of our age is there who dares say that he received at the hands of his contemporaries as many tokens of love, respect, and veneration as Pius IX. ? How often was it that by one kind word falling from his lips, by one affectionate smile of his countenance, the most hardened sinners were converted ! More than once it happened that one conversation was sufficient for him to change his bitterest enemy into his warmest friend. Time and again a single look of his mild eye was enough to win back the erring to the path of duty and to the light of faith.

While the enemies of the Church did all in their power to prepare new difficulties for the Holy Father, the children of the Church were not less ready on all occasions to give him new marks of love and affection.

Under his pontificate many tribes and nations hitherto strangers to Christianity were received into the bosom of the Church. The Catholic nations themselves experienced a revival of faith and piety worthy of the first ages of the Church, and they manifested so firm an attachment to the See of Peter that all the machinations of crafty statesmen and all the seductions of infidel governments were unable to lessen it.

No day commemorative of any important event in the life of the Pope was allowed to pass without being celebrated by the faithful with all the outbursts of joy becoming the sentiments of loyal subjects to their ruler or of dutiful children to their father. Many occasions of this kind offered themselves. Almighty God had permitted the man whom he loved to live to an age but rarely equalled by a successor of St. Peter. Among the popes, Pius IX. was the only one in whom the well-known saying, " Non videbis annos Petri "—Thou shalt not see the years of Peter" —was not verified. This long life gave occasion to the many feasts solemnized in his honor. There was first the celebration of his ordination to the priesthood, then of his elevation to the episcopal dignity, and later on that of his promotion to the papal throne. When his election to the See of Peter was celebrated the pilgrims flocked to Rome from all parts of the world, unmindful of a raging sea, of dreary wastes, of dangerous precipices. And they deemed themselves richly rewarded if, after all their toils, they could but behold the face of the aged pontiff, listen to the sweet accents of his voice, and, in parting, receive his blessing. Where is there, in the whole range of history, a man, an earthly prince, of whom it is said that the eagerness of seeing him was so great among the men of his age, that they flocked to his capital, not only from every country of Europe, but also from the sands of the Sahara, from the pampas of the New World, from the region lying beyond the Rocky Mountains, from the banks of the Ganges, and from the isles of Japan? Did these pilgrims come to see a prince who equalled Solomon in splendor or Augustus in power? Did they come to obtain rich benefices or to be raised to lucrative positions? No, they came to see an aged man who had no kingdom, who lived in his palace more like a prisoner than a sovereign. Him they came to see and to honor, and to him they offered their presents as the tribute of their undying love for the Vicar of Christ. This loyalty of Catholics to Pius IX. is a jewel in his crown which many a powerful king might envy.

Nor was the Pope insensible to the generosity of his faithful subjects. Many of his allocutions bear witness to the fact, and we Catholics of the present age may feel an honest pride in having done so much to sweeten the last years of his checkered life. He told us repeatedly not to be anxious about the future, nor to wish for the triumph of the Church—that is to say, for a triumph consisting in great material power, in unequalled renown for refinement ; because we are already celebrating a most beautiful triumph, to wit, an increase of piety throughout the entire body of the Church, and an intimacy and union between the pastors and the people worthy of the first ages of Christianity.

God, who disposes all things well, had inspired the Catholics of some countries, in which the very existence of their faith was greatly endangered, with a manly courage and a spirit of unyielding firmness. And this, too, was a great source of happiness. Thus Belgium, for a long time fettered by a masonic legislation, roused herself to action and asserted her religious independence. The Catholics of Holland, who had lived for a long time in a kind of religious bondage, succeeded in redeeming both their political and their religious freedom. Denmark and Sweden, after the lapse of three centuries, have in our day for the first time thrown open their territories to the zeal of the Catholic missionary. England, Protestant England, witnesses to-day a religious reaction which bids fair to bring back at no distant period the whole nation to the true fold of Christ. Not less remarkable, as even Protestants will admit, is the progress made by the Catholic Church within the last quarter of a century in our own country. Was not the knowledge of all this like a healing balm instilled into the heart of the much-afflicted pontiff?

Death, which ends all, has also put an end to his many sufferings, but not till he had drained the cup of bitterness to the dregs. He is now with the blessed in heaven, and his tiara is replaced by a crown of glory. How clearly he now understands both what he suffered and why he suffered! He understands the wonderful ways by which God leads His Church, and he sees in many things, in which our troubled gaze perceives only the wickedness of men, the very wisdom and glory of the Most High. Let us, while fondly and sadly perusing the pages of his life, not forget to thank God for having given to our departed Father at once a measure of suffering and a measure of joy, full, shaken down, and overflowing.

THE PAPAL ELECTION.

HISTORICAL SKETCH OF THE ORIGIN AND LAWS OF THE CONCLAVE.

THE PAPAL ELECTION.

CHAPTER I.

THE CATHOLIC HIERARCHY.

OUBTLESS the work of our Divine Redeemer would have in time been forgotten had not He before He ascended into heaven, there to sit for all time at the right hand of His Father, founded a Church, which was to perpetuate among men the memory of His passion and death. Without such an institution there would have remained on earth a mere tradition of a man who during the reign of the Emperor Augustus lived in Judea, who claimed to be the Son of God, and who made good

His word by many miracles. This tradition would have informed us that Christ, on account of His strange doctrine, fell a victim to the jealousy of His enemies, and that He finished His life by dying the death of the cross. Relying on the same tradition, we should have held the opinion that Christ wished to bring our race back to the state from which it had fallen, and that He pointed out the way by which the reconciliation between God and man could be effected.

By degrees, however, the tradition would have been obscured, and before the lapse of many centuries it would have been impossible for the human understanding to know where truth ended and error began.

The history of the Jewish people furnishes us with a strong proof in favor of our hypothesis. For although the religious and the political institutions of the Israelites differed widely from those of other nations, and although the Hebrews had but little intercourse with the Gentiles, and among them the stream of tradition was more faithfully transmitted from father to son than among the European nations, nevertheless the entire history of the Jews is nothing but a continued record of their violations of the divine law. And as God wished that the light of the true faith should never be extinguished among them, He had frequent recourse to extraordinary means: now by raising up a prophet whom He endowed with supernatural powers; now by visiting them with terrible calamities, from which there was neither escape nor relief except in their sincere return to the covenant of the Lord.

The same phenomenon would no doubt have repeated itself among the European nations, especially as the benefits of the redemption were to be bestowed not only on one nation, but on all nations, and this, too, regardless of clime and national prejudices. It cannot be denied, on the other hand, that, independently of a visible Church, God, by way of miracle, might have communicated to every person in particular the grace of redemption and of salvation. God, however, does not govern mankind in general and every individual in particular in a miraculous manner; He rather wishes to manifest Himself to all in a way agreeable to His ordinary providence. For it must be borne in mind that no miracles are wrought or even necessary to preserve and to explain the truths of our religion, but only to prove to the heathen of all lands that the Church is endowed with divine authority.

If, therefore, it was the will of Almighty God that the work of our redemption should be both beautiful in theory and useful in practice, it was absolutely necessary for Him to form a society, divine as to the end intended, human as to its members and ministers, in order that all men might possess and might know that they possess the truth. That this society, this kingdom of God, may not fail of its end, the salvation of all, it must of necessity be a visible kingdom, the laws of which are sanctioned by the Creator Himself.

This kingdom of Christ is the Catholic Church, and as every commonwealth must have powers legislative, judicial, and executive, so also has the Christian commonwealth; and all these powers taken collectively, or rather all the persons in whom these powers reside, form the Ecclesiastical Hierarchy.

The constitution of the Church is not of to-day nor of yesterday. It has stood the test of ages. Many are the men who at returning periods would fain have made amendments to it, would have changed it, or destroyed it altogether. At one time they alleged for their fondness of innovation that the truths of salvation were not transmitted in their pristine purity ; at another they claimed that there should not be any distinction among the members of the Church, but that all should be considered as priests ; or, again, they denied the existence of Christ's visible kingdom on earth.

We readily admit that if these men had received power to fashion out a church after their own fancies they would have given it a constitution far different from that which Christ has given to His Church. But if, on the other hand, we study the pages of history we begin to doubt whether these would-be improvers upon the divine work would in reality have succeeded in their undertaking. Many of them, with the permission of God, were successful enough to carry their plans into execution. But history, again, tells us that they came into existence, that for a time they put the minds of men in commotion, and that in the end they disappeared like dreams. The Church, on the other hand, like the mustard-seed of the Gospel, was constant in her growth ; and to-day, having grown into a mighty tree, she spreads her branches over the whole earth, and is constantly adding new twigs, new blossoms, and new fruits. The roots of that tree go down to purgatory, while its crown, which pierces the skies, reaches up to the throne of God ; and as the Spirit of the Lord rustles through its dense foliage, the spirits of darkness, on the one hand, shudder with fear, and the spirits of light, on the other, striking their golden lyres, sing the rapturous allelujahs of heaven.

But the testimony of history is hardly necessary to show the institutions of the Church in their true light. It is enough for us to know that Christ Himself was the founder of the Church, and that He promised to send to His apostles the Paraclete, who would instruct them in all truth, and that He Himself would be with them all days, even unto the consummation of the world. Whoever is not convinced by these words—words spoken by the Eternal Truth itself; whoever does not see in these words, and in others that are still clearer, and which we intend to quote later on, the intention of Christ to found an organization like the Church—must be one of those proud spirits who, like Lucifer, would place his throne beside the throne of God, or even attempt to place it higher; and should such a one persist in his overweening pride, what wonder if his fate be likened to the fate of him who before the creation of the world unfurled the banner of rebellion in heaven!

Although it were time lost, as we have said, for the faithful to enquire how the constitution of the Church might have been framed differently by Almighty God, still it cannot be denied that it ought to be a matter of interest for every Catholic to have a knowledge of the working of the present hierarchical system. And let it be observed that but a comparatively small number of Catholics have this knowledge, the generality knowing little more than the broad outlines of the system. Thus every Catholic knows that the parish priest has jurisdiction in his parish, the bishop over the whole diocese, and that the pope is the ruler of all—of the priests as well as of laymen. But it is one thing merely to see the stately edifice of the Church from the outside, as it were, and another to understand the principles of order and beauty upon which it is constructed, and by which it is enabled to outlast the storms of centuries and to stand before us, even to-day, in all its original loveliness and perfection.   How is it possible that the Church, without changing her interior organization, could adapt herself to all ages, to all climes, to all forms of government, and to all nations ; in other words, how is it possible for the Church to be, at one and the same time, the handmaid of all by ministering to the spiritual wants of all, and the queen of all by obliging them to obey strictly all and every one of her laws?

Such is the problem which we intend to solve, and we are ready to do this as well as our limited abilities and the narrow compass within which we must necessarily confine ourselves will allow.

Let us begin with the founding of the Church by Christ. Christ had sent His apostles not only to instruct men in the truths of salvation, but also to oblige them to do the works necessary for salvation. Hence He sent His apostles not only as preachers, but also as rulers and as ministers of the sacraments. Now as the Church is to last forever, and as the apostles were to live but for a limited space of time, their power must have been such as could be transmitted to others in the same manner in which they themselves had received it from Christ. Those who did receive this power were called bishops ; nor can any one to-day claim to be a bishop in the true sense of the word unless he can prove that his power was transmitted to him from Christ through the apostles by an uninterrupted succession of bishops. There are no bishops in the Catholic Church who derive their jurisdiction from any other source, and hence all Roman Catholic bishops are deservedly called the successors of the apostles. Theirs it is, and theirs alone, to govern and to rule the Church of Christ.

But, moreover, there never existed a perfect equality among the apostles themselves. Christ Himself made a distinction. He told His apostles on one occasion that Satan had desired to sift them. Now, this permission was really granted to the evil one, and therefore it was not impossible that some would not stand the test. History, alas! proves but too well that many a time this possibility became a reality. This being the case, it follows that but for an admirable provision of divine Providence in behalf of the Church, it might have happened sooner or later that such a confusion of ideas would have taken place among the faithful as to make it utterly impossible for any one to know either where the true Church was, or what graces were granted to the members of that Church. But Christ did not establish a Church which was to be tossed about by the whirlwind of human opinions. He therefore chose one man on whom He bestowed the gift of an infallible faith, and that man was Peter. To Peter our Lord said : " I have prayed for thee, that thy faith fail not." Hence, as far as faith is concerned, Peter enjoyed a privilege which was not granted to the other apostles. But as the powers which the apostles had received in common were to be transmitted to others, so also the power with which Christ distinguished Peter from among his brethren was to be transmitted to his successors ; so that if at any time a difficulty arose in matters of faith or of morals, the bishops, as well as the priests and the laymen, might have recourse to the successor of St. Peter, and be assured that the answer received was, by virtue of the words of Christ, true with the very truth of God, infallible with the very infallibility of God.

But this was not the only distinction conferred

upon Peter by Christ. It was not the intention of the Saviour of mankind to establish twelve Churches, devoid of any other connection among themselves than the source from which all might if they wished draw the truths of faith. Satan by dint of cunning would very soon have succeeded in changing eleven of these Churches into false ones, which in their turn would have combated with relentless fury against the only true Church of Christ. Our Lord prevented this by appointing Peter not only as the fountain of faith, but also as the source of all jurisdiction. The words of Christ to Peter are as follows : " And thou confirm thy brethren." Christ teaches us here in express terms that the other apostles must lean upon Peter not only for perseverance in the true faith, but also for obtaining strength sufficient to withstand the attacks of their enemies. Nor did our Lord hide from them the fact that at times all the powers of darkness would rise up against them, and that in such times they would find no refuge, no security, except by leaning upon Peter, by believing what he be- lieved, by doing what he told them to do. The words of Christ are very clear on this point : " Upon this rock I will build my Church, and the gates of hell shall not prevail against her." Whoever wishes, therefore, to remain victorious over the powers of darkness must be steadfast in his union with the See of Peter. Christ, in order to rouse Peter to the sense of both his dignity and his responsibility, and also to impress upon his brethren the true char- acter of their dependence upon Peter, said to Peter in plain and open terms: " Feed my lambs, feed my sheep." These words reveal to us the plan on which Christ wished to form His Church. Peter is not only a source of truth to his brethren, but also a source of strength ; he is bound to watch over them, and they in their turn are obliged to hearken to his voice. Peter is the shepherd alike of the sheep and of the lambs, of the priests and bishops, and of the laymen. The successors of the other apostles are the shepherds of their respective flocks. Peter is the common pastor of the flocks and of the shepherds themselves.

There are many other texts in Scripture inculcating, if possible more strongly, the same doctrine. One of them, referring to the occasion on which Peter was first called to be an apostle, reads thus : " Thou art Simon, the son of Jonas ; thou shalt be called Cephas"—that is, the rock or groundwork upon which the whole edifice was to be built. At a later period our Lord returns to this idea and enlarges upon it, saying : " To thee I will give the keys of the kingdom of heaven." Now, he that has control over the keys is the master of the house, and as Peter holds the keys of Christ's household, the Church, Peter must needs be the master at least of the visible Church of Christ. In the Apocalypse Christ appears to St. John as the great key-bearer ; indicating that as He Himself holds the keys of the kingdom of heaven, so Peter holds the same keys upon earth in the quality of Christ's vicar.

Such is the original constitution which Christ gave to His Church ; the same it is still, and it will last to the end of time.

So far we have not made any mention of the seventy-two disciples whom Christ gave as helpmates to His apostles. Do we not recognize in them the type of the inferior degrees of the clergy ? The apostles, knowing the mind of their Divine Master better than any others, chose, even during the first year of their apostolical ministry, a certain number of persons, whom they ordained, whom they called deacons, and to whom they entrusted certain special offices. There existed at that time in the minds of many a doubt whether the heathens before receiving baptism should be circumcised or not. The apostles met in Jerusalem in general council, and after a long deliberation Peter stood up and, in virtue of his privilege of infallibility in matters of faith, decided the question, and the controversy was at an end.

That Peter, however, might have acted independently of the council appears from the fact that he had received into the Church the centurion Cornelius, without obliging him to submit to the Jewish rite of circumcision.

The same custom which had obtained in the days of the apostles is still in vigor. Whenever, owing to the perversity of heretics, the Church finds herself in a critical position, and when consequently the successor of St. Peter is obliged to have recourse to extraordinary measures, he first invites the successors of the other apostles to meet in general council, and there deliberates with them as to what enactments are likely to prove most successful.

The pope is not obliged to proceed in this manner. Independent of any council, the pope may pronounce upon matters of faith, and be as assured of speaking in accordance with the eternal Truth as if all the bishops of the earth had been unanimous in the same doctrine. But as other questions besides those relating to matters of faith and morals are to be discussed—such as ecclesiastical institutions, changes in or additions to the laws regulating the external affairs of the Church—it is the part of a prudent ruler, before he gives any decision, to lend an attentive ear to the advice of good and experienced men. The popes do not rule after the manner of tyrants, who make laws to-day and unmake them to-morrow, who to-day demand of their subjects one thing and to-morrow oblige them to the opposite. The pope was made the ruler of all for no other purpose than that he might be the servant of all. He first makes use of human means to determine what is necessary or wholesome to the flock of Christ; and only then, when all natural resources have proved fruitless, he makes use of supernatural ones, being firmly convinced that the assistance of the Holy Ghost will not permit him to go astray. Let him that is unwilling to believe all this, study the history of the last Œcumenical Council, together with its happy results, notwithstanding the sad forebodings of statesmen to the contrary.

Concerning the organization of the Church, we have already mentioned the pope, the general councils, and the apostles or, more properly, the bishops, the priests, and the deacons. All these offices date back as far as the days of the apostles. Nay more, even at that early period the foundation was laid for that admirable division of the Church into patriarchates, primacies, archbishoprics, bishoprics, and parishes, by virtue of which gradation the least member of the Church can almost as easily communicate with the head of Christendom as the cardinal of the pontifical palace himself.

Peter and the other apostles were sent by Christ to convert the whole world. Each one might, therefore, go whithersoever he wished. However, it could not possibly be a correct interpretation of Christ's will if each of them had chosen at random the place to which he would direct his steps, so that an apostle might be at Rome to-day and at Damascus to-morrow, thus making it impossible for his flock to have recourse to him in their greatest needs. But the apostles acted quite differently. According to a venerable tradition of antiquity, they divided the whole known world into twelve parts, of which each took one for his special field of action. In the course of time these parts themselves proved too extensive, even for the zeal of an apostle. They were therefore obliged to form separate congregations, each of which they placed under the jurisdiction of an ecclesiastic endowed with the episcopal dignity. But as little by little the number of the faithful increased in these congregations, it was found necessary to subdivide them and to confide these subdivisions to the care of clergymen belonging to an inferior rank. It is in this manner that we are to understand the gradual formation, not only of the diocese itself with its actual hierarchical government, but also the precedence which, even at the present day, one bishop has over another in the same country.

At the head of the entire Church stands the pope, possessing the fulness of all spiritual power. Next to him are the patriarchs and the primates. In olden times the title of patriarch was restricted to those bishops who filled the sees of Antioch, Rome, and Alexandria. Later on, some other sees were added to this number—for instance, Jerusalem, Constantinople, and Venice. It must, however, be remarked that the patriarchs at present do not enjoy any special privileges, nor do they possess a higher jurisdiction than the other bishops; their title being merely honorary, while during the middle ages much political influence was connected with this dignity. The same may be said concerning primacies. The primate of any country holds the first rank among the bishops of that nation. Thus there was a primate of Germany, of England, of Ireland, and of Poland.

The following suggestions about the government of the Church are of vital importance. The whole domain of the Church is divided into ecclesiastical provinces. At the head of each province stands the metropolitan or archbishop. He ranks foremost among the bishops of that province, and in provincial councils he occupies the first seat ; besides, he enjoys some privileges which are not granted to his brethren in the episcopate ; and in matters of jurisdiction he is, as it were, the connecting link between them and the Roman court. Still, he does not receive any higher ordination than the other bishops, nor is he placed over them in such a manner as to have, strictly speaking, jurisdiction over them ; he is rather " primus inter pares," the first among his equals, having like the others to attend to the government of a diocese, which by way of distinction is called archdiocese. Thus the Archbishop of Baltimore is, indeed, the metropolitan of the ecclesiastical province of the same name ; and yet we cannot say that the diocese of Richmond belongs to the Archdiocese of Baltimore, because they form two distinct parts of the same ecclesiastical province.

The provinces of the Church, then, are divided into dioceses, at the head of each of which is the bishop, holding, as a general rule, the same authority and power over his diocesans as the pope exerts over the entire Church. We say that this holds good as a general rule, because the case may present itself in which the pope, by virtue of his supreme authority and jurisdiction, would find himself obliged to interfere with this general mode of proceeding, and to put limits to the action of a bishop.

The diocese in its turn is subdivided, at least in the Catholic countries of Europe, into deaneries, headed by the dean ; while the deaneries themselves are again divided into parishes, presided over by the pastors or parish priests.

To sum up what has been said till now : We say that the ruler of the entire Church is the pope ; that the ruler of an ecclesiastical province is called archbishop ; that the ruler of a deanery is called dean ; and the parish priest is intrusted with the care of a parish.

Besides, it must be borne in mind that some of the offices mentioned are of such a nature as to make it impossible for any single person to fill them to satisfaction. Hence it is customary that the bishops, who, generally speaking, are burthened with a variety of duties, have a number of ecclesiastical persons, such as coadjutors and vicars-general, attached to their persons, who in one way or another act in the name and with the authority of the bishop himself. On the same principle we explain the introduction into the diocese not only of the cathedral chapters and of the vicars for simplifying the government of the diocese ; but also of chaplains for assisting parish priests in discharging their duties. In most dioceses the ecclesiastical corporations that help the bishop in the government of the diocese have at the same time the privilege to elect a new bishop whenever such an election is necessary.

Now the sovereign pontiff in his quality of ruler over the whole Church, having under his jurisdiction not only all the flocks, but also all the pastors of the flocks, must of necessity have at his side a great number of men, and even of corporations of men, for the purpose of managing affairs ecclesiastic with prudence and promptness. During the early ages the pope when pressed with business had recourse to the principal clergymen in and about the city of Rome. And thus as the bishops had their cathedral chapters, the popes in the course of time created for themselves an organization consisting at first of the suburban bishops and of the Roman priests and deacons. At the present day these counsellors of the pope are known by the name of cardinals, and are called, in accordance with their grade of ordination, either cardinal bishops, cardinal priests, or cardinal deacons. This dignity, at first granted to the Roman clergy only, was gradually extended to other princes of the Church, irrespective of nationality. Although this latter class of cardinals, because of their duties at home and the distance of their sees from Rome, do not take any active part in the government of the Church, they have nevertheless a right to be present at the conclave, and to vote for a new pope.

In the same proportion in which the Church extended her territory and multiplied the number of her children, the ecclesiastical government became more and more complicated. Hence the cardinals, who for a long time, as has been stated, were chosen from among the bishops, deans, and parish priests of Rome, could not possibly at one and the same time share in the general government of the Church, and attend to their parishes, deaneries, or dioceses. They therefore, although preserving their ancient title of bishops, deans, or priests, were relieved of their pastoral charges, and resided under the immediate supervision of the pope in the Lateran palace, or, later, in the Vatican. In this manner the

College of Cardinals resembled very much the cathedral chapter which we mentioned above ; for, as the members of the latter, upon the decease of their bishop, take the government of the diocese into their hands, so also do the cardinals, whenever the Holy See is vacant, govern the whole Church until a new pope has been appointed.

For the better management of affairs, every one of the cardinals (whose number may not exceed seventy-two) is assigned to one or more of the many congregations of cardinals. Thus some cardinals belong to the Congregation of the Index, whose duty it is to examine books and pamphlets in order to decide whether they are beneficial or prejudicial to the faith and morals of the faithful. Others, again, belong to the Congregation of the Propagation of Faith, whose office it is to watch over the interests of the Church in missionary countries. Then, again, as occasions offer, the pope may erect new congregations, which, however, are dissolved as soon as the difficulties in question have disappeared. Every one of these congregations requires a great number of persons, who, although not members of the congregation, are employed either as counsellors, as translators, or as clerks.

Thus far we have given the reader the broad outlines of the system by which the Church is governed. Hasty as our sketch has been, we trust that it will prove sufficient for the reader to understand how, under such a constitution, it happens that the members and the head of the Church are intimately linked together, and that each thought and each word proceeding from the head is communicated to all the members even to the remotest countries.

Still we must confess that our picture is far from

being complete. It represents the Church as she is governed in times of peace and prosperity. But as the Church on earth with good reason is called the Church militant, we cannot be surprised at seeing that the periods of her prosperity are but short and few, while the periods of her struggles and of her sufferings are long and many. In fact, it may safely be asserted that ever since the coming down of the Holy Ghost on the day of Pentecost there has not been a time in which the Church enjoyed perfect peace throughout all the parts of her vast domain. There are even now mighty kingdoms in which the Church of God and her institutions are hardly known ; there are extensive territories in which the Church is hardly tolerated ; there are powerful nations that persecute the Church in the most cruel manner. It is evident that, under such circumstances, the Church finds herself straitened, and that she is unable to display all the beauty and the strength inherent to her wonderful organization. All these countries stand under the immediate jurisdiction of the pope. It is the pope himself who sends the missionaries ; he selects for them a central place from which the whole country is evangelized. In this manner the missions apostolic are formed, which in the course of time are raised to the rank of dioceses. During the pontificate of Pius IX. it happened repeatedly that apostolic missions were erected into regular dioceses—as, for instance, in England and in Holland.

This is not all. It may occur that the maintaining of the regular hierarchy in a certain country would entail much suffering and great molestations on the ecclesiastical dignitaries. In such cases it is but reasonable that the pope should change the hierarchy into an apostolic mission, as was the case in England during the reign of Queen Elizabeth. How easy would it have been for the English pursuivants to apprehend a bishop who is obliged to remain at his see, or a parish priest who is not allowed to leave his parish. The pope, therefore, withdrew all this, and in its stead introduced the missionary system by sending zealous priests into the realm, to whom he granted full powers, and who, under various disguises, went through the land in all directions, strengthening the faltering spirits of the Catholics, administering the sacraments, exposing themselves to all manner of vexation, and not unfrequently sealing their faith by shedding their blood under the most horrible and revolting torments. The Tower of London might bear terrible witness to what we say.

But even without such occasions the pope, in virtue of his plenary power, resorts at times to extraordinary means. The bishops, for example, exercise jurisdiction over the whole extent of their dioceses ; yet the pope has often exempted certain religious orders from this diocesan government.

A more striking instance of this is furnished by the ecclesiastical organization of the Prussian army. At the desire of the crown, the pope constituted the entire army, so long as the soldiers remained under the flag, a separate diocese, at the head of which stood an army-bishop ; so that wherever any corps or regiment of the army might be stationed, its members were subject not to the ordinary of the local diocese, but to their own military bishop.

Thus we see all things ordered for the best in the constitution of the Church. We have a permanent order, without which no organization can preserve its living action. But along with that order we have a freedom of action, which, without disturbing the former, is competent to provide for all extraordinary occurrences. This wise union of order and liberty plainly shows that a more than human wisdom presides over the Church, since that alone could create an institution which far outstrips the duration of any human work. He alone who created the world could create a Church whose birth dates back to the beginning of time, and whose mission will end only with the life of the last of our race.

CHAPTER II.

From what has been said of the office of the pope in the Church, it evidently follows how important it is that the See of Peter should be filled by a worthy successor. It is true that this see is surrounded by divine safeguards ; and we know that, even if it were held by the greatest of sinners, or by the man of the most limited natural ability, no harm could come from this to the preservation and propagation of the faith. Peter would still speak through the mouth of his successor, and as Peter's faith cannot fail, we should have the assurance that the saving truth remained unimpaired. And Christ, who to the consummation of ages will never for a single day abandon His Church, would shield her in her greatest need with His almighty hand, so that the gates of hell should never prevail against her.

But this divine guarantee could not be held as an encouragement to human indifference. It would be a wrong to the majesty of God did men suppose that this divine promise dispensed them from prudent precaution, or that it was of no consequence who was placed upon the throne of St. Peter. As the pope himself, though infallible in teaching, may not neglect the thorough and careful discussion of questions proposed for his doctrinal decision, so may not men appoint as the representative of God one of whose worthiness they have not taken sufficient proof. Even the best will always be, in comparison with God, an unworthy representative ; and when the sovereign pontiffs style themselves so, they use no meaningless phrase, but speak a truth well known to themselves as well as to those whom they address. Men cannot offer to God any thing better than they possess ; but they are bound to give Him the best and the worthiest. To offer less or to offer any thing in a slovenly manner, would be a crime against Infinite Majesty.

But such things have happened in the course of ages ; it has happened that insufficient care was taken, that men were ignorant of the unworthiness of the one chosen, and this ignorance was sometimes wilful, sometimes unwilful. In such cases God still kept His word ; the faith never wavered at Rome ; and never, in the lapse of two thousand years, has a pope defined *ex cathedra* a point of doctrine which a succeeding pope found it necessary to condemn. During the same two thousand years numberless scientific systems have been set up and overturned again, but never a papal definition. The gates of hell have never prevailed against the Church in the cases alluded to ; but she has suffered and suffered severely whenever they occurred. Happily the cases were rare ; and the great majority of the popes, however unworthy they were in comparison with God, were, when compared with men, pious, virtuous, and wise. No dynasty on earth can show so long a line of exemplary princes, so few unworthy rulers as the chair of Peter, and in moral greatness, in masterly ability of government, many a pope stands higher than the greatest of other rulers.

For these qualities, however desirable they may be, and however suited to the sublime dignity of the papacy, we have no divine security. And for this reason, but especially because men owe it to the divine sanctity and majesty, it was necessary to surround the papal election with all possible precautions, so that none but the most worthy and most excellent should be chosen.

Accordingly, the Church has in all ages bestowed the utmost care on this important act ; and the system is no mere mass of ceremonies or formalities, but is the result of the serious study of eighteen centuries. Wherever a deficiency appeared it was supplied, and all measures had no other end in view but that the electors should be irreproachable, that they should be free from all external influence, and should follow only their own conscience in the election.

A very brief historical view of the matter will suffice to prove this. In the earliest ages there was no reason to require any difference in the elections of popes or bishops. There was no fear that any one would covet this dignity through worldly motives ; for how greatly soever the early pontiffs were revered by the faithful, yet they knew that in accepting this pre-eminence, they had to sacrifice whatever might render life pleasant or desirable ; and that they must look forward to a bloody martyrdom in the end. There was then no earthly inducement to stir up the ambition for the tiara in the first popes. And if the candidate had none, much less can we find it in the electors. They had nothing to offer and they had nothing to hope from the one whom they might elect. All Christendom in those days looked forward to martyrdom, and, under such circumstances, men are necessarily virtuous and inaccessible to unworthy motives. Hence, in a vacancy of the Holy See, the bishops of the sees near Rome assembled, and, together with the clergy and faithful people of the capital, agreed on the choice of a successor. There was no definite form of election to be observed under pain of nullity. When the choice had been determined, the newly-elected was consecrated by the Bishop of Ostia, the seaport of Rome.

This continued until the Roman emperors became Christians. Thenceforth the emperors became the protectors of the Church, and as such they received certain rights and privileges. They began by pointing out, in cases of difficulties arising out of a multiplicity of candidates, none of whom could secure a majority of votes, which of them should succeed to the chair of Peter. The papacy now began to exercise an external influence, and then the dangers also came to light, which did not exist in times of bloody persecutions. It is true that time was needed to develop these dangers and to strengthen the Imperial influence, until at length it became necessary to oppose it, and to erect such barriers against it as would restore and preserve the ancient freedom of election.

When Odoacer had secured to himself the possession of Italy, he claimed the same rights which the emperors had exercised before him ; and Theodoric the Great, King of the Ostrogoths, who ruled in Rome after him, went even further, by appointing one pope, Felix III., by his sole vote. His successors were more modest ; they, however, required the election to be referred to them for approval ; they issued an edict of ratification, for which a handsome tribute was expected for the royal treasury.

In later times the eastern Emperor Justinian re-conquered Italy, and then the right of approving the papal election was vested in him and his successors. The emperor's representative held his court at Ravenna under the title of Exarch ; and this officer was to receive immediate notice of a vacancy in the Roman See, whilst the decree of election was to be always subject to the approval of the emperor. The tax on the ratification was first remitted under Constantine Pogonatus, in 680, and as the Imperial power gradually sank lower and lower, the papal election became more and more free.

But now another danger appeared. Parties had been formed at Rome by the various nationalities of which its population consisted ; and these brought their influence to bear, sometimes in unlawful ways, on the election of the pontiff. To counteract this, protection was again sought from the princes ; but this time not from the court of Constantinople, which had lost its hold on western Europe, but from the Carlovingian princes, especially from Charlemagne, who had restored the empire in the West. Thenceforth the election was always to be held in presence of the imperial ambassadors ; a decree not invariably observed, yet giving a recognized right which, on the dissolution of the Carlovingian Empire, passed over to Germany.

The German emperors used the power with all the arbitrary violence of the worst times under the eastern Cæsars. At first they stretched their privilege so far as simply to name the pope themselves without any election. Thus Henry III. alone elevated three German bishops in succession to the papacy. It is granted that he was happy in his choice in each case, and hence the arbitrary use of his Imperial privilege had no bad consequences for the Church. But that was not a condition worthy of God's Vicar on earth; and there was no assurance that all future elections or nominations would be equally fortunate, or that future emperors would be equally favorably disposed towards the Church. A serious danger therefore threatened the freedom of the Church; and since she cannot announce the truth while she is the handmaid of earthly princes, she was threatened even in regard to the fufilment of her mission. And the fact that the emperor's choice fell only on worthy incumbents only enhanced the danger; as this circumstance seemed to approve a measure which attacked the very heart of the Church. But God has promised that the gates of hell should not prevail, and therefore, as this state of affairs was a real danger to the Church, He shielded her with His almighty hand. From that era dates the re-action against every external influence, a reaction which has steadily gained ground even to our own times.

It was the lot of Pope Nicholas II. to inaugurate the movement for the freedom of the papal election. In a decree, "De Electione Pontificis," published in 1059, he points out the evils which had hitherto hampered the election. He mentions even bribes as having been used by ambitious candidates or their supporters. As precautions for the future, he ordains that the cardinal bishops shall first consult together about the future pope; then the cardinal clerics, and finally the lower clergy and the people shall give their vote. The pope thus chosen shall be acknowledged as legitimate by all under pain of excommunication. It is evident that nothing new was hereby ordained, if we except perhaps the clause that the

bishops should have the first voice.   All the rest is
nothing but the method of election which had been
followed from the earliest days.   And even the right
thus given to the cardinal bishops can hardly, in
practice, be considered as a new institution.   For, in
the early times, by reason of the bloody persecutions
of the Church, there was in all its members a wonderful unanimity, which was to some extent lost in
quiet and peaceful ages.   Christians then were one
great family, all the members of which were equally
heroic in self-sacrifice and generosity.   With this
feeling of fellowship was united the most unlimited
reverence for those who, in regard to this family,
held the office of fathers.   When, therefore, the chair
of Peter was vacant, the next in authority were the
cardinal bishops ; and hence it naturally devolved
upon them to seek for the worthiest successor ; from
them all others expected to receive advice.   Pope
Nicholas, therefore, in decreeing that they should
first consult together, only gave a public sanction to
what had been observed from the earliest days, in
almost every election, as something flowing from the
very nature of things.

From this decree it is evident that there is no
longer question of Imperial interference in the election, much less of a nomination of the pope by the
emperor.   It is true that the pope wished to see a
due regard shown to the prince (Henry IV. was still
young at the time and not yet on the throne) ; but
even the words of the decree, " salvo debito honore
et reverentia," plainly show that the pontiff meant
only that regard which was due to the ruler of Germany as protector of the Church.   It was then rather
an instruction to the electors than a privilege for the
prince.   They were not to forget the reverence and

honor due to the monarch. That nothing more was intended is shown by other clauses of the same document, which may be viewed as innovations, the object of which was to guard the election against the power of the emperors as well as against the action of factions in Rome. Thus, the pope ordains that should an election be impossible at Rome, the cardinals shall have the right to elect elsewhere. He ordains moreover that if circumstances prevent the solemn inauguration of the newly elected pontiff, this shall not be a hindrance to him in the full use of his power to govern the Church. The elect was pope by the fact of his legitimate election, and against this no protest could be admitted.

This decree has been to this day the groundwork of the papal election. In unessential matters some alterations have been made by new regulations or the abrogation of old, as the times seemed to require ; but the main point remained firm, that no worldly power has the right of imposing a head on the Church in any form or under any pretext.

By degrees the method of electing was so modified that it was entrusted to the cardinals alone ; and hence the preliminary council of cardinal bishops was abrogated as no longer needed, now that a fixed electoral college existed, composed exclusively of men of the greaest wisdom and virtue. Moreover, the custom was introduced and became a law that the pope should be elected from the college of cardinals. This had been otherwise in ancient ages, when men were sometimes chosen who were not even priests, but who were, of course, first ordained before they could exercise the functions of their high spiritual office. We know that the apostles raised laymen to the episcopate. St. Ambrose was chosen bishop of Milan even before his baptism. It was only after his election that he was baptized, then received the lower orders, and eight days afterwards was consecrated bishop. The groundwork of the hierarchy was laid ; but the solid, well-planned edifice required time for its erection. Hence the decree of Pope Nicholas still permitted, in case of necessity, the choice of an ecclesiastic from another church, that is, of one not a member of the college of cardinals.

Finally, the manifold relations which existed between the pope and Catholic kingdoms gave origin to a certain negative influence exercised by the latter on the election. We have seen that Nicholas required a due regard for the secular power. But care was taken that this should never again lead to the abuses which had formerly existed. No secular power was to choose the pope ; this was and remained the office of the cardinals. It was, however, in the interest of the Church that the future pope should be one against whose person there would be no grounded or ungrounded prejudice in this or that great nation. Now, that the electors might know who would be unacceptable to one or other of the Catholic powers, the privilege of a veto was granted to Austria, France, and Spain. But this veto had not the meaning, as has frequently been asserted, that these nations, or any one of them, could protest against an election once made, or render it null. This would have been a direct return to the old abuses, which it was the object to ward off. Indeed, the difficulties would only have been multiplied. For, instead of one, there were three to control the choice ; and not unfrequently, by reason of conflicting political interests, a candidate would have been most acceptable to one government against whom another entertained the most unconcealed opposition. The veto then was something very different from this. It meant only that each of those nations might depute one of the cardinals to point out the one whom it did not desire to be elected. But this was to be done before the election, in order to hinder the choice. A protest against one already chosen was not allowed. Besides, each of the governments could make use of its veto but once, so that at the most only three cardinals were excluded. It was of course permitted to each of the powers to name several persons, whose elevation would be less agreeable to it, with the understanding that the cardinal who represented its interests could use the veto against any one of them, should he prove a likely candidate during the conclave. Once that this veto had been pronounced against any candidate, the privilege was at an end, and could not be used against any other in the same election. In this manner it was sought to observe all due regard towards the great Catholic nations, whilst, on the other hand, the freedom of the election was secured. This privilege granted to the three leading Catholic governments was termed the "exclusiva." But even this concession does not constitute a formal right to be maintained against the Church, or to which she would consider herself bound to yield unconditionally through a sense of moral obligation. It is nothing more than a grant or concession, grounded on motives of prudence. If a Pope chose to abolish this veto, it would cease ; and if a Pope were elected over the veto, he would still be Pope. But this will hardly happen ; for at Rome such privileges are held sacred, even though there is no strict obligation to regard them.

The formalities and ceremonies connected with

the papal election are the work of a thousand years. It would exceed the limits of our space to give a full account of the origin, the changes, and the development of these formalities. We must content ourselves in this, as in other portions of our task, with merely stating in general terms the principles on which the election is based. In this respect it will suffice to explain how the choice is made according to laws in vigor at the present time.

The nature of the subject suggests its division into three parts :

The first part includes the preliminary steps until the cardinals enter into conclave.

The second regards the election itself in conclave which ends with the conclave itself.

The last part explains the acts that take place immediately after the election and until the government of the Church is restored to its usual form.

Before we pass to the development of these points, we must remark that, owing to peculiar circumstances, the papal election cannot at present be conducted in strict accordance with the method demanded by the usuages and laws of the Church. The presence of the Piedmontese in Rome may yet necessitate other modifications. But we pay little heed to this ephemeral circumstance. In describing the papal election, we do not intend to consider merely how this or that pope was elected : this belongs to the historian ; but we describe the grand acts and forms which, in the intention of the Church, should accompany the election. If now and then, in consequence of the rising of some particular political star, some of the prescriptions can be observed only in their spirit and not in their letter, we may be grieved at this misfortune ; but we must not forget that political stars rise and fall, and the everlasting Church of God outlives them all.

It was for the purpose of preparing the reader so that he might be less sensibly affected by the fact that the conclave has not now its full liberty of action, that we insisted in this chapter on the immovable principles on which the election of a pontiff must proceed. Whatever may be hindered by the pressure of political power, it remains always true that he is our pope whom the cardinals of the Holy Roman Church have chosen. God has stood by His Church in the past ; He will not desert her now.

CHAPTER III.

WE must here repeat that we describe the papal election according to the laws of the Church ; not the modifications enforced by a temporary pressure. How far such pressure may prevail we are not able to foresee ; but we owe this confidence to God, that such forced modifications will never pass into recognized ecclesiastical law ; that after the days of gloom the sun will again shine on the Church, and then the venerable ancient institutions will return to their pristine vigor.

Here, then, we consider the election as it ought to be ; we suppose the Pope to be in possession of his legitimate rights, spiritual and temporal ; and therefore that he is the ruler of Rome. For this he will surely be once more, after the present short-lived usurpation of his dominions by the kingdom of Italy. In order to include all that is connected with this part of our subject, we must go back to the last moments of the dying Pope.

It need hardly be said that, as soon as the physicians declare that the life of the Pope is in serious danger, he receives the last sacraments according to the ritual of the Roman Pontifical. For this purpose he summons the cardinals into his presence, begs their forgiveness, commends to them his household, and gives them all instructions which he may deem necessary in the interest of the Church. He dismisses them with the apostolical benediction.

The Confessor, the Chamberlain, and the domestic prelates remain with the Pope, and when it becomes evident that death is approaching, one of the prelates again and again presents to him the crucifix to be kissed. The officers of the Sacred Penitentiary are summoned to recite the Recommendation for the Dying and the Penitential Psalms; and this is continued till the Pope has breathed his last.

Hereupon notice of the death is given to the Cardinal-Chamberlain of the Roman Church. This functionary, vested in purple robes and accompanied by the domestic chamberlains, approaches the bed of the Pope and calls him aloud three times by his baptismal and family names. Only then, when the notary of the apostolic chamber has been witness that no answer is returned to this threefold call, a declaration of the Pope's death is drawn up in legal form. The cardinal then demands of the chief chamberlain of the late Pope the Fisherman's Ring, with which papal briefs are sealed; and receives from the Prodatarius and the Vice-Chancellor of the Roman Church the seals for the bulls and dispensations. These are then destroyed.

Meanwhile the relatives of the late pontiff, who may have resided in the palace, and the Cardinal-Protector leave the premises with what belongs to them. The Cardinal-Chamberlain then takes formal possession of the palace and orders an inventory of all that it contains.

Finally, the remains of the Pope are intrusted to the clergy of St. Peter's Basilica, who cause the body to be embalmed. The entrails, inclosed in a sealed vessel, are taken in a closed chariot to the Church of Sts. Vincent and Anastasius, where they are buried after the usual funeral absolution. The body of the Pope is vested in the pontifical robes, the tiara is placed on the head and a chalice in the hands ; and thus he is laid out.

Besides the above dispositions, which may be called internal, other measures are taken simultaneously, the object of which is to secure the public tranquillity. For the Pope's death has, on some occasions, given rise to disturbances, and it became necessary to prevent the movements of unruly parties, which were doubly unbecoming at so sad a moment. On this account it was prescribed that the Cardinal-Chamberlain, in concert with the commandant of the troops, should make such arrangements as were needed. The gates and other important posts are guarded by stronger detachments than usual, and patrols are sent through the several wards of the city. These measures having been taken to secure the public peace, the cardinal, escorted by the Swiss Guards, makes a tour through the city in his state carriage. When he sets out the great bell of the capital is tolled as for a funeral. The other bells are tolled in the same manner, and the death of the Pope is then made publicly known.

Simultaneously with this solemn procession, the Cardinal-Chamberlain takes command of the government during the vacancy of the papal throne. As soon as the bells are tolled all the courts are closed, the chanceries cease the writing of bulls, and all ordinary congregations of cardinals are suspended. The Chief-Penitenitary alone, who exercises spiritual jurisdiction in cases of papal reservation continues in the discharge of his office.

The Cardinal-Chamberlain is assited in the government by the respective seniors of the cardinal-bishops, priests, and deacons, as the supreme council of State. These, however, remain in office but three days, after which they are succeeded by the next in seniority, and so on till the new Pope is elected. Furthermore, the Cardinal-Chamberlain is required to summon all the cardinals in Rome to a consultation on the necessary provisions for the time of the vacancy ; and this before the end of the day on which the Pope expired, or on the following day in case the Pope died in the evening. The Roman Senate is also assembled and exhorted to assist in preserving order in the city. In this manner all is attended to that may be necessary under the circumstances.

The first act of the interregnum is an act of grace. Criminals under confinement for minor offences are set free, and prisoners for debt are discharged. All this is done on the day of the late Pope's decease, or on the next day.

We now return to the remains of the pontiff. The first act after the publication of the Pope's death is the solemn laying out of his body. His people's pious duty is to gaze for the last time on the face of their ruler, and hence, after the expiration of twenty-four hours from the death, the body, vested in the white soutane, the mozzetta, and the "camauro rosso," is laid on a bed of state, where it remains till the third day. Near it are placed four lighted tapers ; two of the Noble Guard keep watch, and some members of one of the penitential confraternities kneel in prayer for the departed soul. This takes place in an ante-chamber of the palace, and all that wish are admitted. When the Pope has died at the Vatican, his body is next carried to the Church of St. Peter ; but when his death has occurred in the Quirinal, the remains are first transferred to the Vatican, in solemn procession, under military escort. The hearse is covered with red cloth ; it is drawn by two snow-white mules caparisoned with crimson gold-embroidered trappings, and in front of it walk the brethren of the penitential confraternities with torches. The corpse is vested, as was said, for the exposition, and the face is uncovered. Thus the train moves slowly towards the Vatican, to the sound of muffled trumpets and the tolling of bells, till it rests at the foot of the stairway of Constantine. Four of the brethren then carry the corpse into the Sistine Chapel, where it is clad in full pontifical robes, and again remains lying in state through the night. Lights burn around the couch as before, the brethren recite their prayers, and the Noble Guard keep watch.

On the following morning all the cardinals assemble, with the clergy of St. Peter's, in the Sistine Chapel. The papal choir sings the Response, " Subvenite Sancti," the Pater Noster is recited, the corpse is sprinkled with holy water, and, lastly, is taken into the Basilica.

Here, too, everything is prescribed to the minutest details. The clergy of St. Peter's, preceded by the cross-bearer, accompany the procession with lighted torches. The bier is borne by eight priests, and eight more hold the edges of the pall. The Swiss Guard and the Noble Guard surround it, and the cardinals follow. In this manner the train moves into the nave of the church, where the bier is set down.

The corpse is then once more placed on a bed of state, and again the absolution is pronounced over it. The cardinals retire, and the remains are taken to the Chapel of the Blessed Sacrament, where they lie in state during the day. This chapel is enclosed by a railing, which prevents access to it. But the body is so placed that the feet extend beyond the railing, so that the faithful may kiss them. It is understood that the usual guards are stationed to keep watch over the remains.

As the evening approaches, the cardinals again assemble in the Chapel of the Blessed Sacrament, for the purpose of carrying the corpse into the Chapel of the Choir on the opposite side of the Basilica, where it is to be enclosed in the coffin. This is done in solemn procession, whilst the Miserere is chanted. For the third time the absolution is performed by an archbishop, and in presence of the entire College of Cardinals.

After this the corpse is laid in a coffin of cypress-wood, and with it are deposited as many medals of gold, silver, and copper as were the years of the Pope's reign. These medals are placed in three purses. The face of the corpse is then covered with a white veil, and the whole body with a red cloth bordered with ermine. The coffin is closed and en-cased in a second casket of lead, which bears an in-scription and the arms of the deceased. The inscription consists of the name and age of the Pope, the place and time of his death, and the length of his reign. The following is its usual form :

D. O. M.

. . . . . Papa, Aetatis annorum. . . . . . .

Mensium. . . . . . Dierum. . . . .

Obiit

In Quirinali (Vaticano) Palatio.

Die . . . . Anno. . . . .

Sedit

Annos . . . Menses . . . Dies . . . . . .

Hic requiescit

The casket of lead, when closed, is sealed by the Cardinal-Chamberlain, and then deposited in a third coffin made of common wood. Meanwhile the papal choir chants the Antiphon " Ingrediar," and the Psalm " Quemadmodum desiderat." Finally, an authentic document of the whole proceedings is drawn up by three notaries appointed for the purpose.

Immediately next to the Chapel of the Choir there is a door leading into the vestry-room of the papal chanters. Over this door is a broad and deep niche, into which the coffin is placed ; and there it remains until a monument has been erected for it in a chosen spot within the walls of the Basilica. If the succeeding Pope should die before this monument is finished for his predecessor's remains, the latter are removed to another place to make room in the above niche for its new occupant. But if the late Pope had chosen for his last resting-place a spot outside of St. Peter's, his remains cannot be removed to it for one year after his death. During that year they rest in the above-named niche, or, as the case may be, in the other spot inside the church appointed for the purpose.

Considering the spirit which animates the Church, it is easy to suppose that all the means which our faith affords, would be applied in the richest measure to secure for the soul of the departed pontiff eternal light and everlasting repose in heaven. Surely the Pope needs prayers more than any other mortal. During his life the Church prays without ceasing for him, that God may take him under His special protection and grant him the divine assistance in the direction and government of the faithful committed to his charge. After his death, his people pay him the last tribute of gratitude for the heavy responsibility which for their sake he had taken on his shoulders. In order to fulfil this duty of charity which Christians owe to all men in general and in a special manner towards the vicar of Christ on earth, the Church has ordered nine days' funeral obsequies for the Pope. These begin on the third day after his death, and the solemn services are performed each day by one of the cardinals, whilst all the others assist at them. On the ninth day the cardinals walk in procession around the catafalque erected in the nave of St. Peter's. Five cardinals, after having celebrated Mass for the deceased, sprinkle the bier with holy water, and incense it with the usual prayers. The "Requiescat in pace" is sung for the last time, to which all present answer, "Amen;" and thus the funeral ceremonies are brought to a close.

The Church does not, however, rest satisfied with these nine days' services, but offers, besides, many sacrifices for the repose of the deceased Pope. On the first day alone, two hundred masses are said for him in the church of St. Peter, and one hundred on each of the following days. The same number are celebrated in the several parish churches, besides those said in the churches of the religious orders ; and there can hardly be a single Catholic church or chapel in the whole world, in which there is not a mass offered for the Pope, when he dies, nor a Catholic priest anywhere on earth who does not, of his own accord, pay that tribute of love to the common father.

Every day after the service the cardinals meet in a general congregation, and as one of these meetings had been held on the day before the obsequies, the number of these general assemblies is ten. A minute order of proceedings is laid down for each day, and the business is entirely directed towards the ap-

proaching conclave. In the first meeting a number
of papal bulls are read, which regard the election.
These bulls are of Popes Alexander III., Gregory
X., Clement V., Clement VI., Julius II., Pius IV.,
Gregory XV., Urban VIII., and Clement XII. According to these bulls, the election is to begin ten
days after the death of the Pope. It is not allowed
to wait longer than ten days for absent cardinals, all
of whom have, in the meantime, been summoned.
No ecclesiastical censure can deprive a cardinal of
his vote, and even an excommunication would be of
no force against the one who would be elected. The
election is to be held in secret conclave, and he is
elected on whom two-thirds of the votes are united.
Every ballot which brings no election is cancelled. If
the elect is not yet a bishop, he is first to be consecrated by the Bishop of Ostia. This consecration is
now performed by the Dean of the Sacred College,
even if he is not Bishop of Ostia. As Pope he is
confirmed by no one. Such is the import of the said
bulls, and when the reading of them is concluded,
the cardinals make oath to observe the decrees. Now
follows the breaking of the Fisherman's Ring used
by the late Pope. This is done by the chief master-
of-ceremonies, by order of the Cardinal-Chamberlain.
Next, two prelates are appointed, one to pronounce
the eulogy on the deceased, the other to deliver the
address before the election. The days' sitting is
closed by the selection of two cardinals, whose duty
it shall be to superintend the building of the conclave.

The second congregation is almost entirely devoted to political affairs. The various officers of the
State are confirmed in their positions, the Conservatores of Rome offer a tribute of condolence, and
promise obedience to the Sacred College. There are

four Conservatores, and their office is held in very high esteem. Their official residence is in the Capitol and in the Consulta, and they control the higher department of the police. At the close of this meeting the two cardinals selected on the preceding day give their report on the building of the conclave.

The congregations of the three following days are occupied exclusively with elections for the conclave. Two physicians, one surgeon, one apothecary, two barbers and their assistants are named.

At the sixth meeting the cells of the conclave are assigned by lot to the cardinals, and six masters of ceremonies, besides other necessary attendants, are appointed.

The seventh is the least important of all. Its business is to allow any cardinal, who may desire it, to choose a third attendant in addition to the two allowed by law. These are the so-called conclavists of the cardinals, and they are not to be confounded with other servants. One of them is generally a priest. In virtue of this office they henceforth rank as Roman Knights and enjoy the rights of citizenship.

In the eighth congregation a catalogue is made of all the persons who are to be enclosed in conclave, or of all the conclavists, with name, surname, rank, and birthplace of each.

The last two meetings are occupied with the choice of three cardinals, who are to preside over the entering into the conclave, and over the internal economy of that great family.

But all this does not absorb the whole time and attention of these ten congregations. They serve also for the reception of official deputations and embassies. The ministers of foreign courts and the representatives of the cities of the pontifical States appear before them to express their sentiments of sympathy and loyalty. For these audiences a special ceremonial is laid down. The ambassadors, on entering the hall, bend the knee three times, and then address the cardinals standing and with covered heads ; all others make their address kneeling and uncovered. The Dean of the Sacred College responds in the name of all.

On the day after the obsequies and the last congregation, the Cardinal Dean says the Mass of the Holy Ghost in St. Peter's, at which the other cardinals are present. The discourse before the election is next delivered in Latin, by the cardinal chosen in the first congregation. The drift of this discourse is sufficiently indicated by the nature of the subject, and tends to induce the electors to place a worthy successor in the chair of St. Peter. At the close of the discourse, the cardinals enter the conclave in a most solemn manner. The procession is headed by the conclavists of the cardinals and the papal chaplains, who chant the " Veni Creator." Next comes the master of ceremonies bearing the cross. Then follow the cardinals, according to their three several degrees, and in the order of their creation in each. All wear the purple mozetta. The entire procession is accompanied by the Swiss and the Noble Guards.

In this order, the train advances towards the place where the conclave is to be held. By law it should be in the Vatican, though it has often been held at the Quirinal. The cardinals are not, however, bound to either place. It is for them to select the place for the conclave ; and if they generally chose the Vatican, it was because the long galleries and the large halls of that palace facilitated the preparation of the necessary cells for the electors.

When the procession has reached the place of the conclave, the cardinals betake themselves to the chapel of the election, where they say a short prayer, listen once more to the reading of the bulls on the election, and make oath to observe them. The Cardinal Dean then makes an address to them, and with this closes this portion of the solemnities. For that day the conclave remains open, so that the cardinals may leave it and may also receive visitors in it.

They must, however, all be in it before night, and at the approach of midnight the chief master of ceremonies gives a signal with the bell, on which all who do not belong to the conclave are required to retire. The conclave is then solemnly closed by the marshal of the palace, in the presence of the three cardinals chosen for this purpose in the last congregation.

CHAPTER IV.

WE now come to the most important part of the papal election, or rather to the essential act in it. Thus far we have spoken of the death of the last Pope, of the introduction to the election, which takes place in the conclave. All this was but a preparation for the great act. And since we call this the "preparation" we may designate what we shall describe in the third part by the word "ending" of the conclave. But when the conclave is over the Pope is elected, even though what we are about to describe as taking place after the conclave, has not been exactly performed, but modified or even entirely omitted. As soon as the conclave is over there is a Pope, and this no power on earth, how great soever it may be, can change. The Pope may be killed, then the cardinals choose again ; but it cannot be said that this or that legitimately chosen cardinal is not Pope. From these few premises the reader may judge of the importance of the conclave with regard to the election ; for it is the conclave that chooses the Pope.

First of all let us consider what *conclave* means. Conclave is a Latin word, derived from *clavis*, a

key, to which the syllable *con*, together, is prefixed.
Taking this literal meaning, we see that *conclave* signifies something under key, or under one key, some
things together locked up with one key ; therefore,
in a wider sense, a building with one door. With
reference to the papal election, it is used to designate the building in which this takes place, the entrances of which. as we shall see later, are nearly all
walled up, so that it is almost strictly true to say that
the whole building is locked and unlocked with one
key.

The word conclave, signifying the building in
which the election takes place, was also transferred
to the body of the electors ; so that we understand
by *conclave* the cardinals who are assembled in the
said building to elect the Pope. No other convention
of cardinals is called conclave ; they form congregations. Even the assemblies of cardinals described
above, though connected with the election of the
Pope, are always called congregations. A conclave
exists only when the cardinals are assembled in the
building called *conclave*, without permission to quit
it, and when the real election has begun, which is not
to be interrupted by any other business.

A third, though very improper meaning of the
same word, extends farther, including all those persons who, during the election, dwell in the same
building, namely, the assistants of the cardinals, the
servants, and others ; but it can hardly be said that
all these people taken together form the conclave ;
at most they may be said to pertain to it.

It is evident, therefore, that only the first two
meanings of the word *conclave* are of importance,
namely, that of the building in which the election
takes place, and that of the body of men—the cardinals—who cast votes in the election.

About the building in which the election takes place there was nothing determined. In former times the Pope could be chosen wherever the cardinals assembled for that purpose ; and, in fact, elections were held in various towns of Italy. Nicholas II., at the end of the eleventh century, and Clement IV., in the middle of the thirteenth, ordered that the Pope should be chosen in Rome. Only in case of war, or what comes to the same, when revolution or violence is to be feared, can the conclave take place outside of Rome. But this has seldom been the case. Pius VII. was chosen at Venice in 1800.

In Rome itself no particular place is fixed for the election. This depends on the cardinals, who determine it, at least implicitly, in the first general congregation, when two cardinals are appointed overseers of the conclave to be erected. In the second congregation these two make known what they have done. Hence they must know on the first day where the conclave is to be held.

There are in Rome two places specially adapted to the holding of a conclave, the Vatican and the Quirinal Palaces. The cardinals preferred the former, not only for its immense galleries, but also on account of the proximity of St. Peter's Church, in which, after the election, divers solemnities are performed. But the Quirinal was sometimes selected, as when Pius IX. was chosen Pope.

Next comes the erection of cells for the cardinals. This is done as soon as the building in which the election is to be held has been determined upon. If, as is generally the case, the Vatican has been selected, the cells are put up in the gallery from which the blessing is given. Their dimensions are twenty feet long, twenty broad, and twenty high. They are constructed of light timbers and hung with violet-colored tapestry, if the cardinal has been nominated by the deceased pontiff, otherwise the hangings are green or red. Every cell has a little window facing

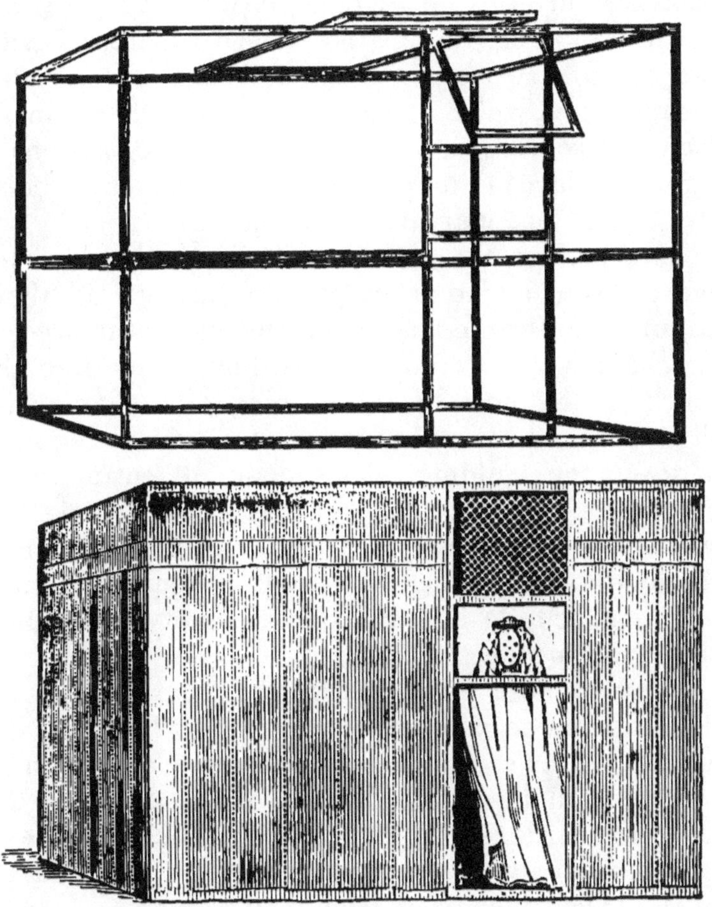

FRAMEWORK AND ROOM OF THE CONCLAVE.

the gallery. But, as the windows of the gallery itself are walled up as far as the upper lights, a kind of dusk prevails in it, which makes itself still more disagreeably felt in the cells. Above every cell is its number and the escutcheon of the cardinal residing there. Each cell is divided into two rooms, the larger of which is occupied by the cardinal himself, the smaller one by his attendants. The space is, therefore, very limited, and when the most indispensable furniture, bed, table, chairs, and press are put into the cell, there is no room to spare. Beside the cell are two other small divisions, one forming the chapel in which the cardinal says or hears mass, the other serving as a refectory. Such is a cardinal's dwelling-place in the conclave, and the suites of rooms are several feet apart from one another.

But besides the erection of these cells, one for every cardinal who takes part in the election, there is work also for the mason. At the end of the preceding chapter we saw how the cardinals enter into the conclave, and how, on the evening of the same day, all persons not belonging to the conclave are required to leave the building. This done, all entrances to the rooms of the conclave, as also the windows, are walled up, one single gate excepted ; but even there all unauthorized going in and out is guarded against with a solicitude almost excessive, notwithstanding the importance of the matter.

We may here mention that the same may be said about a number of other measures to be hereafter described. This care and solicitude exceeds all bounds, and it would be impossible to carry it farther if the college of cardinals were a body of political intriguers against whom too great precautions could not be taken. Such men, it is true, may happen to belong to that august body, just as there was a Judas amongst the apostles. But those elements certainly are exceptions ; they are known, and, humanly speaking, scarcely exercise any influence in the papal election. The vast majority of the Sacred College can safely be admitted to consist of virtuous and intelligent men, who value the good of the Church above every thing else, and whose judgment even the most artful dialectics can hardly lead astray.

But if, neverthless, all communication between the cardinals and the outer world is cut off with a care bordering on excess, we must, to understand this, consider the deeper reasons of it.

First of all, the Pope should not be chosen in the same manner as the ruler of a temporal elective monarchy; for the principal end of the State is to protect the lawful temporal interests of men. Hence it is but natural that these temporal interests should be of great weight in the election, that they should be carefully balanced, and that, as they may change at every moment up to the last, until then also they influence the election.

But in the papal election it is not so. The relation of the Holy See to the Catholic powers deserves indeed fully to be taken into account, and a certain regard is to be had for it in the choice of a new Pope. But all political elements that may enter into this act must exert their influence before the conclave, and the importance given to them has been fixed by what is called the veto of the Catholic powers. We have already explained in what this right consists. Each of the three powers can designate a certain person whose election would not be agreeable to it, and the cardinals will give it due consideration, though not strictly bound to do so. But if these powers, with interests in view entirely different from those of the Catholic Church, were to come during the election with notes, threats, promises, and intrigues, not only would the quiet of the assembly be disturbed, but some of the electors might be so influenced that, even without their knowing or wishing it, worldly considerations would decide a choice which ought to rest only on the rights of God and the welfare of the Church. This is the principal reason for which all communication with the electing body is cut off.

It is, however, not enough that such influences, foreign to the end and life of the Church, be excluded ; not even the slightest ground for suspecting their presence should be given. And here we arrive at one of the most wonderful, really divine regulations of the Catholic Church, which we cannot abstain from briefly describing.

In the nations of the civilized world there are two leading forms of government. The supreme power either proceeds from the people, and in this case the government very frequently presents a sad picture of weakness, and the men in power become the mere instruments of ambitious tribunes ; or the supreme power lies in the hands of a monarch or an aristocracy, and then the people are generally an object of spoliation. Periods of history in which a despot, free from egotism, made his people happy, or a majority of people paid due regard to the rights of a minority, are of rare occurrence. For this reason men even now are yet searching a way of balancing the powers in such a manner that they may prevent each other from doing evil and leave liberty only for doing good. But to this day no one has succeeded in solving the problem, though the greatest minds have made it the study of their lives.

It is not so in the government of the Church. Exteriorly it resembles the monarchy in this, that it is founded on the principle of authority. The pastors feed the sheep, not *vice versa*. Such has been the will of the divine Founder, who possesses all

authority, and from whom all authority of both mon-
archs and people is derived. But the whole authority
finds its scope and its limits not in the well-being of
the shepherds, but in that of the flock. Even Christ
has represented himself under the figure of a shepherd, but not of a shepherd who uses his flock only
for his own benefit, but of a good shepherd who gives
his life for his sheep. Thus in the Church we find
every thing ruled by the shepherds, yet not for the
good of the shepherds, but for that of the flock. We
see the Church provide beforehand for all spiritual
and even corporal necessities. She carefully guards
against all dangers of soul and body, and the shepherd is always ready to stand in the breach to fight
breast to breast against the enemy for the salvation of his flock. Catholics know this spirit of the
Holy Church very well, and therefore feel secure
under her protection. The tendency of laymen to
substitute themselves for the clergy, a fact of frequent occurrence in Protestantism, finds no place
among us, because the interests of both classes do
not oppose each other. The interests of the congregation are also those of the hierarchy. But if, on
this account, one would take us for an indolent and
slavish mass without will and judgment, he would be
greatly mistaken. On the contrary, where human
weakness neglects the interest and salvation of the
congregation, as may be the case, the people
promptly seek help from the superior shepherds,
which they know will not be refused. How far this
foresight of the Church goes is evinced also in the
many precautions taken to secure complete liberty in
the papal election. There should not be left to the
Catholic people any ground of fear lest human considerations and hopes may have influenced the elec-

tion. God's help can certainly not be wanting at that moment, since it is of the greatest import for the Catholic Church ; for He is with her until the end of the world. But men must co-operate as far as it lies in their power, otherwise God may grant only so much of His protection as is absolutely required. The Catholic people must have the satisfaction of knowing that, in this respect, nothing possible to men has been neglected.

It is from this standpoint we must consider the following regulations, which appear to go into the minutest details, and one cannot help recognizing in them the wisdom and providence of the Church.

After this digression, which the reader will excuse, let us return to the papal election.

We have already said that after all persons not connected with the conclave have withdrawn, the entrances, one single gate excepted, are walled up, and that this gate is guarded with particular care. It has two different locks, one inside, the other outside. Both are locked ; the key of the inside is taken into custody by the governor of the conclave, the key of the outside by the master of ceremonies. This gate is the entrance to the conclave itself. In the conclave there is one window, and if an ambassador, for particular reasons, desires to obtain an official audience, he can have it only at this window. All private or secret communication is thereby entirely excluded.

The wall in which the gate is has four openings provided with shutters. Through these the cardinals receive their meals, and whatever else is absolutely required is introduced through them, so that intercourse cannot be had directly as at the window. The carrying of meals is subject to very particular regulations, of which we shall speak later on.

But all this was not yet deemed sufficient. Not only the conclave itself, but also the halls next to it are locked, so that unnoticed access cannot be had. The gate leading into these halls from without, as well as the inner door, are provided with two different locks; the key of the interior lock is kept by the Cardinal-Camerlengo, the key of the exterior by the marshal. Besides all this, a large padlock is added, the key of which is intrusted to the chief master of ceremonies.

Near the main gate is, moreover, a small side-gate, which is also kept locked. It is opened only to let in those persons who are to have an audience at the window of the inner gate, or to let out sick Cardinals who wish to leave the conclave.

Having thus described the arrangement of the building, we now come to the precautions taken during the conclave itself. The marshal of the conclave watches over its security against all danger from without. This is an hereditary dignity, which in former times belonged to the princely house of Savelli, and is now in the possession of the house of Chigi. Prince Chigi is marshal of the conclave. Under his command are the troops, who are stationed near the conclave and occupy all the entrances. During the conclave he lodges in a building near the main gate, and there also the governor of the conclave, who is always a prelate, takes up his abode. The military are distributed over the several quarters of the city to secure tranquillity. Finally, the Cardinal-Chamberlain, together with his assistants, who for the time form his supreme council, remains always in the conclave. The duration of a conclave, as we shall see below when describing the election, cannot be even approximately determined beforehand. The conclave which led to the choice of Gregory X., in 1272, lasted three years, and would then not have ended had not a compromise been effected by which six cardinals were intrusted with the election. Conclaves that lasted several months were frequent. One of the shortest was that in which Pius IX. was chosen, for it lasted but two days.

But whether the conclave be long or short, the greatest precautions are taken that no secret communication may be effected. We have seen that access to the cardinals is rendered difficult, and secret conversation impossible. Even the ambassadors of Catholic powers cannot secretly confer with any cardinal. If an ambassador has any thing to communicate from his government, he must inform the secretary of the Sacred College of it, and also appoint the time at which he desires to be received. Every day three cardinals—a cardinal-bishop, a cardinal-priest, and a cardinal-deacon—are chosen to give audiences, and to these the governor also reports the affairs of the civil administration. At the hour fixed for the reception, the ambassador calls on the marshal and requests him to receive him at the large gate. This reception is always solemn. A numerous suite follows the ambassador, who thus discharges his duty publicly. One of the three cardinals of the council answers the ambassador's address, generally by expressing his thanks for the interest which the power concerned takes in the affairs of the Church.

An easy way of effecting secret communication would be offered by the circumstance that the cardinals' meals have to be carried into the conclave. Wherefore a very exact ceremonial concerning the delivery of meals has been prescribed, the observance of which renders futile all attempts at fraudulent messages,

In the first place the dumb-waiters, by which alone the meals can reach the cardinals, are watched and sealed. Every day at noon the dishes are brought in solemn procession. At the head march two lackeys with wooden staves, bearing their cardinal's arms. If the cardinal was created by the lately

CARRYING FOOD TO THE CONCLAVE.

deceased Pope these staves are violet, otherwise they are green. This also decides the color of the baskets containing the dishes. After the lackeys comes a valet-de-chambre with a silver staff, which is carried inclined if his cardinal belongs to the number of those nominated by the deceased Pope, otherwise it is held upright. Next follow some knights, then the major-domo and the cupbearer ; after them two lackeys, who carry on two poles the basket which contains the food. As the number of cardinals is great, this procession has quite a stately appearance.

When the procession arrives at the dumb-waiter the seals are broken. The major-domo steps forth and calls out the name of his cardinal, and one of the attendants approaches from within to receive the dishes, which are first examined by the appointed

EXAMINING FOOD IN THE CONCLAVE.

prelates to see that they contain no letters. For the same reason the drink is furnished in uncovered crystal bottles. After every thing has been examined, the food is delivered to the cardinal's attendant. This done, the dumb-waiters are again locked and the chief master-of-ceremonies seals them anew.

There are also regulations concerning the kind of food which the cardinals are to receive. Gregory

X. ordained that they should complete the election in three days. If this were not done, for the following five days they should receive but one dish for dinner and supper, and if even after that they had not come to a decision, they should receive nothing but bread, water, and wine. Clement VI. diminished the severity of these prescriptions by allowing broth or fish soup, meat, fish, or eggs, and a dish of salted meat, together with fruits and cheese. Clement XII., to whom this appeared too lenient, though unwilling to forbid it, yet admonished the cardinals anew to observe frugality and moderation. We now proceed to the description of what is done in the conclave itself.

As soon as the inclosure in conclave is accomplished the first act is the oath to be taken by all those who are in any way connected with it. These are, besides the cardinals, their attendants, six masters of-ceremonies, with a servant destined for them, one or several confessors, who must belong to some religious order ; a sacristan and his aid, besides two clerks who help them ; a secretary, with two assistants and a servant ; two physicians and a surgeon ; an apothecary, with two assistants ; two carpenters, two masons, two barbers, with assistants, and thirty-five valets for general service. Ail these persons bind themselves by oath to observe secrecy and fulfil their duties conscientiously. On the same evening, as soon as the conclave is closed, torches are lit, and the Cardinal-Chamberlain with a master of ceremonies examines all the cells that no person not belonging to the conclave may remain. In the same way they make sure that all is locked, and that unobserved correspondence cannot take place. All this is then recorded.

But the conclave is not satisfied with one visit. Twice every day two cardinals walk through the entire inclosure to ascertain that no opening has been made in the walls. To such a degree is carried the solicitude with which the conclave watches over its seclusion. But if, in spite of all these precautions, it should become apparent after the election that a communication from without had been effected in a way of which nothing was known, or which was overlooked, the election already finished is not thereby rendered invalid. It is then supposed that an entrance, which nobody thought of or knew has in reality not been had, especially if no trace of it can be found in the conclave.

The following day begins the election, in which all the cardinals present in the conclave have the right as well as the obligation to take part. They need no longer wait for the arrival of the cardinals out of Rome. But if any arrive after the conclave has been locked, but before the end of the election, they have the right to enter and take part in the election till it is finished. In this case they enter the conclave solemnly, as the cardinals did who are already within. Nothing can prevent a cardinal from exercising the right of election, not even, as has been said already, the censure of excommunication. The only requisite is that he be sound in mind and have received the order of deacon.

But if the cardinals' right of voting is not to be impeded or limited by any thing, the passive right of election, that is, the capability of being elected Pope, is still less limited. The cardinals are free to choose any one whom they deem the most worthy, and it may be said that if, on the one hand they must follow the voice of their conscience, on the other they are not bound to any thing else.

It has been the custom since Urban VI. to choose

the Pope from the ranks of the cardinals, and this is so well established that it is expressed on the ballot, where we find the words, " Eligo Cardinalem," " I choose the cardinal N. N." But a law declaring all other choice invalid does not exist. It is not even required that the person elected be a priest. The celebrated canonist, Phillips, says that even a married layman may be chosen. Only unbaptized persons and heretics are excluded. It need not be said that the cardinals cannot choose a woman, a child, or one that is insane. For though the person elected is not required to be ordained before the election, he must be capable of ordination when elected. An election brought about by simony is void. But even in this case the person elected remains Pope if another has given money for votes against the will or without the knowledge of the candidate, or even with the intention of rendering the election impossible.

The voting takes place twice a day, once in the morning and once in the afternoon. A master of ceremonies gives a sign with the bell ; then he cries out with a loud voice : " Ad capellam Domini." In the morning this is done at six o'clock. As soon as the master of ceremonies has given the signal, an assistant of each cardinal steps forth from his cell and carries his cardinal's writing materials into the chapel. Another assistant holds the cardinal's mantle. This is a garment which every cardinal puts on as soon as he enters the chapel. It resembles in form the ordinary cloak worn by monks, and has a cowl, one end of which is drawn over the head. This mantle is called Croica.

In the chapel each cardinal takes his seat, the first cardinal-bishop occupying the highest seat to the left

of the entrance ; the first cardinal-deacon, the opposite one on the right.   The seats are draped in green,
and the floor of the chapel is covered with a green
carpet.   Before the seat stands a desk, which serves
at the same time for writing and for praying.   It
bears the cardinal's arms.   There is a flue leading
from the chapel to the roof, and when the ballot has
not decided the election, the smoke from the burning
tickets gives notice to the people without that a Pope
has not yet been chosen.

The election itself begins with the Mass of the
Holy Ghost, which is said by the sacristan of the conclave, an Augustinian friar ; after it the cardinals'
assistants must leave, and the cardinals remain alone.

The election can be performed in three ways
only :

1. By quasi-inspiration.

2. By compromise.

3. By ballot, including what is called the " Accessus."

All these three ways have their rules and their
peculiarities, from which it is not allowed to deviate.
If God would choose His representative by means of
real inspiration, and make this direct interference
unmistakably evident by miracle, then all human
ways would be superfluous, and he would be the
Pope whom heaven had thus made known.   But
when such an inspiration is only probable, even
though, according to human reasoning, it may be
evident, the Church is extremely cautious, and calls it
only a quasi-inspiration, subjects it to a number of
tests, and uses with regard to it all possible precautions.

For this as well as every other form of election it
is requisite that the conclave be strictly inclosed.

No canvassing whatever or previous deliberation concerning the candidate must have taken place. As soon as his name is called out by the one who is impelled to nominate him, all the cardinals present must immediately and without further thought give their consent. If a single one hesitates, a quasi-inspiration is not accepted, even though he should assent afterwards. Not even a discussion about using this mode of election is allowed. Like lightning the thought strikes all that the person proposed is the most worthy. Should a cardinal by chance be unable to speak, he must immediately write the name of the elect; and if he cannot even write, this must be done by another cardinal. Not even the shadow of a doubt should occur that the agreement was instantaneous and unanimous. If there are cardinals so sick as to be unable to leave their cells, they are forthwith informed of the result, and must instantly consent. Any objection, hesitation, or deliberation, renders the election by quasi-inspiration invalid. But this nullity would not be caused by previous general consultations held, not about the person thus elected or the form of election, but only about the qualities required in a candidate. If, for example, the cardinals have agreed beforehand to require in the future Pope a special firmness or mildness or erudition or practical acquaintance with public affairs, and then a name is proposed to which all forthwith give their support, such a choice would be valid. In like manner they might agree not to choose this or that one, as is the case when the "exclusiva" is brought to bear. This would not impede the subsequent election of another by quasi-inspiration.

The second form of election is by compromise.

In the case of quasi-inspiration all consultation in regard to this method of election renders the election itself invalid ; but the contrary is the case in the compromise. This method of election absolutely requires a previous agreement about it ; that is to say, all the cardinals must have given their consent to choose the Pope by way of compromise.

The essence of this method of election consists especially in this, that the assembly nominates several persons, to whom the power of electing the Pope is deputed.

Those in whom this power is vested are called " Compromissarii." The number of these is generally more than two. Moreover, it is a law that these Compromissarii be cardinals ; still, if the assembly should delegate others, not of that order, the election would not thereby be rendered invalid. Laymen and excommunicated clerics are excluded from the number of the electors. The assembly gives its instructions to the Compromissarii, on the manner in which they are to carry on the election. These instructions, however, should contain nothing contrary to the customs and laws prescribed for such elections. They could not, for instance, come to a decision by lot.

The electors are to observe strictly the instructions given, provided, as was mentioned, they are not contrary to the established laws and customs. They can raise to the papacy whomsoever they wish, in whatever manner they deem best, whether it be by what is called adoration or by the ballot. They can choose any member of the conclave if they find a worthy candidate. The only restriction is, that he who deposits a ballot may not vote for himself. And hence it follows that if there were but two electors neither of these could be elected, as the votes could

not centre on either of them. When there are three,
one of the three may be elected.

In regard to the manner in which the election
is to be carried on by the Compromissarii, we
find that no more is prescribed than that they solemnly swear that they will give their votes to the
person whom they think best qualified, that they
retire into seclusion and assemble twice each day.
He who is elected by these Compromissarii is the
rightful Pope, provided the electors have exactly
observed all the injunctions.

As an example illustrative of the first method we
mention the election of Clement X., a descendant of
the house of the Altieri, in 1670. As the cardinals
who were assembled in conclave were leaving the
chapel after a fruitless ballot, the populace assembled
without suddenly raised the cry, " Altieri Papa ;"
and thus by a quasi-inspiration, Clement was made
Pope. It has also happened that the vacant see was
filled by a compromise. We have already alluded to
the election of Gregory X. The conclave had been
in seclusion for three years, and no determination
had been arrived at. This long delay was suddenly done away with by the appointment of six cardinals as an electoral committee, who gave the tiara
to the Archdeacon of Liege, Theobald, Viscount of
Piacenza, who at that time was at Acre with the
army of the crusaders.

Such elections, though not according to rules laid
down, are nevertheless valid, being considered as
just departures from the ordinary laws and customs.

The usual manner of electing the Pope is by ballot.
The candidate who receives two thirds of the votes
is elected Pope. If, however, he who has received
two thirds has deposited a vote for himself, and

if independently of this vote he has not the two thirds, he is not considered legally elected. Thus, if there are forty-eight electors, thirty-two votes will be required to form the two thirds. He, therefore, who has thirty-two votes, among which is found his own ballot, has not received the requisite number.

If it should happen that no such majority of votes can be reached, the electors have recourse to another method of balloting, termed the "Accessus." In this all the votes are made to centre upon those who in the previous ballots received the greatest number of votes. Then each of the voters can cast his ballot for one of these candidates. Those, however, who do not wish to change their previous choice, vote for the same, merely adding on their ballot that they do not "accede" to any of the prominent candidates. But if one of the candidates in this mode of election obtains two thirds of the votes he is by that fact elected. However, by thus limiting the number of candidates, it may happen that two of them in the same ballot receive votes enough to elect them. In this emergency he who has the greater number of votes over and above the two thirds is elected. Should there be no majority of votes throughout the election, *i.e.*, should it happen that none of the candidates receives the necessary number, all the proceedings are cancelled, the ballots are burnt, and a new election is entered upon.

The ballot in the afternoon at two o'clock is performed in the same manner which was observed in the morning. The master of ceremonies, ringing his bell, makes his rounds, calling the cardinals "Ad Capellam Domini." The votes are cast, and if the election is not effected, recourse is again had to the *accessus*. In fact, every thing is done in the same manner as in the morning, with this exception, that the " Veni Creator Spiritus" takes the place of the Mass of the Holy Ghost at the beginning of the election.

Thus we see that the conclave meets twice each day until some candidate receives the majority of the ballots.

Before proceeding to particulars, it may be satisfactory to our readers to show how two candidates at the *accessus* can obtain two thirds, or more than two thirds, which at first sight may seem impossible.

Let us suppose that there are forty-eight cardinals in conclave, of whom thirty have given their votes to Cardinal A., and eighteen to Cardinal B. If now, at the *accessus*, two or more give their votes to Cardinal A., and the rest abide by their former votes, it is evident that Cardinal A. would be elected, as he has thirty-two of the ballots, or two thirds ; B., on the contrary, having only eighteen.

Supposing, however, that at the *accessus* eighteen of the cardinals give their vote to B., the others abiding by their given ballot ; Cardinal B. would count thirty-six voices in his favor, whereas A. would have only thirty. The Cardinal B., in this case, would be Pope. But again, it may be that in the ballot Cardinal A. obtains six additional votes, and Cardinal B. twenty ; so that A. would count thirty-six, and B. thirty-eight. Thus both have received two thirds, but B. would be elected, having the greater number of ballots. We see, therefore, that at the *accessus* two candidates may obtain the two thirds, and it is apparent also how they may both have the same number of ballots, and then recourse must be had to another election.

We will proceed now to show in detail how the

election is carried on.   We class the proceedings under the following three heads :

1st. What precedes the balloting.

2d. The ballot itself.

3d. All that follows the ballot, including the *accessus*, if it be necessary to have recourse to it.

In the first place, we will briefly allude to those things which precede the ballot. And first, the formulas or balloting tickets are carefully prepared. A description of these will be given hereafter. These formulas are placed in a silver salver, on a table, in the centre of the chapel where the election takes place. With them is a bag containing as many wooden balls as there are cardinals present in the conclave. Each of these balls has inscribed upon it the name of one of the cardinals. The youngest cardinal-deacon then steps up to the table, takes the bag and draws from it nine balls. The three cardinals whose names are on the first three balls are elected as " Scrutatores" or inspectors. The three following as " Infirmarii," whose duty it is to gather the votes of such cardinals as may chance to be sick in their cells. The last three are to fill the office of " Recognitores," or revisers. It is the duty of these to examine the proceedings and attest the correctness of all that has been done.

These officers being chosen, the formulas or balloting tickets are distributed among the electors. It may be remarked that if these ballots are not printed, it is prescribed that they be all written by one person. They are usually six inches in length and five in width. The cardinals fill up the blanks that have been left, disguising their writing, the better to observe secrecy. The ballot is divided into eight sections. In the first, he who fills the paper signs his own name thus: "Ego N. N. . . . Cardinalis." The second is a blank not to be written upon ; the third contains two spaces for sealing the ballot. The fourth contains the words, "Eligo in summum Pontificem, E. D. meum D. Cardinalem" —that is : "I elect my Lord Cardinal . . . to the dignity of Supreme Pontiff." He who casts the vote, after the word "Cardinal" inserts the name of him whom he deems most deserving of the dignity. The fifth section is again left vacant, and on the sixth are two spaces for seals corresponding to the third. On the seventh the elector writes a motto, generally composed of a number and some verse from the Scriptures. This motto must be retained in the *accessus*. The eighth sec-

Ego	Cardinalis
0	0
Eligo in summum Pontificem E D.. meum D. Cardinalem.	
0	0
Nomen	
Signa	

tion is again a blank. The reverse of this formula is completely covered with devices, so as to render it impossible to read what is written on the inside. On the upper margin is the word " Nomen," and on the lower, " Signa." Each of the electors fills up the formula at the centre table, and there, as it were, in the

DEPOSITING BALLOTS IN THE CONCLAVE.

presence of all, gives his vote. If an elector is not able to write his vote, another having previously taken an oath that what he will hear and write shall be secret, writes the vote of the disabled elector. As soon as a ballot has been filled it is folded in such a manner that nothing is visible but that section on which the word " Eligo" is written. The electors are forbidden, under pain of losing their ballots, to use their ordinary seal. They are required to have a special seal for the occasion.

We proceed now to the counting of the ballots.

The three inspectors take their seats near the altar, upon which a very large chalice and paten are placed. The Cardinal-Dean hereupon rises, takes his ballot, and raising it aloft approaches the altar, kneels and prays ; then rising he says aloud : " Testor Christum Dominum, qui me judicaturus est, me eligere, quem secundum Deum judico eligi debere, et quod idem in accessu præstabo." " I take Christ our Lord to witness that I vote for the one whom, in the sight of God, I judge worthy, and I will do the same in case the *accessus* be used." Having spoken, he places the sealed ballot on the paten and drops it from the paten into the chalice. This done, he retires to his place. After him all the electors in the order of seniority do the same. If there are any of the cardinals sick in their cells, the " infirmarii " place their own votes in the chalice immediately after the dean, and then proceed to the fulfilment of their office. Taking a little casket, which has a small opening in the lid sufficiently large to allow a ballot to be dropped in, they go to the altar, unlock the casket, and having shown that it is empty they relock it, and leaving the key on the altar, proceed to the cells of the sick cardinals. Each of the sick electors receives a formula, fills up the blanks, seals it, and drops it into the casket. The " infirmarii " then return to the chapel, open the casket, and count in a loud voice the number of ballots. The ballots are then dropped from the paten into the chalice. If there are any present who are unable to advance to the altar, the third inspector carries the chalice to them, who, having pronounced the words, " Testor," etc., deposit their vote in the chalice. If a cardinal is so sick as to lose consciousness, he is considered as not being present.

All the ballots now being in the chalice, the first inspector covers the chalice with the paten and shakes it. This action, though not necessary for the validity of the election, is neverthless observed in order to insure still further secrecy.

After this the third inspector counts the ballots, by taking one after another from the chalice into which they had been deposited, and placing them into another. This counting must be done in a loud voice, so that all present may easily hear. If the number of ballots does not agree with the number of electors, the ballots are burnt and a new vote is taken. It may happen that when the number of ballots does not agree with the number of electors, the cardinals do not burn the ballots, but endeavor to discover the cause of the difference. This they may be inclined to do, especially when the conclave has already lasted a long time, and when they see a possibility of the votes concentrating on some very deserving candidate. To cause such a discrepancy between the number of electors and that of the ballots is severely prohibited under sin, and in case the number of ballots exceeds that of the electors, even under pain of excommunication, although the validity of such an election could not be called in question. If the ballots fall short of the number of the electors, he who receives the necessary two thirds independently of his own ballot is elected. Hence if out of forty-eight, one should, without reckoning his own vote, receive thirty-two, he would be rightly elected, even supposing that the full number of forty-eight votes were not deposited in the chalice. If, on the contrary, fifty ballots have been given—two more than the number of the electors—he who is elected must have thirty-four of the votes. It is manifest that both these cases rest on the fact that the elect has evidently secured two thirds of the votes. But when no such result follows, there can be no question of an election by *accessus ;* and the ballots are destroyed.

If the balloting is found correct, the result is published. The first inspector takes up a ballot and reads, though not aloud, the name, which alone is visible ; the second does the same, and passes it to the third, who takes it, and with a loud voice proclaims the name. Every cardinal takes down the name in writing. Should two ballots be found inserted into one another, if they are for different persons they are not counted ; if both bear the same name they count as one ballot. The third inspector having read the name, passes a needle through that part of the ballot where the word " Eligo" is seen, allowing the ballot to slide down the string attached to the needle. This he does with every vote, and then knotting the ends of the string replaces all the ballots in the chalice.

With this closes the ballot. The inspectors proceed to examine more minutely the result of the votes. It may happen :

1st. That the two thirds are absolutely certain ; if so, the closing ceremonies of the election take place.

2d. That the requisite number has not been obtained ; then follows the *accessus.*

3d. That it is doubtful whether the two thirds have been obtained. This doubt must then be settled, to determine whether the closing ceremonies or the *accessus* should follow.

In regard to the last case, it is always uncertain whether he who has two thirds did not in balloting deposit a vote for himself. Hence his own ballot is opened, and if he has voted for himself he is considered as not having received the requisite majority. It may also be the case that an incapacitated cardinal has given a vote. His vote will be opened in order to discover whether he has voted for the cardinal who has just received the two thirds.

Now when all doubt has been removed, and it is certain that two thirds have been obtained, the three "recognitores," or revisers, step forward to review the proceedings, and to compare the ballots with the various signs and mottoes previously made. This having been done, the ballots are burnt.

If the majority has not been obtained, an opportunity is given to secure it by the *accessus*.

The *accessus* is subject to the same formality as the ballot. No oath, however, is administered, as the one taken before the ballot is also binding during the *accessus*. The formula of the ballot differs in this that it is worded, "Ego Cardinalis N. N. accedo Domino meo Cardinali N. N." It is evident that only they give such votes who have received at least one valid vote in the balloting; and they give them for another candidate than the one for whom they voted in the ballot. If a cardinal does not wish to exercise this right of voting, he fills up the formula with the words, "Accedo nemini." The manner of writing, folding, and depositing this vote, and all other ceremonies, are the same as those observed during the regular ballot. If an *accessus*, owing to some circumstance, is declared invalid, it is immediately repeated, otherwise but one *accessus* follows each ballot. The counting of the ballots, however, is peculiar. The votes of the regular ballot and those of the *accessus* are counted together. If the requisite majority is not reached the revisers simply review the counting, and having burnt the ballots declare the *accessus* ended.

If, however, two thirds centre on an individual (and, as we have seen, these two thirds may even be obtained by two candidates), the ballots are examined again in order to verify the proceedings. This can only be done by comparing the seals and mottoes of those ballots given in the morning with those just deposited in the *accessus*. This is generally done as follows :

The first inspector takes the cord upon which have been strung the ballots of the *accessus*, and loosening the first, opens it in such a manner that only the mottoes, seals, numbers, verses and the like become visible. Taking a record of these, he passes the ballot to the second inspector, who does the same, and hands it to the third, who reads them aloud, all the cardinals taking a note of them. The legend of the seal used for closing the ticket is also noticed, and with the help of this it is easy to find a corresponding ballot from the cord holding the tickets of the ballot. This latter is opened and compared with its counterpart, whence it will readily appear whether both ballots have been deposited by the same elector. If these two ballots bear the name of the same candidate, the vote given at the *accessus* is null. If not, then the vote of the regular ballot is published aloud, the name of the candidate it bears, together with the motto. All these are carefully noted down. The ballots having been thus examined and compared, he who has received two thirds, or when several have gained the requisite number, he who has the greatest number of votes, is declared lawfully elected to the dignity of Head of the Church. The ballots are burnt and the conclave is at an end. It yet remains to obtain the consent of the elected cardinal, and when that is ascertained, to give him the honors prescribed.   Hence a great many ceremonies are yet to be gone through before the electors leave the chapel.

As soon, therefore, as it is evident that a cardinal has two thirds of the votes, the inspectors announce the fact, and the junior cardinal goes to the door of the chapel and there rings the bell which summons the master of ceremonies, together with the secretaries of the conclave.   They present themselves to the Cardinal-Dean, in whose company and that of the senior cardinal-priest and the senior deacon they go to the cardinal-elect.   Standing before him, the Cardinal-Dean says : " Acceptasne electionem de te canonice factam in summum Pontificem ?"   " Dost thou accept the election canonically made of thee as Supreme Pontiff ?"   If the cardinal does not immediately answer, the question is repeated three times. Then the elected cardinal kneels down and prays.   If he should refuse, the chair would again be vacant ; if, however, he says, " Accepto," the Cardinal-Dean genuflects, and the first master of ceremonies claps his hands, at which signal all the cardinals rise and remain standing.   The new Pope, when expressing his acceptance of his election, at the same time states the name by which he wishes to be styled as Pope. A record of all these proceedings is taken by the first master of ceremonies.   This is read aloud and is then signed by him and the secretaries of the conclave.

The elect is then conducted by the oldest cardinal-deacons to the altar, and after a short prayer is led to the sacristy.   Having taken off his cardinalitial ring and put on the white stockings, red velvet shoes, white cassock, velvet crimson mozzetta, stole, and white skull cap, he is led forth to the altar, on the

THE ILLUMINATION OF ROME.   Page 197.

platform of which a chair has been placed. Having seated himself he receives "the obedience" of the cardinals, each kissing his foot and hand, and then receiving his embrace. When the Cardinal-Chamberlain pays his homage, he places on the Pope's finger "the Fisherman's Ring," which the Pope immediately returns to him. It is then delivered to the chief master of ceremonies, who is to have engraved upon it the name chosen by the new Pope. The officers of the conclave having been admitted, and having done homage, the senior cardinal-deacon asks the Pope's permission to proclaim the election. Preceded by the processional cross and mace bearers, he goes to the balcony over the main portal of the Quirinal or of the Vatican (the masons having previously removed the wall that had been erected at the beginning of the conclave), the cardinal-deacon steps foward and in a loud voice says : " Annuntio vobis gaudium magnum ; Papam habemus Eminentissimum ac Reverendissimum Dominum N. N., qui sibi imposuit nomen N. N." " I bring you tidings of great joy. We have as Pope the most Eminent and Reverend my Lord Cardinal N. N., who has assumed the name of N. N."

No sooner have the words been spoken than the thundering salutes of St. Angelo's announce the happy tidings far and wide. From the vast populace a deafening " viva" arises, while from every tower of the city the chimes ring out their joyful greetings.

The second grand ceremony of homage takes place in the Sixtine Chapel immediately after the election. Thence the procession moves, chanting the anthem, " Ecce sacerdos magnus," down the stairway of Constantine to St. Peter's, where the Pope re-

ceives the third and public homage.   The Cardinal-
dean then intones the antiphons and prayers prescribed for the occasion, after which the Pope gives
his blessing to the people, and the procession returns to the chapel of the conclave and disbands.
The three days following are given to public rejoic-
ings, congratulatory audiences, and festivities.

CHAPTER V.

PART III.—MINOR PROCEEDINGS CONNECTED WITH THE CONCLAVE.

WHEN all that we have thus far described has been done, he who is elected is Pope, in all right and justice, and no man can in any way call his election in question or endeavor to invalidate it. He governs the Church from that moment, and no other act is required to give him further authority. Some, it is true, assert that the coronation is in some way necessary to the perfection of the election. However, this ceremony is by no means essential, for we find that Clement V. threatens with excommunication those who assert that bulls issued before the coronation are not binding.

If the person elected is only a priest, he must be first consecrated bishop ; if only a deacon, he must receive both ordinations, that of priest and that of bishop. The bestowing of these orders was an honor reserved to the Cardinal-Bishop of Ostia. Of late this duty has devolved upon the Cardinal-Dean. This ordination or consecration must of course precede the coronation. In former days the ordinations took place on the day of coronation ; now they are generally conferred in private. The coronation, usually on the first Sunday or holy-day after the election, is performed with all possible solemnity.

In a festive procession, headed by the papal cross, and composed of all the dignitaries of the Church, the Pope is carried on his sedan-chair under a baldachin, near which march two nobles bearing the "flabelli," or great fans. The chair of the Pope is carried by the highest nobility, and is surrounded by the ambassadors of foreign courts, the officers of the army, the Swiss Guard, and others.

When the procession has reached the basilica, the Pope mounts a throne that has been erected for him. The cardinals take their seats around him to listen to the Latin address that is usually read. After this the canons and clergy of St. Peter's pay their homage to the Pope.

Then follows the solemn entrance of the Pope into St. Peter's. The procession first moves into the Chapel of the Most Blesssed Sacrament, where the Pope offers a short prayer. Thence they proceed to the Clementine Chapel, where he again kneels in prayer. Finally, the procession arrives at the main altar, where the Holy Father ascends his throne and receives the homage of all the dignitaries, after which he gives his blessing to those present.

After this ceremony the Pope intones the hour of Tierce, which the choir continues while his Holiness is being vested. A procession is again formed which moves around the sanctuary, during which one of the masters of ceremonies three times approaches the Pope, carrying on a silver salver a small lock of wool, which he burns, saying at the same time: "Sancte Pater, sic transit gloria mundi," "Holy Father, thus vanishes earthly glory." At the end of this ceremony the high mass begins. After the "Confiteor" the Pope retires to his throne, whilst two cardinals read the orations. Then he returns to

THE CORONATION PROCESSION.—*See next page.*

THE CORONATION PROCESSION.

Page 205.

the altar to receive the pallium. This consists of a white woollen cloth, covering the shoulders, and falling down in front and behind. This was once a peculiar garment of the Jewish high-priest. It belongs peculiarly to the dress of the Pope. The archbishops, however, wear it as a sign of their dignity. They must come to Rome to receive it three months after their election, and are allowed to use it only on certain festivals and in their own churches.

The Cardinal-Dean, after having presented the pallium to the Pope to be kissed, places it upon the pontiff's shoulders saying, "Accipe pallium sanctum, plenitudinem pontificalis officii, ad honorem omnipotentis Dei, et gloriosissimæ ejus Matris et sanctorum apostolorum Petri et Pauli et sanctae Romanæ Ecclesiæ." "Receive the holy pallium, the fulness of pontifical power, in honor of God Almighty, of the ever glorious Virgin Mary, the holy Apostles, Peter and Paul, and of the holy Roman Church." The Pope, clothed in the pallium, rises and incenses the altar, returns to his throne, receives the homage of the cardinals, patriarchs, archbishops, bishops, abbots, and penitentiaries of St. Peter's.

Then the high mass is continued to the collect, when the Pope again retires to his throne. Thereupon the first cardinal-deacon takes the papal crosier and accompanied by the subdeacons, auditors, and secretaries, descends into the chapel of the "Confessio," where repose the relics of the holy Apostles Peter and Paul. Here the deacon begs the intercession of the saints for the new Pope. He repeats three times, "Life to our Lord N. N., whom God has given us as bishop and vicar of Christ." All answer: "O God ! help him ; O Mary ! help him." After this the high mass is continued without any further interruption.

After the mass the Pope is conducted with all pomp to the balcony of St. Peter's, where he is seated upon a throne, and the second in seniority of the cardinal-deacons takes the mitre which the Pope has worn, and the Dean of the Sacred College places the tiara upon his head with the words, " Accipe tiaram tribus coronis ornatam," etc. " Receive the

ST. JOHN LATERAN.

tiara, adorned with the triple crown, and know that thou art the father of princes and kings, the ruler of the earth, the vicar of our Saviour Jesus Christ." After some prayers prescribed for this ceremony the Pope solemnly gives his benediction to the assembled multitude. He then returns to the hall of ornaments, where, being disrobed of the sacred vestments, he receives the congratulations of the cardinals.

The last solemn act connected with the election of the new pontiff is the taking possession of the Lateran basilica. This church is, as it were, the mother of all the churches of Rome and of the world. Formerly the Pope resided in the palace adjoining it. In taking possession of this Church, the Pope, in a manner, takes possession of all the churches. In former days the ceremony took place immediately after the coronation, and the Pope, after a slight repast, set out, riding on a white palfrey, followed by all the officials of Church and State, most of them likewise on horseback, towards the basilica. In later

THE COLISEUM.

times this ceremony is independent of the coronation, and is performed on any convenient day. Nor does he ride on a horse, but is carried . The procession crosses the bridge of Sant' Angelo towards the Capitol. Here a triumphal arch has been raised, beneath which the Senator of Rome, with his ivory staff in his hand, awaits the Pope. He makes an address and tenders his oath of fidelity. The procession passes thence through the Campo Vaccino, under the triumphal arch of Titus, towards the Coliseum, where the Rabbi of the resident Israelites gives over to the Pope the five books of Moses, begging protection for those of his belief. This being granted, the procession moves on to the Church of St. John Lateran.

At the portal the cardinal-archpriest of this church offers the cross to be kissed by the Pope. Here the Pope again mounts his throne and receives the homage of all the clergy of the Lateran.

The keys of the Church—one of gold, the other of silver—are then presented to the Pope by the archpriest, who also reads an address. From this place the procession moves through the church to the council hall, where each of the cardinals and chief prelates receives from the Pope's hand a gold and a silver coin as a remembrance. Then having assumed the tiara, the Pope proceeds to the balcony and blesses the people. The papal treasurer scatters silver coin among the people.

The Pope having laid aside his sacred vestments, is conducted back to the Vatican.

With this end the ceremonies connected with the papal election. We say nothing of the festivities given by the Roman patricians, the foreign ambassadors and others. These not relating to our subject-matter need not be here described.

CHAPTER VI.

THOU art Peter, and upon this rock I will build my Church." These consoling words assure us that the Divine Founder will ever bestow such firmness and stability on all occupants of the chair of St. Peter as will make it evident that He Himself bears the Church upon His strong shoulders, rather than he who holds His place.

We have seen in the foregoing pages all the wise regulations, which, with divine assistance, have been made to place the most worthy person at the head of the Church. And as man has done all in his power to insure success to the work, God has blessed it by giving to his Church a line of popes, which in the history of the world never found its equal, and which will exert its influence on all future times. Eminent among the great men who compose this catalogue stands Pius IX., and his greatness will be more and more clearly manifested as the harvest ripens which was sown by his hand. As yet much is hid from our sight, but when from the seed the mighty tree shall spring and spread far and wide, the memory of the great Pius shall be blessed and every Catholic will glory in his faith, manifest his enthusiasm for its advancement, and confirm its truth by the sacrifice of all that is dearest to him.

We need not then be disheartened. He who sowed the seed now sleeps the sleep of the holy dead ; Leo XIII., who has meanwhile been raised to the papacy will gather in the ripened harvest, and, as the former did not sow for himself or his own glory, so the latter will not reap for his own benefit, but only for the glory of God and the honor of the Church. The chair of St. Peter is filled to-day, but will be again vacant, awaiting another occupant ; but Jesus Christ and His kingdom remain forever.

Christus vincit, Christus regnat, Christus imperat.

LIFE OF LEO XIII.

HIS ELECTION AND THE FIRST ACTS OF HIS REIGN.

THE LIFE OF POPE LEO XIII.

CHAPTER I.

Y words shall not pass away " said our Divine Saviour : " Thou art Peter, and upon this rock I will build my Church, and the gates of hell shall not prevail against it." The Pope dies, but the Papacy lives on ; Peter is immortal. Yesterday Pius IX. gave up his holy soul to God ; to-day he lives anew in Leo XIII. The Supreme Pastor made haste to place at the head of his flock a faithful shepherd, who might console and reanimate it, bearing his staff with glory in the midst of the people of God.

The present vicar of Jesus Christ on earth and the common Father of the Faithful was born on the 2d of March, 1810, at Carpineto, in the diocese of Anagni, in the Papal States. His parents were Count Louis Pecci and Anna Prosperi, the daughter of a noble family whose seat is at Cori, not far from

Carpineto.   In baptism he received the names of Vincent and Joachim.   The Pecci family, of which he is an offspring, belongs to the ancient nobility of Sienna, but in the fifteenth century it removed to the States of the Church.

Carpineto, which has been rendered celebrated by the accession of Leo XIII. to the Holy See, is a town of about 5000 inhabitants.   It is built on a height and flanked by narrow ravines.   The landscape around, though somewhat wild, is beautiful.   Nearly all the houses are small and poor, built of stone and hanging against the rocks.   The palace, in which the Pecci family lives, dates from ancient times.   The apartment of Leo XIII., which lies on the second floor, is furnished in the old style, with a certain richness, but with no eye to comfort.   A portrait of Pius VI. and a few pictures adorn the ante-chamber.   In the great hall is a portrait of the new Pope, in the dress of a Cardinal.   The expression of his countenance is young, smiling, and of striking beauty.   With the advance of years, his features have become more defined, but they have kept that amiable expression which renders the Pontiff so winning to all who know him.   The father of the Pope is there, too, in the uniform of a French colonel, together with his mother, who has all the graces of her descent from patrician blood.   In his bedroom stands a simple iron bed with modest hangings, at the head of which is a silver crucifix on a red ground.   Next to this room is a little family chapel, as there is always in the houses of the ancient nobility.   Cardinal Pecci said Mass here during his stay at the time of his elevation to the Cardinalate.

The tombs of the Peccis are in the Church of the Capuchins.   Their coat of arms consists of a poplar or pine, a bar, two lilies, six roses and a comet on an azure field.

Leo XIII. has three brothers, older than himself, and two sisters. The oldest of his brothers, who is not married, has already reached the age of 84 ; the second, who is 76 years old, has four sons ; the third is a priest, a modest and learned disciple of St. Thomas, who figured conspicuously in the preparatory commissions of the Vatican Council, as one of the theologians of the Holy Father. For six years he taught the philosophy of the Angel of the Schools to the clerics in the seminary of Perugia.

The two sisters are married and both mothers of families.

In 1818, when Joachim Pecci was only eight years old, his father sent him, together with his oldest brother, Joseph, to the college of the Jesuits, in Viterbo. He there made his first communion, on the feast of St. Aloysius, June 21, 1821.

After the death of his mother, in 1824, he removed to Rome and resided with his uncle in the palazzo Muti. He continued the course of his studies at the Roman College, which Leo XII. had just restored to the Jesuits. His professors of rhetoric were Father Ferdinand Minini and Jos. Buonvicini. In the same college he studied philosophy and mathematics, under Fathers Pianciani and Carafa, for three years ; and then theology for four years under Fathers Perrone, Manera, Patrizzi, and others. He sustained, in a most brilliant manner, two public acts or examinations at the Roman College and in the Roman University known under the name of *Sapienza*, and each time gained for himself the warmest applause.

After this, he studied law and diplomacy at the Academy of Noble Ecclesiastics. He there made himself remarkable by a devotedness, zeal and intelligence so great, that Gregory XVI., who was skilled in the knowledge of men, resolved to attach him to himself, and on March 14th, 1837, named him Prelate of his household and Referendary of the Segnatura. Mgr. Pecci was then only 26 years old, but he displayed so many good qualities and such ability for government, that the Holy Father did not hesitate to entrust to him offices of the utmost importance.

He was ordained subdeacon and deacon, in the beginning of the year 1837, by Cardinal Charles Odeschalchi, in the chapel of St. Stanislaus, at Sant' Andrea on the Quirinal. At the end of the same year, on the 23d of December, he was ordained priest by the same Cardinal, and said his first Mass in the same chapel, assisted by his brother, Joseph Pecci, then a member of the Society of Jesus.

He was now fully prepared to run his great career, and it was not difficult to foresee that he would rise to the highest distinction at the Papal Court.

On the 15th of February, 1838, Mgr. Pecci was appointed delegate in the province of Benevento, where it was necessary to restore order. Brigands and smugglers desolated the province to such an extent as to oblige the most powerful families to connive at their evil doings, in order to avoid pillage and murder. The population were terror-stricken and the officers of justice met with obstacles at every step. Once, however, that the public forces had been reorganized, the corps of the customs officers reformed, and that the king of Naples had decided upon repressing the banditti with vigor, Mgr. Pecci pursued the brigands so vigorously, by having them attacked in the very castles where they found a refuge, and by having the families arrested who furnished them with provisions and ammunition, that, within the space of fourteen months, the whole province was completely purged of the malefactors.

Still there remained one band of twenty-eight brigands, the most reckless and notorious known. One day, a marquis, a rich potentate of the province

and the protector of these wretches, came in person to see Mgr. Pecci, and said to him :

" I am going to Rome to get an order for your expulsion from our province, and if that will not do, I will have you carried off."

" Very well," answered Mgr. Pecci ; " but in the mean time, before setting out for Rome, allow me to entrust you to these carabiniers, to whom I give orders to keep you in prison for three months on bread and water."

The very first night that the marquis was in prison, Mgr. Pecci had his castle surrounded, and all of the twenty-eight brigands were either killed or arrested.

This firmness of action was joined to a great love of justice and affability of manners, which gained all hearts. Gregory XVI. praised the delegate highly for the success he had obtained ; the King of Naples, Ferdinand II., congratulated him openly on it. The peaceful inhabitants of the province hailed him as their deliverer, and it was easy to see, from the general grief on the occasion of a serious illness, which threatened a fatal result, how well Mgr. Pecci had known to win for himself the affection of all. Laity and clergy were equally alarmed, and in Benevento there were public processions of penitents, who marched with bare feet, and heads covered with a veil, to implore from heaven the recovery of their delegate.

Three years had sufficed to regenerate Benevento, and this wonderful result induced the Pope to seek the same benefit for another portion of his dominions, through the same means. On June 12th, 1841, Mgr. Pecci was nominated as delegate to Spoleto ; but this destination was soon changed for one of still greater importance, when, on the 17th of the same month, he was appointed delegate for Perugia, the government of which had always presented great difficulties. The young delegate met with the same success as at Benevento. At his arrival in Perugia, a town of about 20,-000 inhabitants, the four city prisons were filled with criminals : five months later there was not one, and the most perfect order reigned throughout the city and its district.

At the time of Mgr. Pecci's appointment to the

government of Perugia, Gregory XVI. expressed his desire to make a journey through his dominions, and as his arrival at Perugia had been fixed for an early day, the delegate hastened from Rome to his province to prepare for a proper reception of his sovereign. A road had been projected from Foligno to Perugia, which would greatly facilitate the approach to the latter city ; but the work was far from its termina. tion. Mgr. Pecci resolved that the road should be finished before the Pope's arrival ; and with his usual energy he accomplished the task, to the wonder of all who knew the difficulties of the enterprise.

Another instance will be of interest. He had received information that the bakers of Perugia gave bread of light weight. The delegate went out, early one morning, with his officers, and inspected all the bakeries of the city. He confiscated all the bread which was found less than the proper weight, and had it distributed to the poor in the market place. One lesson sufficed for the dishonest bakers.

When he had thus governed the province of Perugia for a year and a half, Gregory XVI., who saw that Pecci daily justified more and more the hopes he had conceived of him, preconized him, on the 27th of January, 1843, Archbishop of Damietta *in partibus*, though he was then only 33 years old, and sent him in quality of apostolic nuncio to the court of King Leopold I. at Brussels. He was consecrated bishop, at Rome, in the Church of St. Lawrence, on the Viminal Hill, by Cardinal Lambruschini, assisted by the Bishops Asquini and Castellani, on Sunday, February 19th, 1843, and then set out, by way of Marseilles, Lyons, Rheims, Mezieres, and Namur, to take up his post as Nuncio at Brussels. He held that position for three years ; and the Belgians still remember how great an influence he had gained for himself at the court, and how powerful a patron every Catholic undertaking found in him, not less than his far-sighted judgment, which enabled him to see, even then, the events which from afar prepared the European revolution.

Leopold and all the royal family held him in the highest esteem.

The decree which made him Grand Cross of the Order of Leopold bears the date of May 5th, 1846, and specifies that this royal favor was conferred on him as a particular testimony of good will and esteem.

Mgr. Pecci had a special liking for establishments of Christian education. He frequently visited the celebrated Academy of Saint-Pierre, and always held in the highest esteem the excellent religious of the Sacred Heart, who direct that house. He used to enter their convent without announcing himself, presided at their feasts, and even interested himself in the compositions of the pupils. The ladies that have been educated in that holy house remember to this day with a lively emotion the piety and affability of him who is now the father of Catholicity.

The noble families of Belgium appreciated the great qualities of the apostolic nuncio, who kept up an intercourse with several of them, especially with that of the Count de Mérode, where he used to pay frequent visits during his stay at Brussels. Mgr. de Montpellier, Bishop of Liege, had studied at the Roman College together with his Excellency, and they remained ever after intimately united.

Mgr. Pecci could not long endure the Belgian climate, which is somewhat cold, and his health obliged him to leave Brussels after a sojourn of three years.

In the month of April, 1845, the Nuncio set out from Belgium to visit some of the neighboring countries, before returning to Italy.   His route was from Brussels to Liege, where he spent some days with the friend of his college days, Mgr. Montpellier. Thence he went to Aix-la-Chapelle, Cologne, and up the Rhine to Mainz.   He visited Treves also, and after some delay there, proceeded to Maestricht, whence he returned by way of Liege to Brussels. After reposing from the fatigues of this journey, Mgr. Pecci resolved to pay a visit to England, and spent two weeks in London ; after which he came back to Brussels and took final leave of the Belgian Court.   His journey homeward took him through Paris, Lyons, Avignon and other French cities of renown, to Marseilles, where he took ship for Civita Vecchia.

The King of Belgium had handed him a dispatch for the Holy Father ; but Mgr. Pecci, on his arrival at Rome, did not see Gregory XVI. alive.   The Pope was on his death-bed, and expired on the 1st of June, 1846.   Meanwhile the Bishop of Perugia had died, and a deputation had been sent to Rome from that city to urge the appointment of Mgr. Pecci as his successor. This had been made known to the Nuncio before his departure from Brussels ; and he had been preconized Bishop of Perugia on the 10th of January, 1846.   At the same time the Pope named him Cardinal, thus forestalling the request contained in the above-mentioned dispatch of King Leopold.   As usual, his nomination to the Cardinalate was reserved *in petto ;* and as Gregory XVI. died before he could publicly proclaim the nomination, Mgr. Pecci's elevation to that dignity was delayed.

On Sunday, 26th of July, 1846, the new Bishop

of Perugia took solemn possession of his see, and became the spiritual head of a diocese of which he had already been the civil governor.

He found there still in existence the greater part of the works he had begun three years previously. His only anxiety now was to apply himself to make them prosper and to found new ones in accordance with the needs of the time.   Thus he founded for his priests " the Academy of St. Thomas," and it was his greatest pleasure to preside at its meetings, that thus he might give them a more lively impulse.   One should have been on the spot and have seen Mgr. Pecci living in the midst of the clerics of his seminary, to form an idea of his extreme benevolence and his great spirit of faith.   His brother, Don Giuseppe Pecci, greatly aided him in this undertaking.

Mgr. Pecci brought the ladies of the Sacred Heart, whose singular merit and devotedness he had learned to appreciate at Brussels, to Perugia for the education of young ladies.   He had visited, at Paris, the venerable foundress, Madame Barat, and had promised to take the first opportunity to establish the new order in Italy.   It was only after the lapse of ten years, whilst he was Bishop of Perugia, that he was able to fulfil at once his promise and his earnest desire.   Madame Barat sent a colony of her sisters to Perugia, headed by Madame Lehon, a lady whose merit has since raised her to the highest post in the order.   Another colony of the same order had been established at Rome in 1828, and held possession of the church and convent of the Trinita de' Monti.

During his administration the seminary was re-built and enlarged, and the cathedral repaired and beautified.   In 1849, he presided at a council of the Bishops of Umbria and wrote the acts of the meeting, which tended to the development of religion in that province.   When the Piedmontese invasion absorbed that portion of the Papal dominions, Mgr. Pecci had the honor of suffering imprisonment for the defence of right and justice.   His seminary was seized by the new rulers ; but the bishop lodged his seminarians in his own house, and their studies were not interrupted.

Mgr. Pecci showed in his whole government of

CHURCH OF TRINITA DE' MONTI.

the church of Perugia much firmness and wisdom. He wrote two celebrated letters to King Victor Emmanuel II.   In the first, he reproved the fatal measure of civil marriage imposed upon the people of Umbria ; in the other he protested against the expulsion of the Camaldolese friars of Monte Corona and of other religious corporations.

In 1862, Mgr. Pecci was arraigned by the government for sedition and resistance to its authority. Three clergymen of the diocese had been accused of refusing to sign Passaglia's petition to the Pope urging him to renounce his temporal power. They answered in the public papers that they had refused merely because they had prepared another petition of their own more insulting to the Holy Father than Passaglia's. The bishop wrote to them to recall them to a sense of their duty, and meanwhile suspended them from all functions. The unhappy men, instead of submitting to their bishop, referred his letter to the government, which at once instituted proceedings against Mgr. Pecci. But its own judges were compelled, by the evidence of his innocence, to dismiss the case.

A college had been established at Perugia for the Christian education of young men. The new government seized it and placed its own teachers in it to train the youths in its own principles. Mgr. Pecci at once denounced the measure, withdrew his protection from the college, and took down his arms which had been affixed over the main entrance to the building. On the following day the classes were empty, and the government was foiled.

Seven times he visited the whole of his diocese ; and during his episcopate thirty-six churches were built, and many more were repaired.

All his pastoral letters to his flock are models of ecclesiastical learning, and will serve as perpetual monuments of his zeal. The most remarkable among them are the last two, one of which he published before the Lent of 1877, the other on the 10th of February, 1878. He inveighs strongly against the current errors in regard to religion and Christian life ; the vices which he condemns are blasphemy, the non-observance of feast-days, licentiousness, the reading of bad books and the neglect of education.

Mgr. Pecci had been reserved Cardinal *in petto* by

ARCHBISHOP PECCI RECEIVING THE CARDINAL'S HAT FROM PIUS IX.

Page 227.

his Holiness Gregory XVI. in the Consistory of January 10th, 1846.   The death of the Pope delayed the moment at which he was to receive the purple.   It was only on December 19th, 1853, that he was created Cardinal of the Order of Priests, by Pius IX., with the title of St. Crysogono.

The piety and austerity of Mgr. Pecci were always a subject of great edification for his diocesans.   He practised a special devotion to the Sacred Heart of Jesus, to the Blessed Virgin, and St. Joseph.   "At all times," he wrote in his pastoral of December, 1867, "fervent prayer has been the divine weapon of the Christian ; but, amid the great calamities of the present time, we must more than ever rekindle in souls the love of prayer and fly to the Sacred Heart of Jesus, our Saviour."

He was most simple in his manner of living.   He always rose at daybreak, and after having said his Mass, set to work.   He busied himself much with the study of history and literature, and acquired immense erudition.   He made a profound study of Dante, so far as to be able to recite by heart long passages upon the simple quotation of a line.   His conversation was amiable and sprightly.

Like most of his countrymen, Mgr. Pecci took only one meal a day, at one o'clock.   He was an enemy to delicacies and his fare was most frugal ; it consisted of boiled pastry, which replaced the soup, of boiled or roasted meat, of some greens, and of the cheese of the country, made of goat's milk.   At all seasons of the year, the Archbishop retired at 10 o'clock.

Notwithstanding the simplicity of his life, all those who have known Mgr. Pecci at Perugia affirm that his whole person shows a certain majesty.   He is of tall stature ; his forehead is large, and his penetrating eyes betoken a singular vivacity ; his countenance, which austerity has furrowed from early youth, betrays great keenness.   He has a strong and sonorous voice, and speaks French and German fluently.

At the time of the Council in 1870, Mgr. Pecci, who was then Cardinal, performed a touching ceremony in the church of the French seminary.   He there received the abjuration of a Jewish family of Bologna, and administered baptism and gave holy communion to the converts.   The French bishops, who assisted at the ceremony to the number of fourteen or fifteen, were so struck by the majesty of the celebrant, that they could not refrain from saying afterwards : '' What a fine Pope he would make !''

During the two-and-thirty years of his episcopate he constantly showed himself gentle and benevolent, yet firm and austere.   He admitted no consideration when there was question of principle.

In the Consistory of 21st September, 1877, his Holiness Pius IX. called Cardinal Pecci to Rome as successor of the Camerlengo, Cardinal de Angelis, who had died in the preceding July.   From that time his Eminence inhabited at Rome the palace of Falconieri, his new office obliging him to reside near the Pope.

He was a member of the congregations of the bishops and regulars, of the Council, of the ecclesiastical Immunity, of the Discipline of regulars, and of our Lady of Loretto ; protector of the congregation of the Third Order of St. Francis of Assisi, of the monastery of St. Urban, of that of St. Clare at Assisi, of the conservatory of St. Euphemia, and of the pontifical Academy of Archæology at Rome.

We cannot end this chapter more appropriately than by giving a synopsis of the last pastoral letter which Cardinal Pecci, Archbishop of Perugia, issued to the clergy and faithful of his diocese, a document that would have been considered remarkable even if within a year and a week its author had not been raised to the Papacy as Leo XIII. He took up the question, " Is the Catholic Church hostile to the progress of industry, art, and science ? Is there, as her adversaries declare, a natural and irremediable incompatibility between the Church and civilization ?" These were the questions which the Cardinal set himself to answer, and his answer was, " No ; the Catholic Church is hostile to no phase of progress ; is not incompatible with civilization even in its purely material aspect." He went even further, and took pains to explain to his flock what civilization is, its merits and advantages, and these explanations were not given as a theologian but as a political economist. He said :

"A celebrated French economist, Bastiat, has grouped and shown as in a picture the multiplied benefits man finds in society, and it is a wonder worthy of admiration. Consider the humblest of men, the poorest laborer—he has wherewith to clothe himself, well or ill, and shoes for his feet. Think how many persons, how many agencies, had to be put in motion to furnish this clothing or these shoes ! Daily every man places a morsel of bread to his lips ; behold here what labor ; how many hands it has taken to reach that end, from the husbandman who painfully turned the furrow to confide to it the seed, to the baker who converted the flour into bread ! Every man has rights ; he finds in society lawyers to defend them, magistrates to make them sacred by their sentence, soldiers to compel respect for them. Is he ignorant ? He finds schools, men to write books for

him, others to print and publish them. To satisfy
his religious instincts, his aspirations towards God,
he finds those of his brethren who, laying aside all
other occupation, give themselves up to the study of
sacred lore, renouncing business, pleasure, home, the
better to discharge these lofty duties. But this is
enough to prove to you clearly that society is indispensable in order that our wants, which are as urgent
as they are varied, may be satisfied."

Having thus pointed out the advantages of association and the division of labor, Mgr. Pecci went on
to explain progress and define civilization as follows :

" Society, being made up of men essentially perfec-
tible, cannot remain at a standstill ; it makes progress
and perfects itself. One century inherits the inven-
tions, discoveries, and improvements of its predecessor, and thus the sum of physical, moral, and political
benefits grows marvellously. Who would compare
the miserable huts of primitive peoples, their rude
utensils, their imperfect tools, with all that we of the
nineteenth century possess? Nor is there any more
comparison between the articles produced by our
ingeniously constructed machinery and those toil-
somely wrought by the hands of man. There can be no
doubt that the old highways, unsafe bridges, and long
and disagreeable journeyings of old times were not
the equals in value of our railroads, which, as it were,
fasten wings to our shoulders and have made our
globe smaller, so near to each other have they
brought its nations. Is not our era, by the gentleness of its manners, superior to the rude and brutal
days of barbarism, and are not reciprocal relations on
a more friendly footing? From certain standpoints,
has not the political system been improved under the
influence of time and experience? No longer is pri-

vate vengeance tolerated, or torture; and the petty feudal tyrants, the wrangling communities, the wandering bands of free companions—have they not all disappeared? It is, then, true that man in society goes on perfecting himself in his physical comfort, his moral relations with his fellows, and his political condition. And the different degrees of this successive development to which man in society attains are civilization; this civilization is new-born and rudimentary when the conditions under which man grows more perfect in this threefold sense are but partially developed; it is great and high when they attain a larger development; it would be complete were all the conditions perfectly satisfied."

After this passage, of which G. de Molinari says in the *Debats* that it makes the reader fancy he is listening to one of Michel Chevalier's lectures at the Collége de France, the Cardinal goes on to ask whence proceed progress and civilization. They come, above all, from labor. Labor was despised by the most illustrious of ancient philosophers, but " Christianity elevated, honored, and sanctified it. Jesus Christ, the true Son of God, submitted himself to a poor artisan of Galilee, and in the carpenter's shop of Nazareth did not disdain to set his blessed hand to labor." The apostles supported themselves by their labor, and later, when the barbarian hordes swept over Europe, the monk tilled the soil they had ravaged, and resuscitated industry. Still later the Catholic republics of Italy became the splendid centres of trade, commerce, and arts.

Ionia, the Black Sea, Africa, and Asia were the theatres of the commercial relations and military expeditions of our ancestors; there they made important and fecund conquests; and while abroad their flags floated wreathed with glory and terror, at home they did not remain idle. They cultivated the arts, and their traders, by every honest means, added to public and private wealth. Manufactures of wool, silk, jewelry, colored glass, paper, at Florence, Pisa, Bologna, Milan, Venice, Naples, gave lucrative employment to thousands upon thousands of workmen and attracted to those markets the gold and the competition of strangers.

Of course the Church does not believe that all should be sacrificed to the multiplication of riches, the health and lives of men, the feeble strength of childhood, and Cardinal Pecci protested against the "modern schools of political economy, infested with unbelief, that regard labor as the supreme end of man, and man himself as a machine more or less valuable as it is more or less productive." M. de Molinari, commenting on this, points out that economists do not regard labor as an end but as a means, and that they are thoroughly in accord with their "eminent confrère of Perugia" as to the necessity of limiting the hours of labor and securing days of rest for the artisan as well as of avoiding the exhaustion of children ; they, like the present Pope, believe that charity is necessary ; they favor the widest possible spread of education, detest war and uphold the freedom of commerce, and with sorrow contemplate "the enormous number of the victims made by the privation of education, by physical infirmities, by war, and the convulsions of trade."

After repelling as an odious calumny the accusation against the Church that "she instils into the heart a mystical contempt of earthly things," and commends an asceticism which would exclude all material amelioration of the lot of man, the Cardinal sets himself to refute the still more venomous calumny which causes the Church to be considered the enemy of science. This pretended enmity, he says, is not only absurd, but impious, for it involves the supposition that the Church fears lest science may succeed in dethroning God. So far from dethroning him, science can only make manifest his power and redouble the love he inspires by the full harmony and magnificence of his works.

See and judge for yourselves. What is there that the Church can desire more ardently than the glory of God and the more intimate acquaintance with the divine Workman which is acquired by the study of his works? If the universe is indeed a book on every page of which are inscribed the name and the wisdom of God, it is certain that he will be most filled with love for God, will come the nearest to God, who will have studied this book most deeply and most attentively. . . . What reason can there be that the Church should be jealous of the marvellous progress our age has made by its studies and discoveries? Is there in them anything which, looked at from near or from far, can do harm to the ideas of God and of faith whereof the Church is the guardian and infallible mistress? Bacon, so distinguished in the walks of physical science, has written that a little knowledge leads away from God, but much knowledge leads back to God. This golden saying is always true, and if the Church is afraid of the ruin that might be wrought by the vain ones who think they understand everything because they have a slight smattering of everything, she has full confidence in those who apply seriously and profoundly to the study of nature, for she knows that at the bottom of their researches they will find God, who in all his works displays himself with the infinite attributes of his power, his wisdom, and his goodness."

Then the pastoral letter brings to the support of its author's position the evidence of Copernicus, of Keppler, of Volta, of Galileo, even of the Protestant Faraday, "who saw in the science to which he applied himself with such passion an agency whereby to reach God." Finally it pays homage to the marvellous efforts of science and the sublime spectacle it offers in rendering man master of the forces of nature, in kindling within him a spark of the fire of the Godhead.

"How splendid and majestic does man seem when he reaches after the thunderbolt and lets it fall harmless at his feet ; when he summons the electric spark and sends it, the messenger of his will, through the abysses of ocean, over the precipitous mountains, across the interminable plains ! How glorious, when he bids steam fasten pinions to his shoulders and bear him with the rapidity of lightning over land and sea ! How powerful, when by his ingenuity he seizes upon this force, imprisons it, and conveys it by ways marvellously combined and adapted to give motion —we might almost say intelligence—to brute matter, which thus takes the place of man and spares him his most exhausting toil ! Tell me if there is not in man the semblance of a spark of the Creator when he invokes light and bids it scatter the shades of darkness !

But the Syllabus ? Has not the Syllabus condemned science and civilization ? No ; it has not condemned true civilization—that whereby man perfects himself—but it does condemn " the civilization which would supplant Christianity and destroy with it all wherewith Christianity has enriched us." It is not directed against civilization and science, but against atheism and materialism.''   Having dealt with the material amelioration of the condition of man, he says : '' It would be an agreeable task to cast the same light on those things which concern the amelioration of man's moral and political condition, if, instead of writing a pastoral letter, we had set ourselves to composing a long treatise, *and if we did not intend, if life permits it, to return at a future day to this subject.''*

The Pope of 1878 will conclude the essay begun by the Cardinal of 1877.

CHAPTER II.

THE Cardinal Camerlengo has the most extended rights. He is the head and president of the Apostolic Chamber. At the death of the Pope, he represents, in some manner, the temporal power of the Holy See, in the same way as the Sacred College represents the spiritual power. Hence, to appoint him Camerlengo was to entrust him with the principal authority during the vacancy of the Holy See. The result has shown that it was, so to say, to point him out to the choice of the Cardinals, who were thus given an occasion to appreciate the high qualities of Cardinal Pecci ; and we may safely say that, if Leo XIII. is a Pope after the heart of God, he is no less so after the heart of Pius IX.

On the 7th of February, we find Mgr. Pecci kneeling at the death-bed of the much beloved Pius IX., overwhelmed with grief. When the great and sad event had taken place, and death had deprived us of our beloved father, the Camerlengo, by virtue of his office, found himself charged with the funeral services to be performed. He was to verify the death of the Pope and to receive from the Cardinal-Dean the deposit of the Fisherman's Ring. He was to place in the coffin of Pius IX. the three velvet purses containing the pieces of money that were struck during the late Pontiff's reign, and the parchment on which the events of his life were traced. He was, besides, charged with the direction of all the arrangements to be made for the organization of the Conclave ; and he displayed the highest wisdom in that delicate mission.

The Conclave which was destined to appoint a successor to the immortal Pius IX. was one of the largest in the whole history of the Church and the shortest in duration. The Holy Ghost, whose invisible hand directs and governs the Church, and against whom human calculation and cunning can avail naught, shortened the days of mourning to fill Christendom with new joy.

On the morning of February 18th, their Eminences, the Cardinals went to the Pauline Chapel in the Vatican to assist at the Mass of the Holy Ghost sung by Cardinal Schwarzenberg, Archbishop of Prague. The diplomatic body in full uniform, and the representatives of the Roman nobility, were accommodated in the tribune of the chapel.   At the conclusion of divine service, Monsignor Mercurelli, Secretary of Briefs, delivered an address on the manner in which the election of the Pontiff is to be carried on according to the present regulations of the Church.   All the constitutions concerning the Conclave were observed with the greatest scrupulosity, so that no one might find a pretext to question the validity of the choice. This was also the desire of the Catholic Powers, which they had communicated, through their ambassadors, to the Cardinal Camerlengo.

In the afternoon at four o'clock, the Cardinals assembled again in the Pauline Chapel. Thence they proceeded, between two lines of the Noble Guard, the Swiss Guard and the Palatine Guard of Honor, to the Sistine Chapel, where they sang the " Veni Creator " with the Conclavists. At the conclusion of the prescribed prayers, the Cardinals took the oath required by the Canons. Then the Marshal of the Conclave, Prince Chigi, together with his retinue, stepped in and bound himself by a sacred oath to see that the regulations of the Church were observed during the Conclave. Every one of the Conclavists in like manner took the same oath.

After these last ceremonies, which served as a prelude to the Conclave, were completed, each Cardinal was accompanied by a Noble Guard to the cell assigned him by lot. The cells had been constructed in a part of the Vatican palace known under the name of Cortile di San Damaso.

At eight o'clock, the master of ceremonies went to every cell, rang a small silver bell, and cried out at the third ringing, " Extra omnes." Those that did not belong to the Conclave left the rooms immediately. The Cardinal Camerlengo, accompanied by the senior Cardinal of each order, proceeded to the entrance of the Conclave and gave the keys for the outer door to the Marshal. This the only entrance— all the others had been walled up—was closed by means of two doors. The Marshal kept the keys for the outer, the Camerlengo for the inner door. Thus the closing of the Conclave was completed at nine o'clock in the evening.

The next morning the master of ceremonies rang the silver bell at intervals of half an hour, and cried out " ad capellam Domini." At nine o'clock, the Cardinals proceeded to the Sistine Chapel, where the Dean of the College of Cardinals, Luigi Amat, said low Mass.   The Cardinals who had neither the time nor convenience to offer up the Holy Sacrifice received holy communion.   After Mass, all returned to their cells to take their breakfast.   Towards noon the first ballot took place by sealed tickets.   Cardinal Pecci had twenty-three votes, Cardinal Bilio eleven, Cardinal Franchi* four, Cardinal Panebianco four ; the

CARDINAL FRANCHI.

other votes were scattered among various Cardinals. But this ballot was declared void, because one of the Cardinals had, contrary to the regulation, affixed to his paper a seal which bore the mark of the dignity of a Cardinal.   In the evening at five o'clock the second vote took place, in which Cardinal Pecci received thirty-eight votes out of sixty-one, or more than one

* Died Aug. 1, 1878.

half. But according to the decree of Gregory X. two thirds of the votes are required for the election of a Pope.

In the afternoon, his Eminence Cardinal Moraes Cardoso, Patriarch of Lisbon, arrived in Rome and was admitted, with the customary ceremonies, into

CARDINAL PANEBIANCO.

the Conclave. The double locked doors were opened, and, with the same formality, locked again. A faithful record of the whole proceeding was drawn up by Monsignor Pericoli, Dean of the Apostolic Protonotaries, and by the Marshal of the Conclave, and was signed by the dean, by Prince Philip Lancellotti and Count Astolfo Servanzi.

On the following day, February the 20th, the third

and last ballot took place.   Cardinal Pecci, Bishop of Perugia, was elected Pope by forty-four votes out of sixty-two.   Immediately after the election, the Sub-dean of the College of Cardinals requested Mgr. Martinucci, whose duty it was, to see that the prescribed ceremonies of the succession should be performed. The canopies which had been erected over the seats of the Cardinals were removed, with the exception of the ninth on the Gospel side, which belonged to the elect.

The Dean of the Sacred College presented himself before the newly elected Pope, and asked him : "Acceptasne electionem in Summum Pontificem?" "Do you accept your election as sovereign Pontiff?" The Pope answered that he was unworthy of such an honor ; but since all had chosen him, he submitted to God's will.

The dean put the second question : "Quomodo vis vocari?" "What name will you assume?" The Holy Father answered : "Leo XIII.," in memory of Leo XII., for whom he had ever cherished a great veneration.

In the annals of the Papacy no name stands out more beautifully than that of Leo.   St. Leo the Great stayed Attila, St. Leo III. crowned Charlemagne, St. Leo IV. saved Rome from the Saracens.   St. Leo IX. subdued, by his energy, his courage, and his virtues, even more than by his authority, the raging enemies of the Church ; all the Leos, veritable lions, seem particularly predestined to represent the conquering lion of the tribe of Juda.   Whilst awaiting a new Charlemagne, Leo XIII. stands, from his very accession to the Papal throne, in presence of more than one Attila, and we are well aware that the modern Saracens and other enemies of the Church are to-day both numerous and powerful. Later on, history will say of the present Pontiff : " *Vicit Leo de tribu Juda.*" " The Lion of the tribe of Juda hath conquered."

THE PEOPLE WATCHING FOR THE "SFUMATA."

Mgr. Martinucci, in his capacity of Apostolic Protonotary, drew up the act of acceptance of the supreme Pontiff, whilst the witnesses were Mgr. Lasagni, Secretary of the Sacred College, and Mgr. Marinelli, Bishop of Porphyria.

The newly elected Pope retired immediately to

the sacristy, vested himself in the Papal robes, and
returning again to the chapel, gave the Cardinals the
apostolic benediction for the first time.   The Cardinals kissed his hand and embraced him.   Cardinal
Schwarzenberg, who had been appointed by his Holiness pro-Camerlengo, placed the Fisherman's Ring on
his finger, whereupon the Conclavists were admitted

CARDINAL CATERINI.

to kiss his feet.   The joy was as great as the mourning over the death of Pius IX. had been.   Even on
the first day of the Conclave, the piazza of St. Peter
was crowded with hundreds of persons who came
thither to watch for the " Sfumata," or smoke issuing
from a little chimney which communicates with the
inside of the Sistine Chapel.   When the ballot does
not come to a definite conclusion, the tickets are

burned, and the smoke, which can be observed from without, is a sign that no election has taken place.

Thus it came to pass that most of the people who occupied the piazza of St. Peter at noon, and witnessed the smoke ascending from the chimney had dispersed when, at one o'clock, the bars of the great Loggia on the façade of St. Peter's were withdrawn. The few persons that had loitered in the piazza hastened towards the church. There appeared at the Loggia, preceded by the cross, the oldest Cardinal-Deacon, Caterini, who, notwithstanding his advanced age of 83 years, did not wish to be deprived of the honor of announcing to the Catholic world, the successor of Pius IX., and who now brought to the assembled multitude the glad tidings :

" Annuntio vobis gaudium magnum : habemus Papam Eminentissimum et Reverendissimum Dominum Joachim Pecci, qui sibi imposuit nomen : Leo XIII."

" I announce to you great joy : we have as Pope, his Eminence, the most Reverend Lord Joachim **Pecci,** who takes the name of Leo XIII."

Joyous shouts of applause, indefinitely prolonged, greeted the happy message. The news that a sovereign had been granted to the Church of Christ spread with lightning rapidity throughout the whole city. Just as the peals of the bells of St. Peter's found an echo in the bells of the entire city of Rome, so the joyful news of " Papa Pecci, Leone XIII.," was on all lips in less than an hour. No one that has not witnessed it could believe it possible to unite in one place, and in less than two hours, thousands and thousands of people by one simple word.

Three rows of carriages and princely vehicles, with numerous lackeys, drove up and down the

Borghi.   The Leonine City swarmed with people who poured out of every street and alley like bees from their hives.

About half-past five o'clock the windows of the interior Loggia were thrown open.   A dense mass hung round the entrance of St. Peter's.   In a few moments the new Pope, Leo XIII., made his appearance.   The faith which had remained dormant in the hearts of thousands assembled in St. Peter's broke forth in loud acclamations.   A cry from fifty thousand voices, which the grand structure of St. Peter's alone seemed able to withstand, greeted the new Pope.

The Monsignori and the Cardinals who accompanied the Holy Father, tried in vain to calm the shouts.   The exultation and joy were too great to be silenced.   Then the new Pontiff stretched out his hands over the assembled multitude, and a deathlike silence ensued.   He raised his eyes towards heaven and remained for a few moments in this attitude. His tall, emaciated form towered above all his attendants ; upon the red cape shone the golden stole, and his snow-white hair formed a beautiful contrast with the dark background.   The impressiveness of the moment beggars all description.

Turned towards the high altar of the Basilica, he sang, with a clear and firm voice : " Adjutorium nostrum in nomine Domini ;" to which a choir of thousands of voices answered in unison : " Qui fecit coelum et terram."

The Holy Father leaned somewhat over the railing of the Loggia and imparted to the kneeling multitude his first solemn benediction.

The spectacle which was witnessed in St. Peter's at this moment was sublime in the highest degree.

What is it that makes an innumerable multitude of men of various conditions and stations in life, of different

THE BASILICA OF ST. PETER'S.

habits and tastes, of various countries and nations, without material force, bend their knees in the presence of this venerable old man? Where can you find a spectacle to be compared to this? Thousands

INTERIOR OF ST. PETER'S CHURCH IN ROME.

Page 249.

and thousands on bended knees, thousands and thousands fixing their gaze upon one point, thousands upon thousands whose hearts are exultant with joy, thousands upon thousands down whose cheeks flow tears of joy ; and above them all, the majestic form of the Holy Father blessing his people,

CARDINAL MERTEL.

in the name of the Omnipotent God—all this was a sight the like of which we shall look for in vain outside of the Catholic Church.

The Holy Father retired amid the shouts of : " Viva il Papa ! Viva Leone XIII. ! Viva il Papa Rè !"

When the Marshal of the Conclave had heard the peals of the bells of St. Peter's, he had hastened, with his escort, to the gate which leads to the reception-room of the Cardinals. At the Ruota, Monsignor Lasagni informed him officially of the result of the Conclave ; but the doors were not opened until four o'clock in the afternoon, when the Marshal removed the barriers, and had the honor of kissing the feet of the newly elected Pope outside of the Conclave.

After this first ceremony, his Holiness, passing through the Sistine Chapel, entered the hall of the Paramenti, where he admitted to the kissing of his feet the prelates and personages who had been for that day employed in the exterior service of the Conclave. After this, having again been vested in his pontifical robes, the Holy Father, preceded by two apostolic notaries, having at his sides the Cardinal-Deacons Mertel and Consolini, and followed by Mgr. Ricci, who had resumed the office of Major-domo, and by the Almoner and the Sacristans, advanced to the altar of the Sistine Chapel. After having knelt there and prayed, he rose and seated himself on the *Sedia*, placed on the platform of the altar, to receive the homage of the Cardinals.

After the Dean of the Cardinals had recited the prayers, *super Pontificem electum*, the Pope solemnly gave the apostolic benediction. At last, having descended from the *Sedia* and prayed anew on his knees before the altar, he returned to the hall of the Paramenti. Here he deposited the sacred vestments and went back to his apartments.

During that time, all the bells of Rome continued to ring, re-echoing the joy of the people, and from among the multitudes that returned from the Vatican a long murmur arose which testified to the general gladness.

In the evening, the following proclamation an-

THE SISTINE CHAPEL.   Page 253.

nounced the election of his Eminence Cardinal Pecci to the Papal throne :

"Since God Almighty has deigned to raise to the Papal throne his Holiness Leo XIII., it is ordered that the 'Te Deum laudamus' be sung and the prayer which is found in the ritual under the title : 'Preces dicendæ in processione pro gratiarum actione' be recited in the churches of the Holy City, without any exception, on the 22d of this month, at ten A.M. Moreover, all the bells of Rome shall be rung solemnly at the same time during the space of one hour. Finally we prescribe that in thanksgiving for the exaltation of his Holiness Leo XIII. during the next three days, viz., the 22d, 23d, and 24th inst., the Collect 'pro gratiarum actione' be added in every sacrifice of the Mass.

"Given in our residence, on this the 20th day of February, 1878.

"RAPHAEL, Cardinal-Vicar.
"CAN. PLACIDUS PETACCI, Secretary."

On February the 22d, after the *Te Deum* had been chanted in the Sistine Chapel, his Holiness received the ambassadors of France, Spain, Portugal, and Austria in the pontifical apartments. The ambassador of France, M. le Baron Baude, was the first admitted.

Leo XIII. loves France, and has already given several testimonies of his sympathy for that country. Before entering the Conclave, he received in his quality of Camerlengo, in special audience at the Vatican, the French delegates, who were charged to present to him the address of the Catholic societies. "I thank you warmly," answered his Eminence, "you and all the works which you represent. It is a great happiness for us to see France coming forward first on this occasion ; for, understand it well, we do not confound everything that comes nowadays from France with the French people, who have ever been so much attached to the Holy See and so generous to the Church. We therefore thank France, and we pray that she may prosper with her traditions of faith and greatness. She is at present in a critical position ; but let us hope that the prayers and zeal of her children may draw upon her the graces of Heaven, and that soon she may resume the post of honor which she has always occupied so gloriously."

Some days later, at the moment when the Sacred College rendered its first homage to the Sovereign Pontiff, Cardinal Guibert asked the Holy Father's blessing for himself, for the diocese of Paris, and for the whole of France. Leo XIII. gave his blessing, adding that he loved France much on account of her great generosity and devotedness to the Church.

Lastly, on February the 28th, his Holiness said to the representatives of the French Catholic Universities : " France, in spite of her misfortunes, remains ever worthy of herself and shows that she has not lost her vocation. No one more than the Vicar of Jesus Christ has cause to compassionate the sufferings of France, for in her the Holy See has always found one of its strongest supporters.

" To-day, alas ! she has lost some of her power ; and, weakened by the divisions of party, she is prevented from giving free scope to her noble instincts. And yet, what has she not done for the Holy See, even after her many disasters? She has already given it the pride of her most illustrious families ; the little Pontifical army was to a great extent made up of the sons of France ; and from the time they could no longer serve the cause of the Pope with their swords, France has given proof of her attachment to the Holy See in a thousand other ways ; her offerings always form a considerable part of the Peter's pence.

"So great a generosity cannot remain unrewarded. God will bless a nation which is capable of so many noble sacrifices, and history will yet write many a beautiful page on the *Gesta Dei per Francos.*"

CARDINAL GUIBERT.

From the day following his election, the Sovereign Pontiff received at the Vatican the numerous Catholics that had come from all parts of the world to see him. The audiences lasted for nine hours. In one single day, Leo XIII. spoke to twelve hundred persons that came kneeling one by one before him. At times he had to rest himself awhile, overcome as he was by fatigue. They begged him to suspend his audiences, and he answered with mildness : " No, no, these dear children come from so far !" and he continued his daily labor. How many touching details might be given about these audiences, which the Holy Father grants with an affability and a graciousness to which the majesty of the Pontiff gives a new value. He is a father to all. He receives and blesses the Roman nobility, the representatives of Catholic associations, those of the press, of the Pontifical Zouaves. No one is excluded, and all carry away with them a grateful remembrance of the Vatican. One of the most touching audiences was that given to the deputies of the Perugian clergy, having at their head the mild and pious Mgr. Laurenzi, Bishop of Amata, *in partibus*, and coadjutor of the See of Perugia. The separation was hard. During thirty-two years his Eminence Cardinal Pecci had administered that diocese with an incomparable wisdom, goodness, and vigor. He loved and he was loved in return ; on both sides, therefore, there were tears. The father was forced to abandon the children of his apostolic heart, the children saw themselves obliged to make the sacrifice of their father to the Christian world.

CHAPTER III.

MEANWHILE the day of the coronation, fixed for Sunday, the 3d of March, was approaching. His Holiness Leo XIII. wished to prepare himself for that great act by silence and recollection. The audiences were suspended, and he who was about to put on the highest crown on earth sought in prayer and meditation the strength and courage of which he stood in need to fill in a worthy manner the throne of the glorious Pius IX.

The coronation of Leo XIII. was to take place in the Basilica of St. Peter. Circumstances, which were particularly sad, determined the Sovereign Pontiff, in order to avoid all disorder, to choose the Sistine Chapel for that grand ceremony, which took place with all possible pomp.

The holy father left his apartments, carried on the *sedia gestatoria*, accompanied by all the Cardinals, surrounded by his Pontifical Court.

The cortege was opened by the Swiss Guard and by the bearer of the Papal cross. They were followed by the *sediarii*, or bearers of the *sedia gestatoria*, the *bussolanti*, and the mace-bearers, arrayed in their rich and varied costumes. Then followed the

Noble Guard and the two princes who command this corps, with Prince Colonna arrayed in a costume resembling that of a Spanish cavalier in the time of Philip II.—a white ruff around the neck, black dress, tunic-shaped, black stockings, and on his left breast a large and glittering star. He is Prince Assistant at the Pontifical Throne, and has the privilege of giving the water to the holy father at the lavations during mass. Beside him came the Marquis Sacchetti, also in gala costume as *Foriere maggiore* of the sacred Apostolic palaces. These immediately preceded the Sovereign Pontiff, who was vested in red mozzetta, and was surrounded by his Noble Guard and followed by Mgr. Ricci, Major-domo, Mgr. Cataldi, Pro-Master of the Chamber, Mgr. Samminiatelli, Almoner, Mgr. Marinelli, Sacristan, and others who for the time being hold the places of chamberlains and chaplains. His Holiness entered into the Hall of Tapestries, where he was vested by the two first Cardinal-Deacons in his sacred robes, and on his head was placed a mitre of cloth of gold. When this ceremony was completed, the Pope, preceded by the Penitentiaries of the Vatican Basilica, who hear confessions in so many different languages, by the Archbishops and Bishops in white copes and white mitres, amongst whom were the Greek Deacon and Subdeacon, and finally by the Cardinals, of whom the Cardinal-Deacons wore the *tonacella*, or tunic, the priests the chasuble, and the Archbishops and Bishops the white cope of cloth of silver sown with gold ornaments, and all with white mitres, moved towards the Ducal Hall, which was fitted up as a chapel, and on the arrival of the procession here, his Holiness, after a short prayer, took his place on the throne, which stood on the Gospel side of the altar.

THE PROCESSION IN THE DUCAL HALL.

Page 261.

The Cardinals then approached him one by one and tendered him their obedience. They ascended the steps of the throne one by one and kissed the right hand of the Pontiff. The Archbishops and Bishops kissed the Pontiff's foot. The Holy Father then imparted the Apostolic Benediction and intoned the chant of Tierce, which was continued by the Pontifical choir. At the conclusion of this chant, the Pope was robed in the Pontifical vestments brought to him by the clerks of the Papal Chapel, and the first of the Cardinal-Deacons placed the sacred ring upon his finger. Then Cardinal Mertel, first deacon at the ceremony, with staff ·in hand, rose up, the *Procedamus in pace* was sung, and the procession was formed again and moved in the same order in which it came, except that immediately following the cross-bearer came the consistorial advocates, and in front of the Cardinals came Prince Ruspoli, Master of the Sacred Hospice and the Mitred Abbots. When the cortege began to move, his Holiness ascended the *sedia gestatoria*, under a baldachino of cloth of silver borne by eight dignitaries. The large fans of white ostrich feathers, the *flabelli*, were again seen in procession. The Swiss Guards with drawn swords surrounded the Pontiff. The whole style and arrangement and grandeur of this ceremony equalled, if they did not surpass, the great functions formerly witnessed in the Sistine Chapel during Rome's palmy days. The *Sedia* upon which the Sovereign Pontiff was borne was that presented by the Neapolitan Catholics to the lamented and dearly beloved Pontiff Pius IX.

In the Sistine Chapel the throne was raised upon the marble dais on the Gospel side of the altar. That spot so long bare and unadorned was to-day fitted with its proper ornament. Behind the altar, overshadowed by Michael Angelo's terrible "Last Judgment," with its mighty and muscular figures, was an altar-piece in tapestry representing the fitting subject of Christ giving the keys to Peter. The floor of the chapel was covered with fine green baize, and the steps of the throne and altar with red cloth.

As the procession was about to move, a clerk of the

CARDINAL WISEMAN.

Papal Chapel brought a handful of flax attached to a gilded rod, and having presented it to a master of ceremonies, the latter knelt, and extending the rod, burnt the flax in presence of the Holy Father, pronouncing at the same time in a grave and solemn tone : *Pater Sancte, sic transit gloria mundi.* "Holy Father, thus passeth away the glory of the world." The same act was repeated at the entrance of the Sistine Chapel, and finally a third time within the chapel before the enclosure within which were the seats of the Cardinals. Cardinal Wiseman wrote of this ceremony, "Three times is this impressive rite performed in that procession, as though to counteract the earthly influences of a triple crown." It is to remind the Pontiff that the glory of this world is brief and passing as the flame which finishes in the very act of kindling. The solemn lesson seemed to make a deep impression on the mind of Leo XIII.

A magnificent spectacle was now presented to the eye in the Sistine Chapel. A large number of persons were present in the tribunes. In the Royal gallery were their Royal Highnesses the Duke and Duchess of Parma, with their suite. In the other tribunes were the ambassadors and ministers accredited to the Vatican, with the persons attached to the embassies, and representatives of the Order of St. John of Jerusalem and of the Knights of Calatrava, all in grand uniform and sparkling with decorations. On the same side, in another tribune, were the Roman princes and patricians with their families, and many distinguished personages, Italian and foreign. A tribune to the right was occupied by ladies in black dresses and veils.

When the Pontiff arrived before the Papal altar, he descended from the *sedia gestatoria*, and after a brief prayer began the Introit of the Mass. The *Confiteor* being finished, the Pope sat on the throne, and the three first Cardinal-Bishops, Di Pietro, Sacconi, and Guidi, recited the three customary prayers, *super electum Pontificem*, after which he descended, and, standing before the first step of the altar, the first Cardinal-Deacon removed the mitre from his head, and the second Cardinal-Deacon, Mertel, placed upon his shoulders the Pontifical Pallium, which the Pope first kissed, and which was fastened by three gold pins. Cardinal Mertel, on imposing it, pronounced the following words : *Accipe pallium sanctum, plenitudinem Pontificalis officii, ad honorem omni- potentis Dei, et gloriosissimæ Virginis Mariæ, ejus matris, et Beatorum Apostolorum Petri et Pauli, et Sanctæ Romanæ Ecclesiæ.''* When his Holiness had received the pallium he ascended the altar and thence proceeded to the throne, where he received the full obedience of the Cardinals, who kissed his foot and his hand and then received the kiss of peace, for which his Holiness rose slightly from his throne. The Archbishops and Bishops kissed his foot and his knee and the Penitentiaries his foot only. The Pope then proceeded to the altar and the Mass was continued, with all the prayers proper for the coronation.

On the conclusion of the Mass, the Holy Father removed the maniple, sat again upon the throne, while the choir sang *Corona aurea super caput ejus*, composed expressly for this occasion by the maestro, Signor Pasquali, of Carpineto, the birth-place of the Sovereign Pontiff. The Cardinal-Deacon then intoned the prescribed versicles and the following prayer : *Omnipotens sempiterne Deus, dignitas sacerdotii, et auctor regni, da gratiam famulo tuo Leoni Pontifici nostro, ecclesiam tuam fructuose regendi, ut ab eo qui tua clementia pater regum, et rector omnium fidelium constituitur et coronatur, salubri tua dispositione cuncta bene gubernentur, Per Christum*, etc., to which the cantors replied, *Amen*. Then the second Cardinal-Deacon, who stood at the left of the throne, removed the mitre from the head of the Pontiff, and the first Cardinal-Deacon, who stood at his right, imposed the tiara upon him, at the same time saying in a loud voice these words : *Accipe Tiaram tribus coronis ornatam, et scias Te esse Patrem Principum et Regum, Rectorem Orbis, in terra Vicarium Salvatoris nostri Jesu Christi, cui est honor et gloria in sæcula sæculorum. Amen.*

The tiara placed upon the head of Leo XIII. was that presented to the Holy Father Pius IX. by the Palatine Guard of Honor.

This was the most beautiful and touching part of the ceremony, and produced a deep impression upon the hearts of all present.   Many an eye was wet with tears as the Cardinal placed this crown, this symbol of majesty and power, spiritual and temporal—alas ! the temporal rule is no more—upon the head of a Pontiff who is rapidly nearing the ordinary term of human life.   All seemed so frail, yet it was destined to last forever.   The centuries of the past have but strengthened the Church, the earthly head of which is that aged man sitting before us with the tiara upon his head.   And as the flaming flax signified the transitory nature of worldly glory, so does this feeble Pontiff typify an ever powerful endurance and a perpetual resistance to the mighty ones of the world.

The act of coronation being accomplished, His Holiness imparted the triple benediction to all present.   This was followed by the reading in Latin and Italian of the Bulls of Indulgence by the Cardinal-Deacons.   Then in the midst of a breathless silence and a religious respect, the Pontiff, seated on the *sedia gestatoria*, with the tiara on his head, accompanied by the Cardinals and the procession as before, passed from the chapel, blessing the people kneeling on both sides.   Then having laid aside the Pontifical vestments in the Hall of Tapestries, and surrounded by the Sacred College, by Archbishops and Bishops, and Penitentiaries of St. Peter's, he listened to the following address read by His Eminence Cardinal Di Pietro :—

" Since our votes, inspired by God, have caused the selection for the great dignity of Sovereign Pontiff of the Catholic Church to fall upon your Holiness, we have passed from profound affliction to a lively hope. To the tears which we shed upon the tomb of Pius IX., a Pope so greatly venerated throughout the whole world, and so beloved by us, succeeds the consoling thought that there arises rapidly a new dawn with well founded hopes for the Church of Jesus Christ.

" Yes, Most Holy Father, you gave sufficient proofs of your piety, of your apostolic zeal, of your many virtues, of your high intelligence, of your prudence and of the deep interest you took in the glory and the majesty of our Sacred College, when you ruled the diocese entrusted to you by Divine Providence, or took part in the grave affairs of the Holy See ; so that we can easily persuade ourselves that being elected Sovereign Pontiff you will do as the Apostle wrote of himself to the Thessalonians : *For our Gospel hath not been to you in word only but in power also, and in the Holy Ghost, and in much fulness.*

" Nor, indeed, was the Divine Will slow to manifest itself, that Will which by our suffrages repeated to you the words formerly spoken to David when he was declared King in Israel : *Thou shalt feed my people Israel ; and thou shalt be ruler over them.*

" To which Divine disposition it is gratifying to us to see how suddenly the general sentiment corresponds, and how all concur in venerating your sacred person, as the tribes of Israel prostrated themselves

in Hebron before the new pastor allotted to them by
God. So we likewise hasten, on this solemn day
of your coronation, like the elders of the chosen
people, to repeat to you, in pledge of affection and of
obedience, the words recorded in the sacred pages :
Behold we are thy bone and thy flesh.

" May heaven grant that, as the holy Book of
Kings adds that David reigned forty years—*quadra-
ginta annis regnavit*—so ecclesiastical history may
record for posterity the length of the Pontificate of
Leo XIII.

" These are the sentiments and the sincere wishes
that in the name of the Sacred College I place at
your sacred feet. Deign benignantly to accept them,
by imparting to us your Apostolic benediction."

The Holy Father received these sentiments of the
Sacred College in the most benignant manner, and
replied to them in the following words :

" The noble and affectionate words which your
Most Reverend Eminence, in the name of the whole
Sacred College, has just addressed to us, deeply
touch our heart, already deeply moved by the un-
expected event of our exaltation to the Supreme
Pontificate, which has happened without any merit
of ours.

" The weight of the sovereign Keys, already of
itself so formidable, which has been imposed upon
our shoulders, is rendered heavier still by our little-
ness, which is overburdened by it.

" The very rite which has now been accomplished
with so much solemnity has made us understand
still more the majesty and height of the See to
which we are raised, and has increased in our soul the
idea of the greatness of this sublime throne on earth.

" And since you, Lord Cardinal, have wished to

compare us to David, the words of the same holy King recur spontaneously to our mind, when he said : *Quis ego sum Domine Deus, quia adduxisti me hucusque ?* ' Who am I, O Lord God, that Thou hast brought me here ? '

" Nevertheless, in the midst of so many just reasons for alarm and for comfort, it consoles us to see all Catholics, in unanimous concord, pressing around this Apostolic See to give it a public testimony of obedience and of love.

" The concord and the affection of all the Sacred College, which is most dear to us, and also the certainty of their co-operation in the fulfilment of the difficult ministry to which their votes have called us, consoles us.

" Trust in the most merciful God, who has deigned to raise us to such a height, comforts us ; whose assistance we will never cease to implore with all the fervor of our heart ; and we desire that by all He may be implored, mindful of that which the Apostle says : *Our sufficiency is from God.*

" Persuaded then that it is He who selects the weak things of the earth to confound the strong— *Infirma mundi eligit ut confundat fortia*—we live in the hope that He will sustain our weakness and raise up our humility to show forth His power and to make His strength resplendent.

" With all our heart we thank your Eminence for the courteous sentiments and for the sincere wishes which you, in the name of the Sacred College, have addressed to us, and which we accept with our whole soul.

" We conclude by imparting with all our heart the Apostolic benediction—*Benedictio*, etc."

The Holy Father then arose and went to his apartments in the Vatican. Thus concluded the great event of this day. When the strange conditions under which this coronation took place are considered, it will leave a deep and lasting impression on the minds of those who were present. The majesty and grandeur of the ceremony; all that it represented of the past, and of the present; the long line of illustrious predecessors * of Leo XIII. who have worn this crown; their vicissitudes and fortunes which history relates, and their invincible endurance in the midst of the destruction of crowns and thrones, and the decay of kingdoms and powers, constitute this coronation of the 263d Roman Pontiff an act to which nothing on earth can be compared, and which far surpasses all other coronations.

* The whole number of Popes from St. Peter to Pius the Ninth inclusive is 262. Of these 82 are venerated as saints, 33 of whom are martyrs. One hundred and four were Romans, and 108 natives of Italy; 15 Frenchmen; 9 Greeks; 7 Germans; 5 Asiatics; 3 Africans; 3 Spaniards; 2 Dalmatians; 1 Hebrew; 1 Thracian; 1 Dutchman; 1 Portuguese; 1 Candiot; and one Englishman. The name most commonly taken was John; the 23d and last was a Neapolitan, raised to the Chair in 1410. Nine Pontiffs reigned less than one month, thirty less than one year, and 11 more than twenty years; only 5 occupied the Pontifical Chair over 23 years; these are St. Peter, who was Supreme Pastor in Antioch for about seven or eight years, and twenty-five years, two months, and seven days in Rome; Silvester I., 23 years, 10 months, 27 days; Adrian I., 22 years, 10 months, 17 days; Pius VI., 24 years, 8 months, 14 days; Pius IX., who celebrated his 31st year in the Pontifical Chair, June 16, 1877, had the longest reign except St. Peter, being Pope for 31 years, 7 months, and 20 days.

CHAPTER IV.

LEO XIII., raised to the highest dignity on earth, bearing on his head the triple crown and in his hands the mysterious keys of the Kingdom of God, can now look down, from his lofty throne, on the nations of the globe, the great flock committed to his care. Truly his position is not enviable, nor is his task light. To succeed to Pius IX., than whom no Pope ever won more hearts or wielded a wider influence, was of itself sufficient to dishearten the best of men. But Leo felt that God had placed the burden on his shoulders, and whilst, on the one hand, he acknowledged his own weakness, on the other he filled his soul with boundless confidence in Him who had said that the gates of hell should never prevail against His Church, which he had built on Peter and on his successors.

The new Pontiff had reason to fear that the moderation and regard which had been used towards his venerable predecessor, even by the bitterest enemies of the Church and of the Holy See, would be succeeded by violence and extreme insolence towards himself. The whole world would have cried out against the man, how great and powerful soever he

might be, who would have raised his hand against the
gentle Pius ; but did it not seem that the enemies of
the Papacy had been impatiently awaiting the death
of him whom they durst not touch, to exercise their
wrath on his successor?

The Papacy stands alone, without a friend among
the governments of the world.   It is powerless, without territory, without treasure, without an army, without a voice in the Senate of nations.   Pius IX. had
died a prisoner in his palace ; and Leo XIII. could
not hope to fare better than he.   The prospect must
have been gloomy enough to the new Pope as he cast
a mournful look around.   But he did not lose heart.
Besides looking around him, at the sad spectacle
of human ingratitude, he looked upward to the
source of strength to battle against the world.   Here
all was dark ; but there, on high, was " Lumen in
Cœlo," a ray from heaven, which showed his way
and brought hope of a better future.

The first year of his Pontificate is hardly closed,
and we will briefly review its acts, which will show
how energetically the new Pope addressed himself to his work.   Our sketch must be brief, and it
will limit itself to the principal features of the new
reign ; but enough will be said to console us for the
loss of him whose career was more glorious than
it was prolonged, and whose deeds have already
written his name as Pius the Great in the annals of
the Church.

It is customary for the Sovereign Pontiff, as for
other sovereigns, to announce his accession to the
courts of Europe.   Leo XIII. complied with this
formality, not excluding from his courtesy even the
States which had been most hostile to the Church
under the preceding Pope.   His letters to the Swiss

Confederation, to the Emperor of Germany, and to the Czar, were the olive branch of reconciliation held out to those rulers by the Church they had persecuted, as well as a means by which they might have honorably withdrawn from a false position. We will here give some of these documents, as proofs of the sincerest good faith on the one side, and of the most meaningless professions on the other.

The following is the text of the letter to the Swiss Federal Council :

LEO PP. XIII.

" *To His Excellency the President of the Swiss Confederation.*

"YOUR EXCELLENCY :—Raised by the will of God, and not through any merit of ours, to the high chair of the Prince of the Apostles, we hasten to inform your Excellency, trusting that this our personal communication of the fact will be agreeable and welcome to you. We regret that the friendly relations which formerly subsisted between the Holy See and the Swiss Confederation have for some years been painfully interrupted, and that the condition of the Catholic religion in Switzerland is much to be lamented. With full confidence in the sentiments of rectitude which animate your Excellency and the Swiss people, we hope that some means will soon be found for putting an end to this evil state of things, and, in the pleasing expectation of this, we beseech the Lord to grant you the fulness of His heavenly blessings, and we pray Him at the same time to unite you with us in the bonds of perfect charity.

" Given at St. Peter's, Rome, February 20, 1878, in the first year of our Pontificate.

" LEO PP. XIII."

To this nobly-spoken message the following reply was sent by the Swiss Council :

"*To His Holiness Pope Leo XIII.*

"MOST HOLY FATHER :—Your Holiness has con-descended, by your Brief of February 20, of this year, to acquaint the Swiss Federal Council of your elevation to the Apostolic Chair, which took place on that day. The Federal Council has received this communication with the most lively interest, and will not permit this occasion to pass without offer-ing to Your Holiness their most sincere good wishes, together with their thanks for the Brief with which you have honored them.

" When Your Holiness designates the condition of the Catholics of Switzerland as lamentable, the Coun-cil must observe on its side that your religion, like all others, enjoys a freedom, which is guaranteed to it by the Federal Constitution, and is only restricted by the condition that the ecclesiastical authorities shall not assail either the rights and powers of the State, or the rights and liberties of the citizens.

" The Federal Council will consider itself fortu-nate in being able, within its own sphere of action, to support the exertions of your Holiness to maintain religious peace and a good understanding between the several religious denominations in Switzerland. With this sentiment it avails itself of this first oppor-tunity to convey to your Holiness the assurance of its distinguished veneration, and with you to recommend itself to the protection of the Almighty.

" Bern, April 5, 1878.

" In the name of the Swiss Federal Council.

" SCHENK.

" The Chancellor of the Confederation,   SCHIESS."

It is easy to trace this document to the leaders of the "Cultur-Kampf," which has desolated the Church in Germany and Switzerland, in the name of justice and civil rights. And it is this shameless as well as heartless diplomacy that now rules the world.

The Brief addressed, on the same occasion, to William Emperor of Germany is couched in the following terms :

"Having been, by the inscrutable designs of God, and without any merit of our own, raised to the See of the Prince of the Apostles, we deem it our duty to make this fact known to your Royal and Imperial Majesty, under whose glorious and powerful sceptre live so large a number of the professors of our holy religion.

"We find to our sorrow that the relations which once existed between the Holy See and your Majesty have been broken ; and we therefore appeal to your magnanimity for the restoration of peace and tranquillity of conscience to that portion of your subjects. The Catholics of Prussia, as in duty bound by the faith they profess, will not fail to prove themselves grateful, devoted and faithful towards your Majesty.

"Convinced of your Majesty's equity, we beg our Lord to bestow on you the abundance of His heavenly gifts, and we implore Him to unite us to your Majesty in the bonds of the most perfect Christian charity."

A similar letter, almost in the same terms, was addressed to the Czar of Russia.

The answer from the Court of Berlin did not appear till the 24th of March, and was evidently intended to influence the then approaching elections in Prussia, though it gave little hope of better things for Catholics. After the usual preliminaries, the Emperor is made to say : "Your Holiness with reason observes that our Catholic subjects, like their Protestant fellow-citizens, yield obedience to authority and to the laws, as their common faith in Christ requires. We are happy to perceive, from the friendly expressions of your Holiness, that you are disposed to use the power which your exalted position places in your hands to induce those of our Catholic subjects who have hitherto been forgetful of their duty to obey the laws of the country in which they live."

A letter dictated to the Prince Imperial, in answer to the Holy Father's congratulations to the Emperor on his happy escape from the plots laid against his life, more openly declares the determination of the Imperial Government to maintain the crying injustice of the "May laws." One sentence from the letter will suffice : " In answer to the request of your Holiness, in the letter of the 17th of April, that the constitution and the *laws of Prussia* may be so modified as to be conformable to the dogmas of the Catholic Church [be it remarked that the Holy Father's words are not correctly quoted], I must say that no Prussian monarch can ever accept it, for the reason that the independence of the monarchy would be diminished if the free exercise of its legislation were made subordinate to a foreign power." Socialism, in its worst form, may yet punish the rulers of Prussia for rejecting the only means which might have stayed the decline of their power.

The Czar's answer was dated the 22d of February, which corresponds to the 6th of March in the Gregorian Calendar. It congratulates the Holy Father on his elevation, and then, with the usual truthfulness of modern diplomacy, continues :

" It has not depended on us that the Roman Catholic Church, like all the other churches which exist in our empire, has not fulfilled, in entire security, the mission which religion, strictly independent of all political influence, is called upon to exercise for the edification and moral improvement of the people. Your Holiness may be assured that within these limits the protection compatible with the fundamental laws of our empire will be given to the Church of which you are the spiritual head." One glance at Poland and another at the swarms of exiled bishops, priests, and Catholics in Siberia will suffice to show that it were better for Alexander II. to speak less of the fundamental laws of his empire and to think more of the fundamental law of eternal justice, which no potentate has ever disregarded with impunity.

Let us turn from this sad spectacle of duplicity to more consoling subjects. One of the first objects to which Leo XIII. turned his attention was the perfecting of a great work that had been begun by Pius IX. This was the restoration of the hierarchy in Scotland, in the hope that the true faith would then take deeper root and flourish with greater luxuriance, as had been the case when the hierarchy was established in England.

The Apostolic letters on this subject bear the date of March 4th, 1878, and their tenor is as follows :

LEO, BISHOP, SERVANT OF THE SERVANTS OF GOD, FOR A PERPETUAL REMEMBRANCE.

From the highest summit of the apostolic office, to which, without any merits of ours, but by the disposition of Providence, we have recently been raised, the Roman Pontiffs, our predecessors, never ceased to watch, as from a mountain-top, in order that they might perceive what, as years rolled on, would be most conducive to the prosperity, dignity, and stability of all the churches. Hence, as far as was given them, they were exceedingly solicitous not only to erect Episcopal Sees in every land, but also to recall to life such as had through evil times ceased to exist. For, since the Holy Ghost has placed bishops to rule the Church of God, wherever the state of religion allows the ordinary Episcopal government to be either established or restored, it certainly is not lawful to deprive the Church of the benefits which naturally flow from this divinely established institution.

Wherefore our immediate predecessor, Pius IX., of sacred memory, whose recent death we all deplore, seeing, even from the beginning of his Pontificate, that the missions in the most noble and flourishing kingdom of England had made such progress that the form of Church government which exists in Catholic nations would be beneficial to religion, restored to the English their ordinary bishops by an Apostolic letter, dated 1st October, 1850, beginning *Universalis ecclesiæ;* and, not long after, perceiving that the illustrious regions of Holland and Brabant could enjoy the same salutary dispositions, he there also restored the Episcopal hierarchy by another Apostolic letter, dated 4th March, 1853, beginning *Ex qua die.* The wisdom of these measures—to say nothing of the restoration of the Patriarchate of Jerusalem—has been amply proved by the result which, through the divine grace, has fully realized the hopes of this Holy See; since it is evident to all that a great increase was given to the Catholic Church in each of those countries through the restoration of the Episcopal hierarchy.

The loving heart of the Pontiff was grieved that Scotland could not as yet enjoy the same good fortune. And this grief of his paternal heart was increased by his knowledge of the great progress made by the Catholic Church in Scotland in past days. And, indeed, whoever is even slightly conversant with Church history must have known that the light of the Gospel shone upon the Scots at an early date ; for, to say nothing of what tradition has handed down of more ancient Apostolic missions, it is recounted that towards the end of the fourth century, St. Ninian, who, as venerable Bede attests, had been correctly taught the faith and the mysteries of the truth in Rome ; and in the fifth century, St. Palladius, a Deacon of the Roman Church, having been invested with the sacred mitre, preached the faith of Christ in Scotland ; and that St. Columba, Abbot, who landed there in the sixth century, built a monastery, from which many others sprang. And although from the middle of the eighth century to the eleventh, historical documents concerning the ecclesiastical state of Scotland are almost entirely wanting, still it has been handed down that there were many bishops in the country, ' although some of them had no fixed Sees. But after Malcolm III. came into possession of the sovereign power in the year 1057, through his exertions at the exhortation of his sainted spouse, Margaret, the Christian religion, which, either through the inroads of foreign peoples, or through various political vicissitudes, had suffered heavy losses, began to be restored and spread ; and the still existing remains of churches, monasteries, and religious buildings bear witness to the piety of the ancient Scots. But, to come more directly to our subject, it is known that, in the fifteenth century, the Episcopal Sees had increased to the number of thirteen, to wit, St. Andrews, Glasgow, Dunkeld, Aberdeen, Moray, Bre-

chin, Dumblane, Ross and Caithness, Whithorn and
Lismore, Sodor or the Isles, and Orkney—all of which
were immediately subject to the Apostolic See.   It
is also known—and the Scots are justly proud of the
fact—that the Roman Pontiffs, taking the kingdom of
Scotland under their special protection, regarded the
above-named churches with special favor ; hence,
while they themselves acted as Metropolitans of Scotland, they more than once decreed that the liberties
and immunities, granted in past times by the Roman
Church, mother and teacher of all the Churches,
should be preserved intact ; so that, as was decreed
by Honorius III., of holy memory, the Scottish
Church should be like a favorite daughter, immediately subject to the Apostolic See without any in-
termediary.   Thus Scotland was without a Metropolitan of its own to the time of Sixtus IV., who, re-
flecting on the expense and delays to which the Scots
were subjected in coming to the Roman metropolis,
by an Apostolic letter of the 17th August, 1472, beginning *Triumphans Pastor Æternus*, raised the See of
St. Andrews to be the Metropolitan and Archiepiscopal See of the whole kingdom, the other Sees being
subjected to it as suffragans.   In like manner the See
of Glasgow was withdrawn from the ecclesiastical
province of St. Andrews, by Innocent VIII., in 1491,
and raised to the dignity of a Metropolitan See, with
some of the above Sees as suffragans.

The Scottish Church thus constituted was in a
flourishing condition, when it was reduced to utter
ruin by the outbreak of heresy in the sixteenth century.   Yet never did the anxious care, solicitude, and
watchfulness of the Supreme Pontiffs, our predecessors, fail the Scots that they might persevere strong in
their faith.   For, moved with compassion for that

people, and seeing the wide havoc wrought by the storm, they labored strenuously to succor religion, now by sending missionaries of various religious Orders, again by Apostolic legations and by every kind of assistance. By their care, in this citadel of the Catholic world, besides the Urban College, a special college was opened for chosen youths of the Scottish nation, in which they should be trained in sacred knowledge, and prepared for the priesthood, in order to exercise the sacred ministry in their native land, and to bring spiritual aid to their countrymen. And as that beloved portion of the Lord's flock was bereft of its pastors, Gregory XV., of happy memory, as soon as he had it in his power, sent William, Bishop of Chalcedon, with the ample faculties which belong to ordinaries, to both England and Scotland, to assume the pastoral charge of those scattered sheep ; as may be seen in the Apostolic letter, beginning *Ecclesia Romana*, dated 23d March, 1623. To restore the orthodox faith in the same regions, and to procure the salvation of the English and Scots, Urban VIII. granted ample faculties to Francis Barberini, Cardinal of the Holy Roman Church, as is shown by his brief *Inter gravissimas*, dated 18th of May, 1630. To the same intent also is another letter of the same pontiff, beginning *Multa sunt*, written to the Queen of France, for the purpose of recommending to her good offices the faithful and the afflicted Church of those countries.

Again, in order to provide in the best manner possible for the spiritual government of the Scots, Pope Innocent XII., in 1694, deputed as his Vicar-Apostolic, Thomas Nicholson, Bishop of Peristachium, committing to his care all the kingdom and the islands adjacent. And not long after, when one Vicar-Apostolic was no longer sufficient for the cultivation of the whole of the said vineyard of the Lord, Benedict XIII. gave the aforesaid bishop a companion, in the year 1727. Thus it came to pass that the kingdom of Scotland was divided into two 'Apostolic Vicariates, one of which embraced the southern, the other the northern portion. But the division which had sufficed for the government of the number of Catholics then existing was no longer sufficient, when through the Lord's blessing their numbers had increased. Hence this Apostolic See perceived the necessity of providing additional help for religion in Scotland, by the institution of a third Vicariate. Wherefore, Leo XII., of happy memory, by an Apostolic Letter of the 13th of February, 1827, beginning *Quanta lætitia affecti simus*, divided Scotland into three districts or Apostolic Vicariates—namely, the Eastern, Western, and Northern. It is known to all what a rich harvest the zeal of the new bishops and the anxious care of our Congregation de Propaganda Fide have gathered for the Catholic Church in the said kingdom. From all this it is evident that this Holy See, in its solicitude for all the Churches, has used every endeavor to restore the Scottish nation from the sad calamities of by-gone days.

But Pius IX., of happy memory, had exceedingly at heart the restoration to its pristine beauty of the illustrious Scottish Church. For, the bright example of his predecessors urged him, they having, as it were, smoothed the way for him to the accomplishment of this work. Considering, on the one hand, the condition of the Catholic religion in Scotland, and the daily increasing number of the faithful, of sacred workers, churches, missions, and religious houses, as well as the sufficiency of temporal means ; and seeing, on the other hand, that the liberty granted by the

British Government to Catholics had removed every impediment that might have opposed the restoration to the Scots of the ordinary rule of bishops by which the Catholics of other nations are governed, the said pontiff concluded that the establishment of the Episcopal hierarchy in Scotland should not be further delayed. Meanwhile the Vicars-Apostolic themselves, and very many of the clergy and laity, men conspicuous by noble birth and virtue, besought him earnestly to satisfy their earnest wishes in this matter. This humble request was again laid before him when a chosen band from every rank in the said region, having at their head our venerable brother, John Strain, Bishop of Abila, *in partibus infidelium*, and Vicar-Apostolic of the Eastern District, came to this city to congratulate him on the fiftieth anniversary of his Episcopal consecration. It was then that the said Pius IX. referred the matter, as its importance demanded, to the discussion of our venerable brethren the Cardinals of the Congregation de Propaganda Fide, and their opinion confirmed him more and more in the resolution he had formed. But while he was rejoicing that he had come to the completion of a work so long and ardently wished for, he was called away to receive the crown of justice.

What, therefore, our predecessor was hindered by death from bringing to a conclusion, God, plentiful in mercy, and glorious in all his works, has enabled us to effect, so that we might inaugurate our Pontificate with a happy omen. Wherefore, after having acquired a full knowledge of the entire matter, we have deemed that what had been decreed by the lately deceased Pius IX. should be promulgated. Therefore, raising up our eyes to the Father of Light, from whom comes every good and perfect gift, we have invoked the aid of Divine grace, praying also for the help of the Blessed Virgin Mary, conceived without stain ; of Blessed Joseph, her Spouse and Patron of the Universal Church ; of the blessed Apostles, Peter and Paul, of Andrew and the other saints whom the Scots venerate as patrons, that by their suffrages before God they might bring the said matter to a prosperous issue.

In view of these considerations, by an act of our own will, with certain knowledge, and in virtue of the Apostolic authority which we possess over the whole Church, to the greater glory of Almighty God, and the exaltation of the Catholic faith, we ordain and decree that in the kingdom of Scotland, the hierarchy of ordinary bishops, who shall take their titles from the Sees which by this our constitution we erect, shall be revived, and shall constitute an ecclesiastical province. Moreover, we ordain that, for the present, six Sees shall be erected, and are hereby erected, to wit : St. Andrews, with the addition of the title of Edinburgh, Glasgow, Aberdeen, Dunkeld, Whithorn or Galloway, and Argyll and the Isles.

Recalling to mind the illustrious records of the Church of St. Andrews, and taking into account the present chief city of the said kingdom, and weighing other considerations, we have resolved to call forth, as it were, from the grave, the said renowned See and to raise or restore it, with the addition of the title of Edinburgh, to the rank of the metropolitan or archiepiscopal dignity which had formerly been granted by our predecessor, Sixtus IV., of venerable memory ; and we assign to it, by virtue of our Apostolic authority, four of the above-named Sees, namely, Aberdeen, Dunkeld, Whithorn or Galloway, Argyll and the Isles. In regard to the See of Glasgow, considering the antiquity, importance, and nobility of that city, and especially the highly flourishing state of religion therein, and the archiepiscopal pre-eminence conferred upon it by Innocent VIII., we have thought it proper to give to its bishop the name and insignia of an archbishop; in such manner, however, that until it shall have been otherwise ordained by us or our successors, he shall not receive, beyond the prerogative of the name and honor, any right proper to a true archbishop and metropolitan. We also ordain that the Archbishop of Glasgow, so long as he shall be without suffragans, shall be present with the other bishops in the Provincial Synod of Scotland.

Now, in the aforesaid Archiepiscopal or Metropolitan See of St. Andrews and Edinburgh shall be included the counties of Edinburgh, Linlithgow, Haddington, Berwick, Selkirk, Peebles, Roxburgh, and the southern part of Fife, which lies to the right of the river Eden; also the county of Stirling, except the territories of Baldernock and East Kilpatrick.

In the Archdiocese of Glasgow shall be included the counties of Lanark, Renfrew, Dumbarton, the territories of Baldernock and East Kilpatrick, situated in the county of Stirling, the northern portion of the county of Ayr, which is separated from the southern portion of the same by the Lugton flowing into the river Garnock; also the islands of Great and Little Cumbrae.

In the Diocese of Aberdeen shall be contained the counties of Aberdeen, Kincardine, Banff, Elgin, or Moray, Nairn, Ross (except Lewis in the Hebrides), Cromarty, Sutherland, Caithness, the Orkney and Shetland Islands; and, finally, that portion of the county of Inverness which lies to the north of a straight line drawn from the most northerly point of

Loch Linnhe to the eastern boundary of the said county of Inverness, where the counties of Aberdeen and Banff meet.

In the Diocese of Dunkeld shall be included the counties of Perth, Forfar, Clackmannan, Kinross, and the northern portion of the county of Fife lying to the left of the river Eden ; also those portions of the county of Stirling which are disjoined from it and are surrounded by the counties of Perth and Clackmannan.

The Diocese of Whithorn or Galloway shall contain the counties of Dumfries, Kirkcudbright, Wigtown, and that portion of Ayr which stretches southwards to the left of the Lugton flowing into the river Garnock.

Finally, the Diocese of Argyll and the Isles shall embrace the county of Argyll, the islands of Bute and Arran, the Hebrides, and the southern portion of the county of Inverness which stretches from Loch Linnhe to the eastern boundary of the said county according to the line above described.

Thus, therefore, in the kingdom of Scotland, besides the honorary Archbishopric of Glasgow, there shall be one only ecclesiastical province, consisting of one Archbishop or Metropolitan and four suffragan bishops.

We doubt not that the new prelates, following in the footsteps of their predecessors, who, by their virtues, rendered the Church of Scotland illustrious, will use every endeavor to make the name of the Catholic religion in their country shine with still greater brightness, and to promote the salvation of souls and the increase of the Divine worship. We moreover reserve it to ourselves and to our successors in the Apostolic See, to divide the aforesaid dioceses into others, to increase their number, to change their boundaries, and freely execute whatever else may seem to us in the Lord most conducive to the propagation of the orthodox faith.

And as we see clearly that it will be of great benefit to the said churches, we will and ordain that their prelates shall never fail to transmit to our Congregation de Propaganda Fide, which has hitherto bestowed special care upon the said region, reports upon the Sees committed to their care; and shall inform us through the said congregation of whatever they may deem it necessary or useful to decree in fulfilment of their pastoral duty, and for the increase of their churches. Let them remember, moreover, that they are bound to send in this report, as well as to visit the tombs of the Holy Apostles every four years, as is enacted in the constitution of Sixtus V., of sacred memory, dated December 20th, 1585, beginning *Romanus Pontifex*. In all other matters which belong to the pastoral office, the above-named archbishops and bishops shall enjoy all the rights and faculties given to the Catholic bishops of other nations by the canons and Apostolic constitutions; and they shall be bound by the same obligations which, through the same common and general discipline of the Catholic Church, bind other bishops. Whatever, therefore, may have been in force in the ancient Churches of Scotland, or in the subsequent missions by special constitutions or privileges or particular customs, now that the circumstances are changed, shall no longer convey any right or impose any obligation. And, in order that no doubt may arise in future on this head, we, by the plenitude of our Apostolic authority, deprive the said special statutes, ordinances, privileges, and customs, at however remote or immemorial a

time they may have been introduced, and now in
force, of all power of inducing any obligation or conveying any right.

Wherefore it shall be in the power of the Scottish
prelates to decree whatever is requisite for the execution of the common law and whatever is competent
to the Episcopal authority according to the general
discipline of the Church.   Let them feel assured that
we shall willingly lend them the aid of our Apostolic
authority in whatever may seem conducive to the increase of the glory of God's name and the welfare of
souls.   And as an earnest of our good-will towards
the beloved daughter of the Holy See, the Church of
Scotland, we declare that these prelates, when they
shall have been invested with the title and rights of
ordinary bishops, shall not be deprived of the special
and more ample faculties which they formerly enjoyed as Vicars of the Holy See.   For it is not right
that they should suffer any loss from what, in compli-
ance with the wishes of the Scottish Catholics, has
been decreed by us for the greater good of religion in
their country.   And whereas the condition of Scotland is such that means are still wanting for the support of the clergy and the various needs of each
church, we have a certain hope that our beloved sons
in Christ, to whose earnest wish for the restoration of
the Episcopal hierarchy we have acceded, will continue to aid those whom we place over them with
alms and offerings, to provide for the Episcopal Sees,
the splendor of the churches and of the divine worship, the support of the clergy and the poor, and the
other needs of the Church.

And now we turn with most humble prayer to Him
in whom it hath pleased the Father in the fulness of
time to restore all things, beseeching Him who has

begun the good work to perfect it, confirm it, and strengthen it, and to give to all those whose duty it is to execute these our decrees, the light and strength of heavenly grace, so that the Episcopal hierarchy restored by us in the kingdom of Scotland may be for the greater good of the Catholic religion. For this end, also, we invoke, as intercessors with our Saviour Jesus Christ, His most blessed Mother, the blessed Joseph, his reputed father, the blessed Apostles Peter and Paul, as also St. Andrew, whom Scotland venerates with special devotion, and the other saints, especially the blessed Margaret, Queen of Scotland, that they may look with benign favor upon this Church now born again.

Finally, we decree that this our letter shall never be impugned by reason of omission or addition or any defect in expressing our intention or any other defect, but shall always be valid and obtain effect in all things, and shall be inviolably observed; notwithstanding Apostolic edicts and general or special sanctions published in synodal, provincial, and universal councils, and the rights and privileges of the ancient Sees of Scotland, and of the missions and apostolic vicariates afterwards constituted therein, and of all churches or pious institutes, and all things to the contrary whatsoever. We expressly abrogate all these things in so far as they contradict the foregoing, although for their abrogation they would require special mention or any other particular formality. We decree, moreover, that whatever may be done to the contrary, knowingly or ignorantly, by any person, in the name of any authority whatsoever, shall be null and void. We will also that even printed copies of this letter when subscribed by a public notary, and confirmed by the seal of an ecclesiastical dignitary, shall have the same credit as would be given to the expression of our will by the exhibition of this diploma itself.

Let no man, therefore, dare to infringe or rashly gainsay this our decree of erection and restoration. If any one should presume to attempt this, let him know that he shall incur the indignation of Almighty God and of His blessed Apostles Peter and Paul.

Given at Rome at St. Peter's, in the year of the Lord's Incarnation one thousand eight hundred and seventy-eight, the fourth of the nones of March (4th March, 1878), in the first year of our pontificate.

F. CARDINAL ASQUINI.
C. CARDINAL SACCONI, Pro-Datarius.

On the 5th of March, the parish priests of Rome, with the preachers appointed for the coming Lenten sermons in the several churches of the city, were, according to custom, admitted to an audience with the Holy Father. They were introduced by the Cardinal Vicar, Monaco la Valetta. Leo XIII. received them in the throne-room, and addressed them in the following memorable words :

" It is a most agreeable thing for us, My Lord Cardinal, to see gathered around us, to-day, this assembly of the pastors of Rome, together with all the preachers for the approaching season of Lent. Overwhelmed as we are, especially during these the first days of our Pontificate, by continual thoughts and cares, we have little time to gather our ideas together, so as to say a few words to you, excellent pastors, who are called upon to share the pastoral anxieties of the Bishop of Rome, and to you, also, who are charged with preaching.

" Still, we have not wished to allow the present opportunity to escape without giving you a few of our thoughts.

" We will say to you, in the first place, then, that, if all the faithful of the world are the objects of our paternal solicitude, this beloved flock of Rome in the midst of which we live, and which is bound to us by so many ties, is, in a measure, especially so. It is one of our most fervent prayers and the most ardent desire of our heart, that the people of Rome preserve the old faith pure and entire, that their morals may escape corruption, that we may see their love for this Holy Apostolic See, and their docile obedience to the laws and instructions they receive from it, increase more and more. We know too well that in all parts of the world the enemies of the Church are trying, by every means, to wrest these inestimable treasures from the minds and hearts of the faithful ; but we also know that they aim, in an especial manner, at this city, which is the centre of Catholicity, and that every influence is brought to bear to lead it to infidelity and immorality.

" It is, therefore, necessary that you, our beloved pastors, be awake to the exceptional condition of the times in which we live, and to the most fearful dangers to which the faith and morals of the Roman people are particularly exposed. It is necessary that your zeal increase and multiply in proportion as these perils increase, and as the efforts of the enemy are redoubled. If the ministry of pastors has been always and everywhere laborious and difficult, it is certain that in the times in which we live, and within these walls, you will have to call forth all your energies in an especial manner, that you fail not in the high object of your mission. You must bring to it, moreover, and as an indispensable condition, a spirit of full and entire sacrifice, that will always lead you to place the glory of God and the salvation of souls above every consideration of convenience or interest. Rest assured that if you are animated by this spirit, you who are the laborers of the mystic vine, your apostolic labors will be crowned with priceless and abundant fruits.

" The Roman clergy have always given magnificent examples of zeal and self-denial that have made them the model and admiration of others ; therefore do we promise ourselves the most happy and consoling results from your labors, persuaded that these will be all the greater in proportion as your cares are more assiduous, your sacrifices more generous and more entire, your zeal more enlightened, your conduct more blameless.

" It is now a pleasure to us to address you, heralds of the Gospel, who will to-morrow commence to sow the good seed of the Divine Word among the faithful. Remember that this Word, proclaimed in bygone times by the apostles, under the inspiration of the Spirit of God, with which they were filled, was strong enough to root out of the world the bad weeds of false doctrines, to enlighten minds, and to rekindle in hearts a sincere love for the good and the beautiful ; it sufficed to convert the world and to gain it whole and entire to Jesus Christ. This Word can now also save the world from the abyss to which it is hastening, wash away its stains, and again subject it to Jesus Christ.

" It is, then, indispensably necessary that sacred speakers, walking in the footsteps of the apostles, relying on divine virtue more than on their own strength and their persuasive eloquence, preach to the faithful Jesus Christ, the mysteries of His life and death, His doctrines and His heavenly counsels, the Church and her sublime prerogatives, the divine authority of her visible head, her greatness and her beneficent influence for the true welfare of nations ; they must meet with simple and solid reasoning all the most pernicious and most prevalent errors of our times, by seeking to penetrate to the very bottom of men's hearts, and to inspire them with truth and virtue.

" But that all may succeed according to our prayers and desires, we invoke upon all pastors of souls, and upon all heralds of the Gospel, the abundance of heavenly lights and the efficacious aid of divine grace. We desire you to find an earnest of these favors and a proof of our paternal good-will in the Apostolic Benediction which from the bottom of our heart we bestow upon all pastors of souls, and upon their flocks, upon Lenten preachers, and upon their Apostolic labors.

" *Benedictio Dei*," etc.

These are precious words and lessons of more than human wisdom, the full understanding and practical observance of which would go far to cure the many evils under which society is groaning in our times.

More than a month had elapsed since the election of Leo XIII., and the world was still waiting with anxiety for his first official utterance to define his course and declare his principles. The world could not appreciate the wisdom of this delay ; but its anxiety was relieved at length on the 28th of March, when the Holy Father held his first consistory in the Vatican, and again, a little later, when the first Encyclical was published to all the bishops of the Church in communion with the Holy See.

The consistory was unusually solemn, as Leo XIII. on that occasion resumed all the ceremonial which had been discontinued by Pius IX. since the invasion of Rome.   Seated on his throne, vested in his pontifical insignia, with the golden mitre on his head, Leo XIII. delivered the following magnificent allocution to the assembled cardinals :

VENERABLE BRETHREN : As soon as we were called, through your suffrages, in the past month, to assume the government of the Universal Church, and to hold here on earth the place of the Prince of pastors, our Lord Jesus Christ, we felt ourselves moved by the greatest apprehension and fear, on account of the knowledge of our own unworthiness, as well as the inadequacy of our strength to bear such a burden, which appeared the greater on account of the splendid and illustrious fame of our predecessor, Pius IX. That great pastor of the flock of Christ, always combating energetically for truth and justice, and sustaining the great burden of the administration of the entire Church, not only rendered this Apostolic chair more resplendent by his virtues, but filled the Church with love and admiration.   And in the same manner as he surpassed the whole series of Roman pontiffs in the length of his reign, so, may we say, he surpassed all in the public testimonials of sympathy and veneration which he received.   On the other hand, our heart was filled with sorrow at the sad condition in which we find not only human society, but also the Catholic Church, and in an especial manner this Apostolic See, violently despoiled of its temporal dominions, and so reduced as to be completely unable to enjoy its full, free, and independent power.

And although we felt ourselves inclined to refuse the great honor offered us, yet with what heart could we resist the will of God, so evidently made known to us through the harmony of your suffrages, seeking only the welfare of the Catholic Church, and succeed-

ing so promptly in completing the election of the new
pontiff ? For this reason we thought ourselves obliged
to accept the burden presented to us, in obedience to
the will of God, in whom we place all our trust, firmly
hoping that He who has elevated us to so high a position will support our weakness.

Now, venerable brethren, as this is the first time
that we address you, we declare that nothing shall
be held more sacred by us, with the aid of divine
grace, than the inviolable preservation of the Catholic
faith, the defence of the rights of the Church and the
Holy Apostolic See, and the promotion of the salvation of all men.

For the fufilment of this part of our ministry, we
confide in your counsel and wisdom, which we trust
will never be wanting to us, and this we wish you to
understand, not as a mere compliment, but as a solemn
declaration of our will.   For we bear in mind what is
narrated in Holy Writ, when Moses, terrified at the
great weight laid upon him, called together seventy
of the ancients of Israel, that they might divide with
him the cares of the government of his people. Having this example before our eyes, now that we are
called as leader and governor of the whole Christian
world, we cannot do less than ask help in our fatigues,
and comfort in our cares, from you who hold in the
Church of God the same position as the elders of
Israel.

Besides, we know that the sacred Scriptures say
that "there is safety where there is much counsel;"
we know that the holy Council of Trent attests that
the sovereign pontiff should find assistance in the wisdom of the cardinals ; and finally that St. Bernard calls
the cardinals the assistants and counsellors of the
sovereign pontiff. We, who for five-and-twenty years

had the good fortune to form a part of the Sacred College, bring to this throne not only a heart full of affection and sympathy for you, but still more the consolation of having, in the exercise of our duties to the Church, companions and co-operators in our obligations, and sharers in our glories and honors.

Moreover, it is with the greatest pleasure that we communicate to you, venerable brethren, the completion of a work which was undertaken by our glorious predecessor, Pius IX., and which had already been discussed by those among you who form a part of the Sacred Congregation for the Propagation of the Faith, namely, the establishment of the Episcopal hierarchy in the illustrious kingdom of Scotland. We, by the grace of God, had the consolation of issuing the apostolic bull for this purpose, on the fourth day of the present month. We rejoiced that we were able to answer the fervent prayers of those beloved children of Jesus Christ, the clergy and faithful of Scotland, who have ever shown the greatest devotion towards the Catholic Church and the chair of St. Peter, and we most firmly hope that this work of the Holy Apostolic See may be crowned with heavenly fruits, and that through the mediation and prayers of the patron saints of Scotland, *suscipiant montes pacem populo, et colles justitiam;* her mountains may receive peace and her hills justice for her people.

Finally, venerable brethren, we doubt not that you, united in the same spirit with us, will work unceasingly for the defence of the holy Apostolic See and the increase of the glory of God ; knowing that our reward in heaven shall be the same, if our trials in the interest of the Church shall have been the same on earth. Pray, therefore, humbly with us that God, rich in mercies, through the powerful intercession of

His Immaculate Mother, of St. Joseph, Patron of the Universal Church, the Holy Apostles SS. Peter and Paul, may be propitious, and happily direct our minds and actions through the days of our pontificate, that we may conduct the Bark of Peter, which has been confided to us, through the fury of the winds and the waves, to the desired port of tranquillity and peace.

His Eminence Cardinal Di Pietro, in the absence of his Eminence Cardinal Amat, and in the name of the Sacred College of Cardinals, replied as follows :

" Your Holiness, in your great goodness, has expressed to us in this allocution your thanks for the unity of our votes in raising your sacred person to that elevated position of sovereign pontiff of the Holy Roman Church, and you have deigned to add words of comfort for our Sacred College, from which you justly expect help in these turbulent times.

" Yes, it is indeed true, most Holy Father, that it was our suffrages that elevated your worthy person to a sublime dignity ; but making use of the words of the holy Apostle St. Peter, I will say, *God who knoweth the hearts gave testimony, giving unto you the Holy Ghost as well as to us.*

" It was through the inspiration of the Holy Spirit that we have placed you on ' the lofty tower,' as St. Bernard writes to his dear friend Eugenius when raised to the pontificate. In that eminent position in which you have all things under your eyes and subject to you, you can uproot and destroy, scatter and undo, build and plant anew—a difficult task, forsooth ! But indeed that view from above requires you to be always prepared, and to take no repose, as there is no time for repose when you have the general direction of the Church.

" A continual solicitude and vigilance are required

of him who holds this inheritance, which, although great and magnificent in its external appearances, consists in reality of the cross and innumerable cares.

" We could not possibly doubt that your Holiness would always continue to have at heart, as you have just declared to us, the dignity of our Sacred College, and, in reply to such courteous words, we promise that you will always find us prompt and obedient to give you all possible assistance, so as to render less burdensome that great weight which, in resignation to the Divine will, you have deigned to bear ; though we are aware that while our promises are a comfort to you, yet they can take but little from the greatness of your anxiety.

" Notwithstanding the burden which you have to bear, turn your eyes to heaven, and confide in the Divine promise that each one shall receive a reward according to his labor.   Take courage, then, and confide in God, and repeat to yourself those words of St. Bernard, *Si labor terret, merces invitat*.   But besides the reward which your Holiness expects in heaven, receive from my lips, in the name of our Sacred College, a wish that you may enjoy even on earth that reward which consists in seeing your pontificate always increase the number of the faithful children of the Catholic Church, and that they may continue obedient and respectful towards the chair of Peter, and bound to the Apostolic See, in the words of St. Ambrose, not with the ties of perfidy, but with the bonds of faith."

In the same consistory, Cardinal Camillo di Pietro was named Camerlengo of the Holy Roman Church, and several vacant sees were provided with bishops. The Holy Father made the customary profession of faith and took the oath to observe the apostolic constitutions.

The hall was then thrown open for a ceremony of peculiar interest for the Catholics of the new world. It was the conferring of the cardinal's hat on the Archbishop of New York, John McCloskey, who had been declared cardinal by Pius IX., on the 15th of March, 1875.

As the cardinal's hat can only be conferred by the Pope in person, this final ceremony was, of course, to be delayed until the new cardinal was summoned to Rome. Cardinal McCloskey sailed from New York, February 9th, two days after the death of Pope Pius, arriving in Rome two days after the election of Pope Leo. On proceeding to Rome to receive the hat at the hands of the Pope, a member of the Sacred College wears the short violet robe proper to such occasions, exchanging it for a longer one of the same color when he pays his formal visit to the Pope. Thereafter, according to the strict etiquette of the Vatican, he should not appear in public till the day appointed for the consistory, when he proceeds in a carriage with all possible pomp to the Vatican, and in the Sistine Chapel awaits the assembling of the Sacred College. Meanwhile, the cardinals enter the great hall of the consistory ; and at a given signal two cardinal-deacons, after kissing the Pope's hand, proceed to the chapel, whence they conduct the new cardinal to the presence of the pontiff. Thrice the cardinal makes a profound reverence to the Head of the Church—once at the threshold, once in the middle of the hall, once at the foot of the throne ; then ascending its steps, he kisses the feet of the Pope, who also bestows upon him the kiss of peace. He then embraces all the other members of the Sacred College.

Now, while the Te Deum is chanted, the cardinals

CARDINAL McCLOSKEY.

Born in Brooklyn, N. Y., March 10, 1810.
Ordained January 12, 1834.
Consecrated Bishop, March 10, 1844.
Transferred to diocese of New York, May 6, 1864.
Created Cardinal, July 15, 1875.

procced, two by two, to the Papal Chapel, where they pass around the altar with their new comrade.   Kneeling upon the altar steps, the new cardinal is approached by the master of ceremonies, who covers his head with his *capuchon* or hood ; when the "Te ergo" is reached, the new cardinal prostrates himself on the floor, and thus remains till the end of the canticle, and of the prayers which are to be recited by the Cardinal-Dean.   He rises, and his hood is thrown back. The Dean of the Sacred College, attended by two other cardinals and the Cardinal-Camerlengo, receives from the new cardinal the oath of office, by which he declares that he is ready to shed his blood for the Holy Roman Church and the maintenance of the Apostolical college to which he belongs ; then the whole company return in due order as before to the Consistorial Hall.   Here the new cardinal kneels before the Pope ; the master of ceremonies covers his head with the hood, on which the Pope places the red velvet hat, pronouncing at the same time the prescribed prayers. The Holy Father then withdraws, and the cardinals form a circle about their new brother, who salutes and thanks them.   At the first consistory the Pope closes the mouth of the new cardinal, which ceremony—it is merely a ceremony, and does not affect the cardinal's status or rights—signifies that he is not to speak without permission of what he has heard ; at the next the Pope opens his mouth, gives him the cardinal's ring and confers his title—that of one of the churches of Rome, a sort of ecclesiastical fief—upon him.

The cardinal's hat is of red cloth with a very small crown and broad brim.   Two ties, each ending in five rows of red silk acorns or tassels, three in each row, are fastened to the crown and fall on either side, being long enough to meet under the wearer's chin.   Originally, instead of this fringe each tie had but a single tassel, because the hat was then used on all solemn occasions.   At present the hat is not worn, and therefore the fringing may be more elaborate. Indeed after the hat has been conferred it is not again seen till the cardinal's death, when it is placed upon his bier, and, as a rule, suspended in the church above his tomb.   The red hat of the cardinals is of felt, of the same shape as those of simple ecclesiastics.   On ordinary occasions they wear a black hat with a red ribbon, gold-embroidered.   The ring given to the cardinal to consecrate his marriage with the Church is a sapphire set in gold.

Such was the first consistory of the new Pope, and the Catholic world rejoiced to see Pius IX. live again in the noble and fearless words and acts of his successor.   This joy on the part of the loyal sons of the Church was enhanced, whilst the hate and fear of its enemies were stirred up afresh, by the first Encyclical published by Leo XIII., which is too important to be omitted or even abridged.   We give it entire :

TO THE VENERABLE BROTHERS, ALL THE PATRIARCHS, PRIMATES, ARCHBISHOPS AND BISHOPS, HOLDING GRACE AND COMMUNION WITH THE APOSTOLIC SEE :

POPE LEO XIII.

Venerable Brothers : Health and Apostolic Benediction.

As soon as, through the inscrutable counsel of God, we were raised, though unworthy, to the summit of the Apostolic dignity, we immediately felt ourselves impelled with the desire and almost the necessity of addressing you by letter, not only to express to you our sentiments of sincere love, but also, by the office divinely entrusted to us, to strengthen you, who are called to a part of our solicitude, to sustain with us the struggle of these times for the Church of God and for the salvation of souls.

For from the very beginning of our pontificate the sad spectacle presented itself to us of the evils with which the human race is everywhere oppressed ; this widespread subversion of the supreme truths upon which, as foundations, human society rests ; this insubordination of minds, impatient of all legitimate authority ; this perpetual cause of discords, whence intestine struggles, cruel and bloody wars spring ; the contempt of the laws which regulate morals and defend justice ; the insatiable cupidity of transient goods and the utter forgetfulness of eternal things, even to that mad fury in which many hesitate not to lay violent hands upon themselves ; the thriftless administration, the squandering of the public moneys, and the impudence of those who, when most guilty, give out that they are the vindicators of country, of liberty, and of every right ; finally, that deadly poison which works itself into the very vitals of human society, never allows it to be quiet, and presages for it new revolutions with calamitous results.

We are convinced that the cause of these evils lies principally in the rejection of the august authority of the Church, which presides over the human race in the name of God, and is the safeguard of all legitimate authority. The enemies of public order, knowing this full well, thought that nothing was more conducive to uproot the foundations of society than to attack the Church of God pertinaciously, and by foul calumnies bring her into odium and disrepute, as if she were the enemy of real civilization, and destroy the supreme power of the Roman Pontiff, the champion of the unchangeable principles of eternal justice. Hence have come those laws destructive of the divine constitution of the Church, which we grieve to see enacted in many countries ; hence emanated contempt for Episcopal power, impediments to the exercise of the ecclesiastical ministry, the dissolution of the religious corporations, and the confiscation of the goods with which the ministers of the Church and the poor were supported ; hence public institutions consecrated to charity were taken from the salutary administration of the Church ; hence sprang that license to teach and print every iniquity, while, on the other hand, the right of the Church to instruct and educate youth is violated and trampled under foot.

This too is the end and object of the usurpation of the civil principality which Divine Providence gave to the Bishop of Rome many centuries ago, that he might use freely the power given by Christ for the salvation of souls.

We have called to mind this sad accumulation of evils, venerable brothers, not with a view of increasing your grief, which this most wretched condition of things of itself produces in you, but because we know that thus you will clearly see how serious is the situation of affairs which calls for our zealous solicitude, and how assiduously we must labor to defend and vindicate to the best of our power the Church of God and the dignity of this Apostolic See, charged with so many calumnies.

It is evident, venerable brothers, that human civilization lacks a solid foundation, unless it rests upon the eternal principles of truth and the unchangeable laws of justice, and unless sincere love binds the wills of men together and governs their mutual relations.

Now, who can deny that it is the Church that, by preaching the gospel to the nations, brought the light of truth among barbarous and superstitious people, and moved them to recognize the Divine Author of things and to respect themselves ; that, by abolishing slavery, recalled men to the pristine dignity of their noble nature ; by unfurling the banner of redemption in every clime of the earth, by introducing or protecting the arts, by founding excellent institutions of charity which provide for every misery, cultivated the human race everywhere, raised it from its degradation, and brought it to a life becoming the dignity and the destinies of man? And if any one of sound intelligence will compare this age in which we live, so hostile to religion and the Church of Christ, with those happy times when the Church was regarded by nations as a mother, he will clearly perceive that this our age, full of disorders and revolutions, is going rapidly to ruin ; whereas those ages advanced in the excellence of their institutions, in tranquillity of life, in wealth and prosperity, in proportion as the people were more subject to the authority and laws of the Church. And if the many benefits which we have cited, effected by the ministry and salutary assistance of the Church, are the real works and glories of civilization, the Church, so far from abhorring and repudiating it, rather makes it her glory to be its nourisher, teacher, and mother.

But that kind of civilization which is opposed to the holy doctrines and laws of the Church is only a shadow of civilization, an empty name without reality, as appears from the example of those people upon whom the light of the Gospel has not shone, and in whose life a glimmer of civilization is to be seen, but its real and solid benefits do not exist. That cer-

tainly is not to be regarded as the perfection of civilization which contemns legitimate authority, nor is
that to be reputed as liberty which basely and miserably thrives on the unrestrained propagation of
errors, on the free indulgence of every wicked desire, on the impunity of crimes and offences, on the
oppression of good citizens of every class. For since
such things are false, wicked, and absurd, they certainly cannot render the human family prosperous,
for *sin maketh nations miserable* (Prov. 14 : 34), for
when the mind and heart are corrupt, they drag men
down into every misfortune, disturb all order, and
destroy the peace of nations.

Moreover, considering what has been done by the
Roman See, what can be more unjust than to deny
the eminent services rendered by the Bishops of
Rome to the cause of society? Certainly our predecessors, in order to provide for the good of the people, never hesitated to undertake struggles of every
kind, to perform great labors and expose themselves
to serious difficulties ; and, with their eyes fixed upon
heaven, they neither quailed before the threats of the
wicked, nor suffered themselves to be led astray from
their duty by flattery or promises. It was this Apostolic See that gathered up and united the remnants of
ancient society ; it was the torch to shed light on the
civilization of Christian times ; it was the anchor of
safety in those violent tempests by which the human
race was tossed about ; it was the sacred bond of concord which united nations of diverse customs together ; finally, it was the common centre whence all
men derived, together with the doctrines of religion,
encouragement and counsels to peace. It is the
glory of the sovereign pontiffs that they ever threw
themselves into the breach, that human society

might not sink back into ancient superstition and barbarism.

Oh, that this salutary authority had never been
neglected or repudiated ! Certainly the civil power
would never have lost that august and sacred glory
which it received from religion, and which alone rendered obedience noble and worthy of man ; nor would
so many seditions and wars have raged, which rendered the earth desolate with calamities and slaughter ;
nor would once flourishing kingdoms, now fallen from
the height of prosperity, be oppressed with the weight
of misfortune.   A signal proof of this are the people
of the East, who, having burst asunder the bonds
which joined them to this Apostolic See, have lost the
splendor of their former greatness, the glory of the
sciences and arts, and the dignity of their empire.

But the distinguished benefits, which the illustrious monuments of every age declare to have been
bestowed by the Apostolic See upon every clime of
the earth, were particularly experienced by this land
of Italy, which, being nearer to the source, received
more abundant blessings.   For to the Roman pontiffs
Italy is indebted for the glory and greatness in which
she surpassed other nations.   Their paternal authority
and solicitude often protected her from the assaults
of her enemies, and brought her assistance, that the
Catholic faith might always be preserved entire in the
hearts of the Italians.

These services of our predecessors, to pass over
many others, are recorded in the history of St. Leo
the Great, of Alexander III., Innocent III., St. Pius
V., Leo X., and other pontiffs, by whose zeal and protection Italy escaped from the utter ruin threatened by
the barbarians, retained the old faith incorrupt, and
amid the darkness and degradation of an uncultured

age nourished and maintained the light of science and the splendor of the arts. This fair city, the seat of the pontiffs, bears witness to these benefits, of which it received so great a share, becoming not only the fortified citadel of faith, but also the asylum and home of the fine arts and of learning, which have won for her the admiration and respect of the whole world. And as the greatness of these things is consigned to eternal remembrance in history, it will easily be understood that nothing but base calumny and malice could have published, by word of mouth and in print, that the Apostolic See is a hindrance to the civilization and happiness of the people of Italy.

If, then, all the hopes of Italy and of the whole world repose in that useful and salutary power, which is the authority of the Apostolic See, and in that bond which unites all the faithful with the Roman pontiff, we can deem nothing more important than to preserve the dignity of the Chair of St. Peter entire, and to render more intimate the union of the members with the Head, of the children with the Father.

Wherefore, in the first place, that we may assert to the best of our power the rights and liberty of this Holy See, we shall never cease to contend for the obedience due to our authority, for the removal of the obstacles which hinder the full liberty of our ministry, and for our restoration to that condition in which the counsels of the Divine Wisdom first placed the Roman bishops. We are not moved, venerable brothers, to demand this restoration by ambition or the desire of dominion ; but by our office, and by the religious oaths which bind us ; and because this principality is necessary to preserve the full liberty of the spiritual power, and it is most clear that in the question of the temporal principality of the Apostolic See, the cause of the public good and the safety of society are involved. Hence we cannot omit, because of our office, by which we are bound to defend the rights of the Holy Church, to renew and confirm by these our letters all the declarations and protests which our predecessor of holy memory, Pius IX., published and reiterated against the occupation of his civil principality, and against the violation of the rights of the Roman Church. At the same time, we turn our discourse to the princes and supreme rulers of the nations, and we adjure them again and again, by the august name of the Most High God, not to reject the assistance of the Church offered to them in such a critical time, but to gather in a friendly manner around this centre of authority and safety, and be united more inseparably with it in the bonds of sincere love and obedience. God grant that they may recognize the truth of what we have said, and may know that the teaching of Christ, as St. Augustine says, *if it be observed, will be very salutary to the Republic;* and that in the preservation of the Church and in obedience to her their own prosperity and peace are included. Let them turn their thoughts and cares to removing the evils which afflict the Church and her visible Head, so that the people over whom they preside, entering upon the way of justice and peace, may enjoy a happy era of prosperity and glory.

And finally, that the harmony between the entire Catholic flock and the supreme pastor may be more lasting, we appeal to you with particular affection, venerable brothers, and we warmly exhort you in your sacerdotal zeal and pastoral vigilance to inflame with the love of religion the faithful entrusted to you, that they may cleave more closely to this chair of truth and justice, and receive all its doctrines with the full assent of their mind and will ; rejecting all opinions which they know to be opposed to the teaching of the Church. The Roman pontiffs, our predecessors, and especially Pius IX., of holy memory, in the Œcumenical Council of the Vatican especially, mindful of the words of St. Paul, *Beware, lest any man cheat you by philosophy and vain deceit, according to the tradition of men, according to the elements of the world, and not according to Christ*, never neglected, when it was necessary, to condemn current errors and brand them with the Apostolic censure. Following in the footsteps of our predecessors, we confirm and reiterate all these condemnations, and at the same time we earnestly beg the Father of lights that all the faithful, united with us in the same sentiments, may think and speak in accord with us. But it is your duty, venerable brothers, to use sedulous care that the seed of heavenly doctrines be scattered widely through the vineyard of the Lord, and that the teachings of the Catholic faith be early instilled into the minds of the faithful, strike deep root there, and be preserved incorrupt from the contagion of error. The more earnestly the enemies of religion try to instil into the unwary and especially into youth those things which becloud the mind and corrupt morals, the greater should be your efforts to obtain not only a solid method of education, but also to make the teaching itself agreeable to the Catholic faith, particularly in philosophy, upon which the right study of the other sciences depends, and which, far from destroying revelation, rather rejoices to point out the way to it, and defends it against those who attack it, as the great Augustine, the Angelic Doctor, and other teachers of Christian wisdom prove by their example and writings.

Moreover, it is necessary that the proper training of youth to insure the true faith and good morals, should begin with the earliest years in the family itself, which, being miserably disturbed in these our times, can be restored to its dignity only by those laws according to which it was instituted in the Church by its Divine Author. He raised the contract of marriage, by which He wished to signify His own union with the Church, to the dignity of a sacrament, and thus not only sanctified that union, but also prepared both for parents and children the most efficacious aids, by which, through the observance of their mutual duties, they may more easily obtain temporal and eternal happiness. But when impious laws, setting aside the sanctity of this great sacrament, reduced it to the level of civil contracts, the consequence was that, the dignity of Christian union being violated, citizens live in legal concubinage, instead of legitimate union, and neglect the duties of mutual faith ; children refuse obedience to parents, the bonds of domestic love are loosened, and, to the destruction of public morals, foolish love is often succeeded by pernicious and disastrous separations. These wretched and deplorable facts cannot, venerable brothers, but arouse your zeal, and move you to admonish the faithful entrusted to your vigilance, that they may observe the doctrines which concern Christian marriage, and obey the laws by which the Church regulates the duties of parents and children.

It is thus that you will bring about a desirable reform in the morals and manner of life of individual men ; for as from a corrupt root bad fruit cannot fail to spring, so the poison which depraves the family produces vice in individual citizens. On the contrary, when the family circle is regulated by the rules of a Christian life, the individual members begin by degrees to love religion and piety, to abhor false and pernicious doctrines, follow virtue, obey their elders, and suppress that selfish interest which enervates and enfeebles human nature. For this purpose it will be very useful to promote those pious associations which have been established to the great advance of Catholic interests especially in this age.

Great indeed and superior to human strength are these things which we hope and desire, venerable brothers ; but since God has made the people of the earth capable of being reclaimed, since He has founded His Church for the salvation of nations, and promised to be with her unto the consummation of the world, we firmly trust, with your co-operation, that the human race, sensible of its many calamities, will finally seek salvation and prosperity in submission to the Church and the infallible teaching of this Apostolic See.

Meanwhile, venerable brothers, before we close, we must congratulate you on that admirable union and harmony which unite you together and join you with this Apostolic See. We deem this perfect union not only an impregnable bulwark against the enemy, but also a happy omen of better days for the Church ; and while it brings great comfort to our weakness, it also lifts up our soul, that in the arduous office which we have accepted we may sustain every labor and every struggle for the Church of God.

Moreover, these motives of hope and joy which we have expressed to you cannot be separated from the tokens of love and obedience which, in the beginning of our pontificate, you, venerable brothers, and, together with you, many ecclesiastics and laymen, have given us, by letters, by offerings, by pilgrimages, and by other offices of piety, showing that the love which they had felt for our worthy predecessor remains so firm, so lasting, and entire, that it wanes not even towards the person of so unequal a successor. For these splendid testimonies of Catholic piety we humbly praise the Lord because He is good and merciful, and from the bottom of our heart we publicly profess the sentiments of our gratitude to you, venerable brothers, and to all the beloved children from whom we received them, while we cherish the confidence that in these sad and critical times your zeal and affection and those of the faithful will never fail us. And we doubt not that these excellent examples of filial piety and Christian virtue will avail much, and move the most merciful God to look more propitiously upon His flock, and grant peace and victory to the Church. But as we believe He will give this peace and victory more readily if the faithful pray for it with constant fervor, we earnestly exhort you, venerable brothers, to excite the zeal of the faithful to ask for it through the intercession of the Immaculate Queen of Heaven, of St. Joseph, patron of the Church, and of the holy princes of the Apostles, Peter and Paul, to whose powerful patronage we suppliantly commend our own humble person, all the orders of the ecclesiastical hierarchy, and the entire flock of the Lord.

For the rest we pray that these days, on which we celebrate the resurrection of Jesus Christ, may be to you, venerable brothers, and to all the faithful, blessed and full of holy joy, while we beseech the most merciful God, through the blood of the Immaculate Lamb, by whom the handwriting which was against us was erased, to pardon the faults we have committed, and remit the punishments we deserve for them.

The grace of our Lord Jesus Christ, and the charity of God, and the communication of the Holy Spirit be with you all, venerable brothers ; to all whom, as to all our beloved children, the clergy and faithful of your churches, as a pledge of particular benevolence and a token of heavenly protection, we most lovingly impart the Apostolic Benediction.

Given at St. Peter's, Rome, on the solemn day of Easter, the 21st of April, in the year 1878, the first year of our pontificate.

LEO XIII., Pope.

This noble document, which is as strong in matter as it is moderate in form, gives us the complement to the celebrated Pastoral Letter of the Cardinal-Bishop of Perugia on the subject of the Church and civilization, of which mention was made in its proper place. The rights of the Holy See to its temporal power are held up with all the firmness of him whose " Non possumus" will never be forgotten. Obedience to the teachings of the sovereign pontiff is proclaimed as the true and only safeguard of civilization ; and the religious constitution of the Christian family is pointed out as the necessary guardian of public morals. Modern ideas are denounced and reprobated as a very destruction of both rulers and nations. Would that the rulers and nations now tossed about in the throes of never-ending revolutions, instead of devising remedies of their own or following the baseless theories of demagogues or world-reformers, which can only lead them further astray, would listen to the divinely appointed guide, and return to the truth which alone can make them free !

Besides the Encyclical which we have just seen,

Leo XIII. has already published several other re-markable documents, one of which we will place here, because of its special importance. We owe it to an event which caused great grief to the pontiff's heart, closing prematurely a career of unusual brilliancy. This was the death of Cardinal Alexander Franchi, who had been selected by the holy father as his Secretary of State. His appointment dated from the 3d of March, and on the 31st of July following Car-dinal Franchi died after a brief and severe illness. Leo XIII. then chose Cardinal Lorenzo Nina to the vacant post. The appointment was accompanied by a brief of the holy father to the new Secretary, which has been read with admiration by friend and foe:

"Our heart received a severe blow and our soul was filled with the deepest sorrow at the sudden death of Cardinal Alessandro Franchi, our Secretary of State. Called, as he was, to so exalted an office by the confidence he awakened within us by his uncommon gifts of heart and mind and the long service he had rendered to the Church, he so fully came up to all our expectations in the short time we had him with us that his memory will never fade from our mind and his name in the future as well as in the past shall be held by us in affection and benediction.

"But, since it has pleased God to visit this trial upon us, we bow with submissive soul to the Divine counsels, and we now turn our thoughts to the selec-tion of a successor. We have fixed our eyes on you, Signor Cardinal, whose great experience in the man-agement of affairs, whose firmness of purpose, and whose spirit of generous sacrifice in behalf of the Church are so well known.

"It seems proper to us, on your entering upon the duties of your new career, to address you this letter, to open our mind to you on some very important points to which you will be called upon, in an especial manner, to devote all your care.

" Already in the first days of our pontificate, from the height of the Apostolic See, we cast our eyes upon the society of the present day to learn its condition, to ascertain its wants, and to consider its remedies. And at that time, in the encyclical letter written to all our venerable brethren of the episcopate, we deplored the decay of truths, not only of supernatural truths taught by faith, but also of natural truths, whether practical or speculative ; also the reign of the most fatal errors and the most grave danger that threatens society from the ever-growing disorders into which it is plunged.

" We have said that the principal cause of so many calamities was the separation proclaimed, and the apostacy of the society of the present day, from Christ and his Church, which alone possesses the virtue necessary to remedy such evils. By the startling light of facts, we have showed that the Church founded by Christ to renovate the world, from her very first appearance upon the earth began to make it feel the great comfort of her superhuman virtue, and that in the darkest and most sorrowful days she was the only beacon that showed the true way, the only refuge that promised tranquillity and salvation. Hence it is very easy to infer that if, in those times, the Church was able to spread such signal blessings throughout the earth, she can most assuredly still do so to-day ; that the Church, as every Catholic holds as a matter of faith, ever animated by the spirit of Jesus Christ, who promised her his infallible aid, was constituted the mistress of truth and the guardian of a holy and immaculate law, and as such she still possesses all the strength necessary to cope with the moral and intellectual corruption that poisons society, and redeem it to salvation.

" And since most wily enemies, to make her hated and suspected, circulate grave calumnies against her, we have, in the first place, endeavored to dispel prejudices and to confound accusations, confident that when the people know the Church as she really is in her gentleness, they will return from all quarters to her bosom.

" Guided by such intentions as these, we have desired to make our voice heard by those who rule the destinies of nations, earnestly calling upon them not to refuse, in these times when it is so much needed, the most solid aid that the Church holds out to them ; and urged on by apostolic charity, we have also turned to those who are not united to us by the bond of the Catholic religion, anxious that their subjects may enjoy the beneficent influence of that divine institution.

" You are well aware, Signor Cardinal, that, in pursuance of this impulse of our heart, we wrote also to the powerful emperor of the illustrious German nation, which, on account of the difficult position of the Catholics in that country, called for our special solicitude. This step on our part, solely inspired by the desire of seeing religious peace restored to Germany, was favorably received by the august emperor, and had the happy result of bringing about friendly negotiations, in which it was not our intention to obtain merely a truce, that would leave the door open to new conflicts, but to bring about, by the removal of all obstacles, a real, solid, and durable peace. The importance of this object was justly estimated by the wisdom of those in whose hands the destinies of the empire are placed. We are confident that they will extend to us a friendly hand to attain it. The Church, without doubt, will be happy to see peace restored in that noble nation, but such a result will be fortunate also for the empire, which, with Catholic consciences at rest, will find, as in times past, its most faithful and devoted subjects among the sons of the Catholic Church.

"Our paternal vigilance could not allow us to forget the East, where grave events in progress are preparing a better future for the interests of religion. Nothing shall be wanting on the part of the Apostolic See to secure this, and we have the hope that the illustrious churches of those regions will finally arrive at the enjoyment of a fruitful life, and shine forth with all their wonted splendor.

"As you will readily see, from these brief hints, Signor Cardinal, that since our design is to carry the beneficent action of the Church and the Papacy into the heart of the society of the present day, it is necessary that you also bring to bear all your lights and all your energies to this design that God has placed in our heart. Moreover, you must give all your attention to another point of the highest importance—that is, to the very difficult position created for the head of the Church in Italy and in Rome, since he has been despoiled of his temporal dominion which Providence conferred upon him, so as to secure the independence of the spiritual power. We will not pause here to reflect that the violation of the most sacred rights of the Apostolic See and of the Roman pontiff is fatal even to the well-being and tranquillity of the peoples, who, seeing most sacred and ancient rights violated with impunity in the person of the vicar of Jesus Christ himself, find all ideas of duty and justice destroyed in themselves, respect for laws diminished, and the social and civil laws of society overthrown.

" And we desire to call your attention to the fact that Catholics in all countries can never be tranquil until their chief pontiff, the master of their faith and moderator of their consciences, is surrounded by true liberty and real independence.   We can not, however, refrain from observing that this spiritual power, which, because of its divine origin and its superhuman destiny, should exercise a beneficial influence in favor of the human race and enjoy the fullest liberty, is, on the contrary, by the actual condition of things, so hampered that the government of the universal Church has become most difficult to it.

" This is well known, and is confirmed by daily events.   The solemn complaints of our predecessor, Pius IX., of holy memory, in his consistorial allocution of March 12th, 1877, may be repeated by us with the same reasons, and with the addition of others no less grave, growing out of new obstacles placed in the way of the exercise of our supreme power.   Most assuredly, not only must we lament with our illustrious predecessor over the suppression of religious orders that deprives the pontiff of a powerful aid in the congregations in which the most important affairs of the Church are discussed, but we have also to regret that divine worship has been despoiled of its ministers by the law regarding military service, which compels all, without distinction, to do military duty ; we have to deplore that we and our clergy are deprived of institutions of charity and benevolence erected in Rome either by the Roman pontiffs or by the Catholic people who placed them under the protection of the Church ; also, to the great sorrow of our heart, as father and pastor, we are constrained to see, under our very eyes, the progress of heresy in the very city of Rome, the centre of the Catholic religion, where, with impunity, heterodox temples and schools are opened in large numbers, and to witness the perversion that results from it, especially among a large proportion of young people, to whom is offered a godless education ; and, as if all this were a trifling matter, they attempt even to render the very acts of our spiritual jurisdiction fruitless.

" It is well known to you, Signor Cardinal, how, since the occupation of Rome, in order to pacify as much as possible the consciences of Catholics deeply interested in the fate of their head, a willingness to allow the sovereign pontiff full liberty in the nomination of bishops to the different sees of Italy was loudly and publicly proclaimed ; but subsequently, under the pretext that the act of their canonical institution had not been submitted to the *placet* of the government, the new bishops were refused their revenues, thus entailing a heavy expense upon the Apostolic See, which was compelled to provide for their support, as well as a great injury to the souls committed to the care of these prelates.

" The government has also refused to recognize acts emanating from their episcopal jurisdiction, such as the appointment to parishes and other ecclesiastical benefices. And when, to obviate these great evils, the Apostolic See permitted the newly-elected bishops of Italy to present their bulls of appointment and institution, issued according to the canons, the condition of the Church did not, on that account, become less intolerable. Notwithstanding the presentation, the rulers continued to refuse their salaries and to ignore the jurisdiction of many bishops. Then, again, those who are allowed to exercise their functions see their claims sent from one bureau to another, and subjected to indefinite delays ; and men, respected for their virtues and learning, deemed by the pontiff worthy of exercising the highest duties of the ecclesiastical hierarchy, are compelled to submit to all manner of humiliations, and to be subjected to private and minute inspection, as if they were vulgar or suspected persons. Our venerable brother, chosen by us to rule over the Church of Perugia in our name, though already charged with the government of another diocese, where he was lawfully recognized, is vainly waiting an answer. Thus it is that, with a deplorable astuteness, they take with the left hand from the Church that which, for political reasons, they pretended to give her with the right.

" To render the state of things in many dioceses of Italy more aggravated, the right of royal patronage has been put forward with such exaggerated pretensions and such odious measures that they not only judicially notified our venerable brother, the Archbishop of Chieti, that his jurisdiction was interdicted, but that his appointment was declared null and his episcopal character not to be recognized.

" It is not our intention to stop to show the flimsy foundation for any such rights, even in the opinion of many minds in the opposite camp. It will be enough for us merely to state that the Apostolic See, to which is reserved the appointment of bishops, has not been in the habit of yielding the right of patronage except to such princes as have deserved well of the Church by defending her privileges, favoring her extension, and increasing her patrimony ; and those who combat it by attacking her rights and usurping her property become, by the very act, by virtue of the canons, incapable of exercising it.

"The facts we have here touched upon clearly indicate the intention to continue in Italy a system of increasing hostility towards the Church, and likewise demonstrate the sort of liberty reserved for her, and the kind of respect with which it is proposed to surround the head of the Catholic Church.

"Under such deplorable circumstances we are not unmindful, Signor Cardinal, of the sacred duties imposed upon us by the apostolic ministry, and with our eyes fixed on heaven, and with our soul fortified by the certain hope of divine assistance, we shall study never to fail in our duties. You, who, by reason of our confidence in you, are called to share in our exalted cares, will bring, like your illustrious predecessor, to the accomplishment of our designs, the concurrence of all your energies, and you may rest assured that our co-operation will never be wanting.

"In the meantime, as an earnest of our special affection, receive the apostolic benediction, which we most heartily bestow upon you.

"From the Vatican, August 27th, 1878.

"LEO XIII., Pope."

Here is the language of truth and deep conviction—language as moderate in its tone as it is powerful in its significance. It is a document that will stand in its noble simplicity, and the day will come when the rulers of the world will regret that they neglected its wisdom. It will then be felt that the revolt of the temporal against the spiritual, of Cæsar against Pontiff, is a perversion of all order, a loosening of all the bonds that hold society together, and that its consequences recoil with destructive reaction on its authors. Such is the warning given to the world by him to whom God has entrusted the guidance of nations, and who speaks in sorrow, not in anger, at the sad prospect before him of evils that threaten those whom he loves.

It is generally believed that the documents emanating from the Vatican during the present reign are the productions of the learned Pontiff himself, whose eminent natural gifts, cultivated by a long life of study, have given a depth to his thought, a keenness to his expression, and an irresistible power to his reasoning which rank him among the best scholars of the age. We have already seen how earnestly he labored in his diocese of Perugia for the elevation of ecclesiastical studies to a high standard of excellence, especially by a return to the doctrine and method of Aristotle and St. Thomas. We shall not be surprised to find him, now that he is placed over the universal Church, using his influence and his power for the same noble end, and urging on all those who direct seminaries and universities the importance of depth and thoroughness of philosophical and theological learning, especially in these days when so much false science is arrayed against the Church. The Academy of St. Thomas, which Cardinal Pecci had established at Perugia, has been established at Rome by Leo XIII. This was, as might have been expected, one of the new Pope's first cares. Every opportunity is seized for promoting this object. Thus, when the Bishop of Lecce, Mgr. Zola, was admitted to an audience, on the 18th September, the Holy Father said to him : " I greatly desire to see introduced into the seminaries the philosophical text-books of Canon Sanseverino. This great scholar, the glory of the Neapolitan clergy, labored efficaciously to bring philosophy back to the true and solid form which is that taught by St. Thomas. We rejoice that his works are already used in the seminary of Lecce, and we desire that in all seminaries the method and the doctrine of the Angel of the

CARDINAL LEDOCHOWSKI.

Schools should be followed. It is to be deeply regretted that Sanseverino died young, but he has left zealous disciples after him to continue his work, such as Prisco and Signoriello.''

In all seminaries and schools of ecclesiastical sciences, immediately subject to the Holy See, the doctrine of St. Thomas has been made obligatory. A memorable audience granted by Leo XIII. to the professors of the Gregorian University, better known as the Roman College, founded and munificently endowed by Gregory XIII., but at present expropriated by the Italian government, is thus narrated by the *Civilta Cattolica* : " On Wednesday, November 27th, His Holiness Pope Leo XIII. was pleased to admit to an audience at the Vatican the professors of the Gregorian University in the three faculties of theology, canon law, and philosophy, whose classes, driven from the Roman College, are continued in the Germanico-Hungarian College. The Rector of the College, Rev. A. Molza, and the Prefect of Studies, Rev. Jos. Kleutgen, accompanied the professors to the Throne-Room, where the Holy Father met them in company with Cardinals Bartolini, Ledochowski, and Parocchi. An address was read by the Very Rev. V. Cardella, Provincial of Rome, to which the Pope made the following eloquent reply in Latin :

" Most delightful to every cultivated man is the remembrance of his youthful days when his mind was imbued with letters ; the recollection of that first scene of his labors, and of those great and good men who devoted themselves with such ardor to his improvement. For this reason your presence here, and the words you have spoken, have given us no small pleasure, since you recalled the happy days when we were a student of the Roman College. With joy do we remember the happy tranquillity of those days, and the far-seeing and profuse liberality of Leo XII., our predecessor, who, for the promotion of literature and science, had just then restored the Roman Col-

lege to the fathers of the Society of Jesus; the
throngs of students, their public displays of learning,
their disputations on philosophical and theological
theses, and the profound scholars who presided at
them, John Curi, John Perrone, Francis Manera,
Antony Ferrarini, Andrew Carafa, John B. Pianciani,
and others, by whose learning and kindness we
profited; and we now gladly and publicly declare that
our heart has been ever since so closely bound to the
great men whom we have named, and to your institution, that it has never been, nor ever shall be, es-
tranged.

"Not less is the pleasure you have caused us by
the docility and hearty submission with which you
have responded to our desire in regard to the method
of teaching the sacred sciences and that of philosophy. None of you surely can fail to perceive how
important it has now become to imbue the minds of
youth, especially of those who are destined to serve
the Church, with sound and solid learning, to refute
the numerous and widespread errors by which not
only supernatural truth is attacked, but even natural
verities are torn from their very foundations; to ban-
ish from the schools a false science which is hostile to
faith and to reason, and which has usurped an almost
universal sway; and to replace it by a science based
on sound principles, explained in a proper and correct method in conformity with faith and revelation.

"Now this true science, we think, is no other
than that which, coming from the early fathers of the
Church, and brought into a complete system by the
scholastic doctors, especially by the leader of them
all, the angelic St. Thomas of Aquin, has been ex-
tolled by general councils and by Roman pontiffs, and
has been the law of learning for many centuries in

Catholic universities.   And as it is our earnest desire to restore this science to its ancient glory for the advancement and the honor of studies, we could not but turn our eyes to the Gregorian University, which, though driven from its own and ancient seat, much to our grief, and not crowded with the same numbers of students as of old, is yet so renowned and so frequented that it can contribute powerfully to the restoration and advancement of studies which we desire.

"We have no doubt that you will, according to your promise, devote all your energy to this object. This is a duty imposed on you by the obedience which, by your rule, you vow to the Holy See ; and by the constitutions of your society, which decree that philosophy and theology shall be taught according to the doctrine and method of St. Thomas.   This is further required by the very nature and spirit of the Gregorian University ; for, as it receives its students from every country, the salutary stream of human and divine wisdom which they will draw here will be easily and rapidly diffused over the whole world.

"With this hope in our heart, we pray God, the Father of Lights, in whom and from whom is all wisdom, that he would enlighten your minds and give you courage to battle for the truth.   As a pledge of these divine blessings and an earnest of our special favor, we give to you, to your entire society, and to all the students in your classes, the apostolic benediction."

At the close of this discourse the Holy Father permitted the fathers present to kiss his foot and his hand, and conversed with each one of them with great kindness, congratulating this one on the learned volumes he had published, encouraging another to publish other works, and others to persevere in the pursuit of their several studies. Among these fathers was the venerable Patrizi, well known for his exegetical works, who had formerly been the teacher of the young Pecci now seated on the throne of St. Peter, and whom His Holiness had always held in kindly remembrance. When the Pope saw the old man approaching, he arose, and, descending from his throne, warmly embraced him, remembering the many happy days spent at his feet in early youth. What a touching lesson this furnishes to our rising generation !

From such beginnings in the matter of sound Christian education we may anticipate other and perhaps more weighty lessons on the same subject, of wider bearing and more general usefulness. It can not be denied that the serious evils which weigh upon the world to-day are mainly the effect of bad education—of education emancipated from the Church, and controlled by men who have neither faith in the supernatural nor regard for the Author of the natural. Our Pontiff knows this but too well, and though he may not be sanguine of a speedy return to true principles, he feels it his duty to raise his voice, in season and out of season, to warn the nations of their fatal mistake. We have already heard him as Cardinal of Perugia, and also as Pope in his first encyclical ; we shall hear him again in his brief to the Archbishop of Cologne, and in the encyclical published on the 28th of December, two noble monuments to his wisdom and to his zeal for the welfare of misguided men. We will give these documents entire, because every sentence is full of wisdom and of lessons worthy of eternal remembrance.

The following is the brief to the Archbishop :

" Venerable Brother, health and apostolic benediction.

"We derived great consolation and pleasure from the friendly letter in which you conveyed to us your good wishes and auguries of happiness on the approach of the solemnity of our Lord's Nativity; for in it was clearly apparent your devotion to our person, and your inviolable attachment to this apostolic see.   And these sentiments, while they increase our affection for you, redound greatly to your honor, and confirm with still stronger proof the perfect and reverent obedience paid to us by the flock of the Church of Cologne committed to your care.   We are convinced that it is through a merciful dispensation of God, who rules and governs all things, that similar signs of affection and devotion have been manifested towards us by you and others of our venerable brothers, the bishops of the Catholic world; for in the present sad condition of affairs, this wonderful unanimity gives us the greatest joy and refreshment, and causes us to say from our heart with the apostle, 'Blessed be God, who comforts us in all our tribulations.'   And, indeed, as soon as ever, on our exaltation to the height of this apostolic throne, we turned to address ourselves to all our venerable brethren in the episcopate, we found in their replies such an identity of thought, of opinion, and almost of words, that we not only rejoiced at the marvellous unity which flourishes in the Church of God, but had manifest proof that the bishops of the whole world are the interpreters of the sound doctrine which is derived from the apostolic see, and that they will be our cheerful helpers in our pastoral care and labors.

"And now this unity in doctrine, in counsel, and in action, gives us ground for hope that our desires will be fulfilled, and that from this fulfilment the Church will derive the greatest advantages and civil society also will reap the most abundant fruits. For you well know, Venerable Brother, that we entertain the most intimate conviction—a conviction which we have often expressed and publicly declared —that the cause of the dangers which threaten society is to be sought principally in the fact that the authority of the Church is on all sides intercepted, and prevented from exercising its salutary influence for the public good, and that its liberty is so fettered that it is scarcely allowed to provide for the private necessities and welfare of individuals. And this persuasion is generated in our mind not only by the knowledge which we have of the nature and powerful influence of the Church, but also by unquestionable historical proofs from which it is manifest that the condition of civil society is then most prosperous when the Church enjoys full liberty of action, and that whenever she is shackled by restrictions, those principles and doctrines which tend to the fall and dissolution of all human society begin to prevail.

" Since, then, this has been long our settled opinion, it was natural that, from the very beginning of our Pontificate, we should strive to call back princes and people to peace and friendship with the Church. And to you, Venerable Brother, it is certainly well known that we have for some time directed our efforts to the end that the noble nation of the Germans may see the end of its dissensions and obtain the blessings and fruits of a lasting peace without injury to the rights of the Church ; and we think that you also know that, as far as we are concerned, we have neglected no means of arriving at an end so noble and so worthy of our solicitude. But whether that which we have undertaken and are striving to effect will at last be prosperously accomplished He knows from whom comes everything that is good, and who has implanted in us so ardent a desire and longing for peace.

" But whatever may be the ultimate issue, resigning ourselves to the divine will, but animated by the same desire, we will persevere in the arduous task committed to us, so long as life shall endure.   For so great a duty can not lawfully be postponed or neglected, while by the perverted teaching of perfidious men, who have thrown off all restraint of law, religious, political, and social order, is threatened with destruction.   We should hold ourselves to be neglecting the duty of our apostolic ministry if we did not offer to human society, in this most dangerous crisis of its existence, the efficacious remedies which the Church provides.   From this purpose, therefore, of saving all, and particularly your nation, Venerable Brother, no obstacles, from whatever quarter they may come, will turn us aside.   For our heart will never be able to rest as long as, to the great loss of souls, the pastors of the Church are condemned or exiled, the ministry of the priesthood fettered in every way, the religious communities and pious congregations overthrown and scattered, and all education, not even that of the clergy being excepted, withdrawn from the authority and watchful care of the bishops.   And that this work of salvation undertaken by us may be more perfectly and speedily accomplished, we call upon you, Venerable Brother, and the illustrious bishops of your country, to strive together with us, with united desires and efforts, that the faithful committed to your charge may show themselves more and more docile to the teachings of the Church, and may more exactly observe the prescriptions of the divine law, so that ' the communication of their faith may be more manifest in the acknowledgment of every good work, which is in them in Christ Jesus.' Thence will result that moderation and that obedience to laws (not repugnant to the faith and duty of a Catholic) by which they will show themselves worthy to receive the blessings of peace and to enjoy its happy fruits.

" But you are perfectly aware, Venerable Brother, that our endeavors in so grave a matter will be altogether vain, unless we have the blessing and help of God ; for ' unless he build the house, they labor in vain who build it.'

" Wherefore we must pour forth before him fervent supplications and prayers, earnestly beseeching him to enlighten his Vicar on earth and the bishops ; and, since the hearts of kings are in his hand, we should implore him to incline to more gentle counsels the illustrious and powerful Emperor of the Germans, and the distinguished personages who are his advisers.

" Lastly, since the united prayer of many hearts offers a kind of violence to the divine goodness, we desire that the bishops of Germany should by a common exhortation excite the flocks over whom they preside to pray that the divine help may be present and propitious to our efforts.

" In the meanwhile, as an augury of heavenly gifts, and as a pledge of our love, we impart to you, Venerable Brother, and also to the other bishops of Germany, and to the faithful entrusted to your vigilance, with the deepest affection of heart in the Lord, the apostolic benediction.

" Given at Rome, at St. Peter's, the 24th day of December, 1878, in the first year of our Pontificate.

" LEO PP. XIII."

The encyclical, which we shall now give in full, has created a ferment in all the political circles of Europe. The leaders of the anti-Christian and anti-social parties feel the truth of its utterances, and see the end to which their schemes must bring society. The mask is torn from their faces, and they stand before the world, not, as they pretended, its benefactors, but, as they are, its worst enemies. May the lessons here so paternally and so forcibly conveyed be of service to prevent the sad issue of modern infidelity !

ENCYCLICAL LETTER OF OUR MOST HOLY FATHER, LEO XIII.

VENERABLE BRETHREN : Health and apostolic benediction.

From the commencement of our pontificate, and in fulfilment of the duty of our office, we addressed you in an Encyclical Letter, to point out that deadly poison which is creeping into human society and is leading it to ruin. We then also indicated the efficacious remedies by means of which society may be restored, and escape the serious dangers that threaten it. But the evils we then deplored have increased so rapidly, that we are compelled once more to address you, as though the words of the prophet were ringing in our ear : "Cry, cease not ; lift up thy voice like a trumpet."

You understand, venerable brethren, that we allude to that sect of men who call themselves by various and almost barbarous titles—Socialists, Communists, and Nihilists—and who, scattered all over the world, closely bound together in an unholy league, are no longer satisfied with lurking in secret, but boldly come forth into the light with the determination to uproot the foundation of society. It is surely these men that are signified by the words of Holy Writ, "who defile the flesh, and despise authority and blaspheme majesty." They will not leave any thing intact that has been wisely decreed by divine and human laws for the security and honor of life. They refuse obedience to the higher powers, who hold from God the right to command, and to whom, according to the apostle, every soul ought to be subject, and they preach the perfect equality of all men in every thing that concerns their rights and duties. They dishonor the natural union of man and woman, sacred even among barbarians, and endeavor to relax or even to break asunder that bond which chiefly cements domestic society. Seduced by the lust of earthly goods, which is " the root of all evil," and through the coveting of which "many have erred from the faith," they assail the right of property sanctioned by the natural law, and under the pretence of supplying the wants of men, and satisfying their lawful desires, they aim at making a common spoil of whatever has been legitimately acquired by inheritance, by skill, industry, or economy. They publish these monstrous doctrines at their meetings, they urge them in pamphlets, and spread them far and wide by means of the press. The result of this is that, within a short time, the majesty and authority of kings, which should be revered by all, has been rendered so odious to a seditious rabble, that traitors, breaking loose from all restraint, have more than once lifted their hands against the rulers of kingdoms.

These attempts of perfidious men, who threaten to undermine civil life and fill all thinking minds with alarm, had their origin in the poisoned doctrines broached long ago, like seeds of corruption, which are now producing their destructive fruit. You are aware, venerable brethren, that the warfare raised against the Church by the reformers in the sixteenth century still continues and tends to this end, that by the denial of all revelation and the suppression of the supernatural order, the reason of man may run riot in its own conceits. This error, which unjustly derives its name from reason, flatters the pride of man, loosens the reins to all his passions, and thus it has deceived many minds, whilst it has made deep ravages on civil society. Hence it comes that, by a new sort of impiety, unknown to the pagans, states constitute themselves independently of God or of the order which He has established. Public authority is declared to derive neither its principle nor its power from God, but from the multitude, which, believing itself free from all divine sanction, obeys no laws but such as its own caprice has dictated. Supernatural truth being rejected as contrary to reason, the Creator and Redeemer of the human race is ignored and banished from the universities, the lyceums and schools, as also from the whole economy of human life. The rewards and punishments of a future and eternal life are forgotten in the pursuit of present pleasure. With these doctrines widely spread, and this extreme license of thought and action extended everywhere, it is not surprising that men of the lowest order, weary of the poverty of their home or of their little workshop, should yearn to seize upon the dwellings and possessions of the rich ; that there remains neither peace nor tranquillity in private or public life, and that society is brought to the brink of destruction.

The supreme pastors of the Church, on whom the duty rests of preserving the flock of the Lord from the snares of their enemies, have not neglected to point out the danger and to provide for the safety of the faithful. Indeed, from the moment that secret societies began to be formed and to cause the evils of which we have just spoken, the Roman Pontiffs Clement XII. and Benedict XIV. unveiled the iniquitous designs of these sects, and warned the faithful of the whole world of the serious evils which would result from them. When men who gloried in the name of philosophers had asserted for man an unlimited independence, and had devised what they called a new code of right in opposition to the natural and the divine law, Pope Pius VI. immediately raised his voice against these false and wicked doctrines, and with apostolic foresight predicted the calamities which would flow from them. And when, in spite of this warning, these principles were still maintained and even made the basis of public legislation, Pius VII. and Leo XII. solemnly condemned secret societies and again gave warning of the perils

that menaced the nations.   Lastly, every one remem-
bers with what authority and firmness our glorious
predecessor, Pius IX., in his allocutions and ency-
clicals, combated the projects of these associations,
especially of the Socialists, who were just then beginning to appear.

But to our great grief, those who are charged
with the care of the public welfare have allowed
themselves to be blinded by the arts of the wicked or
intimidated by their threats, whilst they have always
treated the Church with suspicion and injustice, for-
getting that the efforts of the sects would have been
powerless if the teaching of the Catholic Church and
the authority of the Roman Pontiffs had always been
duly respected by princes and people ; for it is " the
Church of the living God, the pillar and ground of
truth," which teaches the doctrines and principles
on which society can rest secure, without fear of the
fatal effects of Socialism.   For although the Socialists
pervert the Gospel to deceive the unwary, and wrest
it to their own sense, yet in truth there cannot be
two things more at variance with one another than
their depraved ideas and the beautiful teachings of
Christ. " For what participation hath justice with
injustice, or what fellowship hath light with darkness ?" They never cease proclaiming that all men
are equal in all things, and hence kings have no right
to command them, nor laws any power to bind unless made by themselves and according to their own
inclinations.   But, on the other hand, the Gospel
teaches that all men are indeed equal, inasmuch as
all have the same nature, all are called to the sublime
dignity of children of God, are destined to the same
end, and will be judged by the same law which will
decree the punishment or the reward deserved by

each one. But an inequality of rights and powers emanates from the Author of nature Himself, " of whom all paternity is named in heaven and on earth." According to the Catholic doctrine, princes and people are bound together by a mutual relation of rights and duties in such a manner that a check is laid on the excess of power, and obedience is rendered easy, constant, and noble. To the subjects the Church constantly repeats the apostle's precept : " There is no power but from God ; and the powers that are, are ordained of God. Therefore he who resisteth the power, resisteth the ordinance of God, and they that resist purchase to themselves damnation." And again, she bids them " be subject of necessity, not only for wrath, but also for conscience sake ;" and to render " to all men their dues, to whom tribute, tribute ; to whom custom, custom ; to whom fear, fear ; to whom honor, honor." For He who has created and who governs all things has wisely ordained that the lowest should depend on the middle, and the middle on the highest, that all may reach their end. And as even in heaven He has decreed a distinction among the angels, so that some are inferior to others, and as in the Church He has instituted a diversity of degrees and offices, so that not all are apostles, not all are doctors, nor all pastors ; so too He has established in civil society different orders in dignity, in right and power, so that the state, like the Church, might form one body composed of many members, some more noble than others, but all necessary to one another, and all laboring for the common good.

But that princes may use the power vested in them " unto edification and not unto destruction," the Church appropriately warns them that they too are responsible to the supreme judge, and she addresses to them the words of divine wisdom : " Give ear, ye that rule the people and that please yourselves in multitudes of nations ; for power is given you by the Lord, and strength by the Most High, who will examine your works and search out your thoughts ; for a most severe judgment shall be for them that bear rule. For God will not accept any man's person, neither will He stand in awe of any man's greatness ; for He hath made the little and the great, and He hath equally care of all. But a greater punishment is ready for the more mighty." If, however, at times it happens that public power is exercised by princes rashly and beyond bound, the Catholic doctrine does not allow subjects to rebel against a ruler by private authority, lest the peaceful order be more and more disturbed and society suffer greater detriment. And when things have come to such a pass that no other hope of safety appears, it teaches that a speedy remedy is to be sought from God by the merit of Christian forbearance and by fervent supplications. But if the ordinances of legislators and princes sanction or command what is contrary to the divine or the natural law, then the dignity of the Christian name, our duty, and the apostolic precept proclaim that " we must obey God rather than men."

This salutary influence which the Church exercises over civil society for the maintenance of order in it and for its preservation, is felt also in domestic society, which is the foundation of the state. You know, venerable brethren, that the constitution of this society has, by virtue of the natural law, its foundation in the indissoluble union of the husband and wife, and its complement in the mutual rights and duties of parents and children, of masters and servants. You know also that this society is totally annihilated by the theories of Socialism ; for when the firm bond is broken which the religious marriage throws around it, the authority of the parent over his offspring and the duties of children towards their parents must necessarily be relaxed. On the contrary, the marriage, " honorable in all," which God Himself instituted from the beginning for the propagation and perpetuity of the race, and which He made indissoluble, has become in the teaching of the Church more firm and more holy through Christ, who conferred on it the dignity of a sacrament, an image of His own union with the Church. Hence, according to the apostle, " the husband is the head of the wife, as Christ is the head of the Church ;" and as the Church is subject to Christ, who honors her with a chaste and perpetual love, so wives should be subject to their husbands, who in return are bound to love their wives with a faithful and constant affection.

The Church likewise regulates the powers of the parent and master in such a way as to keep children and servants in their duty, and yet not allow those powers to be abused. For according to Catholic teaching, the authority of parents and masters comes to them from the authority of our heavenly Father and Master ; and therefore it not only derives from Him its origin and its force, but it should also be imbued with the nature and character of that divine authority. Hence the apostle exhorts children " to obey their parents in the Lord," and " to honor their father and their mother, which precept is the first that hath a promise." And to parents he says : " And you, fathers, provoke not your children to anger, but bring them up in the discipline and correction of the Lord." In like manner, the divine commandment is given by the apostle to servants and masters ; the former being told " to be obedient to their masters according to the flesh, as to Christ ; serving with a good will, as to the Lord ;" whilst the latter are " to forbear threatenings, knowing that the Lord of all is in heaven, and that there is no respect of persons with Him." Now, if all these precepts were observed by each of those whom they concern, according to the disposition of God's will, surely each family would be an image of heaven, and the benefits arising from this would not be confined within the family circle, but would spread abroad over the nations themselves.

But Catholic wisdom, resting on the principles of natural and divine law, has provided for public and private tranquillity by those doctrines also which it maintains in regard to the ownership and distribution of property held for the necessities and conveniences of life. The Socialists denounce the right of property as a human invention, repugnant to the natural equality of men ; they claim a community of goods, and preach that poverty is not to be endured with patience, and that the possessions and rights of the rich can be lawfully disregarded. But the Church more wisely recognizes an inequality among men, of different degrees in strength of body and of mind, also in the possession of goods, and ordains that the right of proprietorship and of dominion, which comes from nature itself, is to remain intact and inviolable to each one. For she knows that God, the author and asserter of all right, has forbidden theft and rapine in such a manner that it is not allowed even to covet another's goods ; and that thieves and robbers, as well as adulterers and idolaters, are excluded from the kingdom of heaven. But the Church, like a good mother, does not therefore neglect the care of the poor or the relief of their wants. On the contrary, embracing them with maternal tenderness, and remembering that they bear the person of Christ Himself, who esteems as done to Himself whatever is done to one of His little ones, holds them in high honor, comforts them in every way, raises up for them, protects and defends, asylums and hospitals to receive them, to nourish and heal them. She urges the rich, by the most pressing commandment, to distribute their superfluity among the poor, and threatens them with the judgment of God, by which they shall be doomed to eternal punishment, if they refuse to relieve their afflicted brethren. Finally, she consoles and rejoices the hearts of the poor, now by presenting to them the example of Jesus Christ, " who, being rich, became poor for our sakes ;" and again by recalling His words by which He declares the poor blessed, and bids them hope for the happiness of eternal life. Who does not see that this is the best means of appeasing the long quarrel between the poor and the rich ? For the very evidence of circumstances and facts shows that, if this means is rejected, one of two alternatives must follow : either the greatest portion of mankind will be reduced to the ignominious condition of slaves, as they were long ago among the pagans ; or human society will be agitated by continual troubles and desolated by robbery and pillage, as we have seen even in our own days.

This being the case, venerable brethren, we on whom the government of the Church has now devolved, after having shown, from the first days of our pontificate, to princes and peoples tossed about by the violence of the tempest, the only harbor where they can find a safe refuge, moved to-day by the extreme peril which threatens, we again raise our apostolic voice, and we conjure them, by their desire for their own security and that of the common weal, that they would listen to the teaching of the Church, which has done so much for the welfare of states, and would remember that the interests of the state and of religion are so united, that every loss inflicted on the latter diminishes by so much the submission of subjects and the majesty of the ruler. And since they know that for the repression of Socialism the Church possesses a power which is not to be found either in human laws, or in the restraints of magistrates, or the arms of soldiery, let them restore to the Church that freedom which will enable her to wield her power for the common good of human society.

And do you, venerable brethren, who know the origin and the nature of the threatening evils, labor with all the energy of your souls to impress the Catholic doctrine deeply on the minds of all. Let it be your endeavor that all may accustom themselves, even from their tenderest years, to cherish a filial love for God and reverence for His name ; to yield obedience to the majesty of princes and of the laws ; to curb their passions, and to observe the order which God has established in civil and domestic society. Do all that you can to prevent the children of the Church from uniting themselves with that abominable sect or to favor it in any manner. Let them, on the contrary, by noble deeds and by their honorable conduct in all things, show to the world how happy society would be if it were entirely composed of members like them. Lastly, as Socialism seeks its disciples chiefly in that class of men who follow trades or hire their labor, and whose weariness of work more easily tempts them with the desire of wealth and the hope of possessing it, it will be of great use to encourage those associations of artisans and laborers which, founded under the patronage of religion, teach their members to be content with their lot, to endure their toils, and to lead a calm and tranquil life.

May our endeavors and yours, venerable brethren, be prospered by Him to whom we are in duty bound to refer the beginning and the end of every good undertaking! The hope of a speedy help is raised within us by these very days in which we celebrate the birth of our Lord, who gives us also the hope of that salutary restoration which He, at His birth, brought to a world grown old in evils and fallen almost to the abyss of misfortune, and promises us the peace which He then announced to men by the voice of His angels. The arm of the Lord is not shortened so as not to be able to save us, nor is His ear become heavy so as not to hear. In these sacred days, therefore, we wish you, venerable brethren, and the faithful of your churches all happiness and joy ; and we fervently implore of Him who gives all good gifts to men, that there may appear anew to us the goodness and humanity of God our Saviour, who snatches us from the power of our enemy and lifts us up to the dignity of His children. And that we may more speedily and more fully enjoy these blessings, join your prayers to ours and add to them the intercession of the Blessed Virgin Mary, Immaculate in her origin, of St. Joseph, her spouse, and of the holy apostles Peter and Paul, in whose assistance we confidently trust. Meanwhile, as a pledge of the divine gifts, we impart from the depths of our heart the apostolic benediction to you, venerable brethren, to your clergy and to all the faithful people.

Given at St. Peter's, Rome, 28th December, 1878, the first year of our pontificate.   LEO PP. XIII.

CHURCH OF ST. MARY MAJOR.

Page 347.

Such documents as we have reprinted in this volume, and such acts as we have briefly sketched, fill up the first year of this already glorious reign ; we cannot, however, close our book without the mention of the solemn services performed by the Holy Father in person or by his order, to commemorate the anniversary of the death of his predecessor, Pius IX. These were attended in the Sistine Chapel, in the Basilicas of St. Peter, St. John Lateran, and St. Mary Major by an immense throng of pious Christians, as well as by the cardinals and other dignitaries both of Church and State.

To crown the first year of his pontificate, and to implore the divine blessings on the future, Leo XIII., in imitation of preceding popes, proclaimed

A GENERAL JUBILEE

on the 15th of February, 1879, by a Bull which we should insert here but for the fear of extending this volume beyond its proper bounds.

We had hoped to add the creation of new cardinals as a part of the events of this year ; but this has been delayed, though not without giving us sufficient indication of a design which fills many hearts, especially in England, Germany, and America, with joy and consolation.   We refer to the proposed elevation of John Henry Newman, D.D., the celebrated English Oratorian, and of Doctor Hergenröther, the learned Professor of Ecclesiastical History in the University of Würtzburg, to the Cardinalate— an honor which both deserve the more as they have the less expected or sought it.

Here we close our rapid sketch of the first year of the new Pontificate. We might have brought in other

subjects, such as the discourse of Leo XIII. to the pilgrims from persecuted Poland ; the words addressed
by him to various delegations of Catholic associations,
to students and seminaries ; to pilgrims from all lands
who came to render homage to the successor of the
beloved Pius ; the hopes born of the Kissingen confer-
ences between Prince Bismarck and the Nuncio of the
Holy See—hopes which seem to have been already
blasted by the haughty obstinacy of men who will not
acknowledge that they have erred : all these matters might have filled the outlines of the sketch.   But
it is hard to speak of present acts and of living actors,
and we have said enough to prove that the first year
of Leo's reign is one full of great deeds and of greater
promise, and to establish the thesis with which we
set out, that though we may grieve for the death of
Pius the Great, we have also reason to rejoice that he
has been succeeded by Leo XIII.

PICTORIAL
LIVES OF THE SAINTS,

WITH REFLECTIONS, FOR EVERY DAY IN THE YEAR.

WITH A PREFACE BY
Rev. EDWARD McGLYNN, D.D.

PASTOR OF ST. STEPHEN'S CHURCH, NEW YORK

ST. BRIDGID RECEIVING THE VEIL.

The present volume offers in a compendious form the lives of many eminent servants of God, forming, as it were, **A BOOK OF DAILY MEDITATIONS.** It is embellished with a beautiful **Chromo Frontispiece of the Holy Family** and a full-page **picture of St. Patrick the glorious Apostle of Ireland**, made, expressly for this work, from a fine steel engraving. In addition the book contains an illustration for almost every life given, altogether **NEARLY FOUR HUNDRED ILLUSTRATIONS,** making it the most attractive book now published. To crown all, there is a Preface by the learned and eminent **Dr. Edward McGlynn,** in which is set forth in burning words the great benefit to be gained by reading and meditating on the Lives of the Saints, those shining stars of heaven, the glory of the Church, who shed an ever-luminous ray o'er the narrow and stormy path which all must travel in order to reach the haven of eternal bliss.

The work has been greatly admired by **OUR HOLY FATHER, POPE LEO XIII.,** who sent his special blessing to the publishers, by the hands of Very Rev. Dr. Hostlot, Rector of the American College, Rome. It is approved by **His Eminence the Cardinal, Archbishop of New York; The Most Reverend Archbishops of** Milwaukee, Oregon, Philadelphia; **The Right Reverend Bishops of** Arizona,—Buffalo,—Chicago,—Cleveland,—Columbus,—Detroit,—Erie,—Fort Wayne,—Galveston,—Grass Valley,—Greenbay,—Leavenworth,—Louisville,—Marquette,—Nesqualy,—Ogdensburg,—Peoria,—Providence,—Savannah,—Scranton,—St. Cloud,—St. Paul,—Wheeling.

The work is issued in the best style on highly calendered tinted paper, and the side is beautified by a symbolical design of the Coronation of the Blessed Virgin, the Queen of All Saints. **Sold only by Subscription.**

Elegantly bound in extra cloth, full gilt side, $3.50; elegantly bound in extra cloth, full gilt side, gilt edges, $4; elegantly bound in French morocco, full gilt side, gilt edges, $5.50.

BENZIGER BROTHERS,
Printers to the Holy Apostolic See,
NEW YORK, 311 BROADWAY.

CINCINNATI, 143 Main Street.   ST. LOUIS, 204 N. 5th Street.